MAKING MAN

JOHN DRAKE

MAKING MAN Copyright © 2018 by John Drake.

For information contact;

info@makingmanbook.com

www.makingmanbook.com

Published by John Drake

Book and Cover design by Colin Brennan

ISBN: 978-1-9164314-0-9

First Edition: July 2018

For Charlie

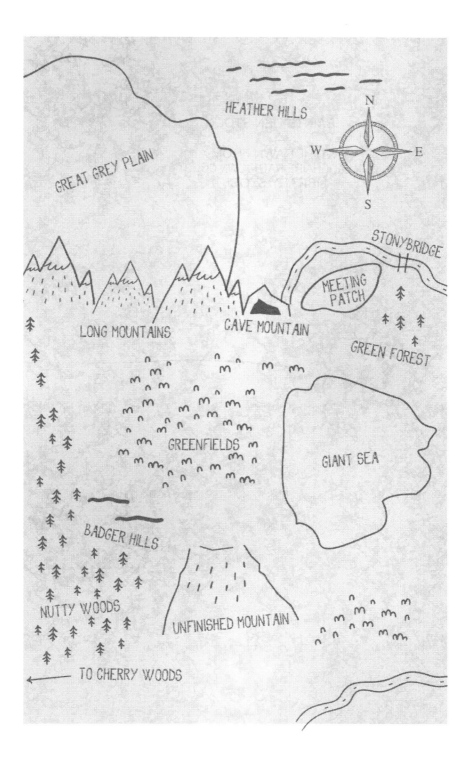

If you can trust yourself when all men doubt you,
 But make allowance for their doubting too;
If you can dream and not make dreams your master;
 If you can think and not make thoughts your aim,
Or watch the things you gave your life to, broken,
 And stoop and build 'em up with worn-out tools;
Yours is the Earth and everything that's in it,
 And, which is more, you'll be a Man, my son!

If ~ Rudyard Kipling

PROLOGUE

The last thing the goat expected to see was the arrow flying towards him. It was, in fact, the very last thing he expected, full stop. He expected no more. Had he a dark sense of humour he might have given a little chuckle. As it was he was a slow-witted character, as goats go, so there was no chuckle. He did, however, possess a wonderful sense of balance and so was surprised, for a brief period, to find himself falling to the valley floor far below.

'Bugger,' he thought, as he passed his familiar crags in the mountainside.

Thud.

Cobble sat on his rocky outcrop on the rumbling Cave Mountain and looked out over the Boardom tribeland. Their lands were vast, but not because they had marauded around the place causing general pillage-like mischief. It was rather because there was nobody else there. It stretched as far as he could see, right up to the Heather Hills in the far north. To the south was the Giant Sea, in reality actually a large lake that acted as a natural boundary for the tribe. It was named long ago, before the memory of any living Boarder and legend tells of a great battle with a giant, three times the height of a man and fists the size of a chicken. This was completely untrue, naturally, though it did help to put Dornak The Giant Slayer at the top of the food chain for several moons before his ambitious brother performed a ruthless cost benefit analysis on the subject, the upshot of which was the most infamous case of sibling regicide in Boardom's history.

The tribesfolk were not famous for their imagination, particularly when it came to naming places or people. The forest that bordered the eastern end of Boardom was largely made up of tall evergreen trees. It was known as Green Forest. Cave Mountain was the last peak in the Long Mountains, a range running off into the distance to the west. To its right was the Great Grey Plain, so named because it was a large, expansive plain and mostly grey. Cobble wasn't sure if any of the tribe had ever ventured past the horizon that way, certainly none of the current incumbents seemed capable of it. They regularly struggled to move from the fire pits to their caves at sunset, instead often sleeping where they found themselves, even in the depths of winter.

Laziness was their third most irritating trait, Cobble decided.

The day was bright and breezy, just like his mind, but living in Boardom was suffocating. He was surrounded by people with the ambition of rocks. To the tribesfolk nothing was so important that it couldn't be done after a good nap and this infuriated him. There was so much that could be achieved, so many improvements that could have been made to people's lives. He had spent his life creating these things; from roughly hewn wooden bowls to help bring water from the small stream that ran across the north and west sides of the village, to the complex stone stand that would allow simultaneous cooking of multiple items at the fire pits, but no-one shared his vision, no-one cared. Not even his father, Block, who was respected like no other before him. The tribe loved his father and he loved them in return. After all, he slew the giant boar of Rockslide that gave the tribeland its current name. It had been the go-to story for years for young parents trying to control mischievous children. 'Now, you're not to leave the Meeting Patch on your own, young man. The giant boar is out there and will eat your arms for dinner before you can blink, and then how will you draw on the cave wall? Do you hear me?' and 'Remember little Pebble? He went playing too far away after dark and all they found of him the next day was his big toe, twitching in the pine needles.' Left unchecked, the stories developed into darker and darker tales of children coming to gruesome ends in a variety of ways, some more deliberately comical than others.

What nobody knew, not even Cobble, was that his father was asleep during this gallant slaying. The boar had simply fallen down the hillside, missing him by inches and landing on a stubborn branch protruding nonchalantly from the floor. The curdling squeal had woken him and a future filled with meat and adulation flashed in front of his eyes. He had tied up the unfortunate animal with some thin, waxy branches and dragged him back to the Meeting Patch.

For a brief time Cobble thought he had a future he could look forward to. People began to show an interest in his inventions, even visiting him in Green Forest, a place that most avoided but was his favourite place to realise his ideas, to see the next contraption to sprout from the mind of Cobble the Stout. It was a false interest, Cobble knew, but he ignored this inconvenient truth. It was the first time anyone had properly noticed him and he wallowed in the attention his father's reputation had gifted him. The pleasure was short lived, however. The lethargic ambition of the ignorant can destroy the spirit of the curious.

As he looked out over the Meeting Patch, Cobble wondered if his time in the limelight was coming to an end. The false interest was waning, the lustre of impressing the chief's son diminishing as his lack of influence with his father became more apparent. Gradually, he realised, he was returning to his status as the forgotten member of the tribe. He was like the sprouts that nobody ate at the annual Rock Festival dinner. They had to be there. It was traditional, and tradition was important, but nobody knew quite why.

He was never able to put a finger on why the tribe was so against him. It seemed to him to be most unfair. He should be lauded as a son of the famous Block. Instead he felt like a stranger at a wedding. He decided it was his disposition, his tendency to look for, and find, new ways of doing things. Boardom's population was only small, about two dozen people in all, and almost all of them were quite happy doing what they had done for moon after moon. Eat, shout, scratch, sleep, repeat.

He thought back to the night when everything had changed for him. He had been sitting at the same spot he was at now, on the outcrop at Cave Mountain. He remembered again the commotion at the fire pit far below him. Old Shankswill had made his famous fermented pear juice again and the older tribesfolk were shouting and cursing more loudly than usual. The latrine pit, which had been dug far away from the fire pit for obvious olfactory reasons, was no longer the first choice for many of those requiring relief. Any bare patch of grass would do. Cobble remembered rolling his eyes judgmentally. 'Where is their sense?' he had muttered. He would have thought they would regret it in the morning, had he not known that they would neither care nor remember. These were Neanderthals in every sense of the word.

As he watched the collective staggering and swaying of his raucous tribe, he had seen two figures making a circuitous route towards the sewage pit. He had recognised the pair, even from that distance; the rotund, bloated silhouette of his father, Block, and the strong, confident gait of Cobble's only brother, Chip. As it happened, they were walking to their drunken, stinking deaths. Not that anyone knew.

That was a long time ago now, but his memories from those days still scarred his thoughts. His father had always favoured Chip. If Block was prone to introspection, which he emphatically wasn't, he would have known that it was because Chip was everything he aspired to be; competitive, extroverted and able. In a society where apathy and shouting are core skills, competitiveness can get you a long way up the social ladder. If there was something to be done then Chip wanted to be the one to do it first, fastest and best.

In a rare family outing during their childhood, long before the boar slaying, Cobble and Chip were foraging for mushrooms in Green Forest with their father. As part of the traditions of the Rock Festival, each family was given a task to complete ahead of the day and it was one of the few occasions when any of the male adults ventured more than a few dozen paces from their fire pits. Inertia was a most powerful force in Boardom. Block had been given 'Mushroom Gathering' and had decided that this year he would create an impression. When indolence is a virtue, great fame can be made expelling the smallest amounts of energy.

He wanted the biggest, most pungent mushrooms to bring back for the feast. To an outsider it may have looked like a show of community spirit, a grand effort by one to benefit the whole. For Block, it was a chance at immortality. He wanted to be part of a story, the story, the oral history of the tribe. He might even get his own song. Block wanted to be in a song. Last year Slate the Sharp had produced a pile of apples half as tall as his cave opening. For days afterwards he was the focus of the tribe's attentions. There were stories regaled about him, adding it to the compendium of tales told around the fire pits. Block would have to sit through it that night and he was damned if he was going to go through another year without having his own.

'Boys!' he shouted ''ere!'

Cobble and Chip turned to their father.

'Yes Dad?' said Chip, sidestepping in front of Cobble.

'These little blighters are all you should be thinking about between now and sunset. Short fat stalks, wide flat tops. No spots, do you 'ear me? No spots.'

'Yes Dad,' said Chip, trundling off before Cobble could react.

He followed his infuriating brother to a clump of ferns near a large conifer.

'Let's divide the jobs up, Chip,' said Cobble, instinctively trying to solve a problem that wasn't really there. 'One of us can pick the mushrooms while the other one carries an armful back to the cave.'

Without the slightest pause Chip saw an opportunity and pounced. 'Great idea brother, you're a clever little boy, ain't you. You pick 'em and I'll do all the 'ard work going back and forth to the cave. How about that?'

There were three reasons why Cobble raised a single, hairy eyebrow.

Firstly, Chip had agreed to one of his ideas. This simply never happened. Never. Even when Chip thought Cobble had suggested something reasonable he would argue against it, just for entertainment.

Secondly, Chip had offered to do the harder of the two jobs. He must have been at Old Shankswill's pear juice, Cobble thought.

Thirdly, and most importantly, Cobble raised one eyebrow because Chip couldn't. Never waste an opportunity to show off a unique skill, Chip himself had taught him that.

By sunset there was a mound of fat mushrooms in the mouth of the family cave worthy of any bard's time. The brothers had worked together to produce something special for their father. Cobble felt good, part of something. Perhaps the tides of this sibling relationship were changing. Perhaps they could form a unique rapport. He might even reveal some of his latest ideas to him. He would like that, he had decided.

He needn't have dreamt so hard. As he finally approached the Meeting Patch under a darkening red sky, he could just make out a group of men clapping a round figure on his ample back and rocking him by the shoulders as if congratulating him. As he neared the tribal fire pit he began to hear the voices, catching more of them as he got closer.

'...impressive...'

'...on your own too...'

'You and your ol' man 'ave raised the bar with this one.'

'I would never 'ave thought there were so many mushrooms in all of Green Forest.'

'Where is Goober? Oi! Goober! Come 'ere! You need to sharpen your story stick, Block has produced a memorable crop!'

'Well my son 'elped me out a bit too.'

Cobble recognised his father's voice. Son? son? Cobble had felt like throwing himself from a tree, just to be sure he was real.

'Like a chip off the ol' block, eh? Eh?' said Granite the Ordinary, nudging Old Shankswill with a knowing elbow. It was an old joke, but there was nothing quite like familiar ground with Neanderthals. They knew this joke, it was like a comfortable pair of slippers. The whole group roared with laughter, holding on to each other for fear they may fall over with merriment.

That was it. That was the moment Cobble knew he no longer belonged to the tribe. The betrayal of his brother, taking the glory because the dumb-witted tribesfolk couldn't imagine there being another person foraging in the forest, and the betrayal of his father, and Cobble was sure that his father had forgotten Chip had a brother rather than forgetting he had a son. That was the subtle knife to Cobble's heart. He didn't feel betrayed by the tribe, there needs to be a certain sense of accountability for betrayal, and only Block and Chip had relinquished theirs for Cobble.

Cobble wanted his own story. It was the only thing he shared with his father, although their motivations travelled from opposite directions. His father wanted to listen to a bard regaling tales of the famous mushroom mountain, knowing the size would increase as the years went by. He wanted the small amount of fame and adulation it would bring. Cobble wanted a story because it meant he had done something memorable. Something worthwhile.

Cobble wanted his own story.

CHAPTER ONE

THE BENCHMARK

Cobble scooped up the cold water and splashed the dust from his face. He had been working in Green Forest for two full weeks on his contribution to this year's Rock Festival.

'You can make one of your... things. Something to... you know?' they had instructed, helpfully.

He was used to this, a member of the tribe in location only. The more they neglected him the more he tried to win their favour. One day it would be worth it and they would bring him into the fold. Perhaps one of the women would show an interest in him and he could settle down with his own young family. His motivation was born out of an absence of alternatives, Boardom was all he knew – it was all any of them knew. He had decided he must fit in if he was to live a halfway happy life. He was like a cricket who didn't like chirping but rubbed his wings together anyway because everyone else seemed to think it was a good idea.

For the most part he made simple, imperfect and unappreciated inventions for the tribe. For the most part the tribe nodded politely with an occasional and condescending pat on the head, quickly turning their attentions back to the important task of the day, usually picking bugs from a range of body parts. And so it went on, with the tribe thinking that Cobble was not quite deserving of their respect and Cobble thinking that they were not quite deserving of his inventions.

He worked alone and savoured every minute, as only one who has an inherent dislike of other people can. Not that Cobble was an unpleasant sort. He was, in fact, a most congenial young man. It was the absence of congeniality in most of his tribe that made him feel this way. They didn't understand him. They were old fashioned Neanderthals who refused to see the value in his modern thinking. Some of the elder tribesfolk still thought fire was new-fangled and wouldn't last the summer.

He had spent most of his childhood inventing. Not in the usual 'Look at my magic stick Daddy' kind of way, more in the 'How can I make my life easier with this stick' kind of way – an altogether more practical approach to invention. It was a serious business for Cobble and gave him an escape from the dreary life of a cave-dweller. There were no whirring gizmos with bells or cuckoos, partly because gizmos and bells didn't exist, but mostly because Cobble didn't believe in showboating. That kind of exhibitionist behaviour was for the alpha males and Cobble wasn't one of them. He barely got away with being a delta male. When people were asked to recall the tribe members he was the one they couldn't quite remember. He was that niggle in the back of your mind when you've forgotten something.

He had busied himself by looking for a problem to solve, as usual, picturing the Rock Festival in his mind. There was the large line of boulders starting at the Obelisk and diminishing in size, punctuated by a black pebble at the far end. An outsider may have considered this a thought provoking artistic installation, right up to the point they watched large hairy men running up them and leaping over the Obelisk to a new broken bone below. His mind's eye moved to the Rock Competition area, where lines of smooth, white rocks were laid out for the judges' inspection. Each judge had their own rigorous process, some even licking the rocks to establish their quality. He lowered his eyelids at the thought. The prize was an armful of carrots. Carrots were special, only grown by the most skilled and active of the tribesfolk. Her name was Moss. She, along with her dutiful daughters and a handful of the women, were the only other members of the tribe to display any enthusiasm for practical tasks. In any group of people there are those who act and those who act. It's how the world balances. None of the men knew, nor cared, how they did it. All they knew was they had turnips, and occasionally carrots, without doing anything to make them appear. Perfect.

Then there was the main event, the Song Contest on the raised area at the Obelisk and one of the few occasions the tribe could be described as something approaching energetic. The important men of the tribe would take it in turns to roar their lyrics as many times as they could manage before passing out. He could hear them in his memories; Deaf Tiger's gritty number 'I Want To Shout All Day', 'The Ballad of Boardom' by The Trolling Stones and last year's winner, the touching love song from Log Jam and the Splinters, 'You Make Me Want To Eat Turnips'. None had more than twelve unique words. He pictured the crowd, bouncing up and down like a drunken pancake, and the circle of women around them, sitting dutifully next to the food. As each song finished the men would march over and take whatever they wanted. It was like watching a termite army finding a forest in the desert. The choice was limited, usually mushrooms, fruit and a small selection of dried meat. Meat was a rarity and was often left for weeks beforehand on the drying stones at Moss' storage cave before it was selected for dinner.

Then came the drinking. Cobble had never understood its appeal. He had tried a few times growing up but always ended the night with an emptier stomach than he started with. The older men, and some of the more dominant younger ones, seemed able to drink large quantities without any change to their input/output ratio. The longer the drinking went on the more they sang and danced, with a rapid descent towards shouting and staggering.

While all this went on, the women of the tribe sat in the filthy mud of the Meeting Patch distributing the food, and later the drink, from their places in the circle. Cobble wondered how they did it. The aches and pains from the day would trouble them for weeks afterwards and they got nothing in return. Time for that to change, he decided.

He settled on a bench, so to speak. He knew if he only made something for the women then he may as well not return at all so he would make one long bench for some of the older men to rest on during the more active segments of the festival. This would buy him some grace to give each of the ten women a small stool to lift them from the dirt. Little victories could start a revolution, he dreamt pointlessly.

He dried his face with a hairy arm and looked at his offerings proudly. Now to get them back to the Meeting Patch, he thought. He picked up one end of the heavy bench, dragged it across the pine needles and out into the open grassland. It was some time before he walked through the crowd of men, red-faced and glistening. He waited for praise but expected none as he left the bench at the edge of the circle.

Before beginning his trek back to the forest he stopped at his cave and stored away his tools. He wondered what the women would say when he brought the stools to them. He knew they would show more gratitude than the men, but that was like saying eagles had a better understanding of the solar system than jellyfish because they were closer to the stars. He preferred the women, and while they could never be accused of being friends of his, Moss and Plum at least showed an occasional interest in his wellbeing, if not his inventions. He hoped one of them would say something. Anything.

Cave Mountain spoke with its signature rumble as he made his way back to the forest. It was a much easier walk without the bench and he reached his clearing quickly, but came to a sharp stop as he took in the view. There was a distinctly unstool-like quality to it. His mind raced. Someone had taken them. They were too heavy to have been dragged by any small woodland creature and too awkward for anything bigger. They could only have been taken by something with a thumb. He sat on the floor and stared at the emptiness.

He had become accustomed to being ignored and was well equipped to cope with it. He had always found it easier to deal with the absence of emotion rather than the existence of it. This was new territory altogether and he wasn't sure he knew how to react. Why would they steal them? He wasn't even sure that anyone knew what he had been doing, so they must have been watching him. It worried him to think that his place in the tribe had now sunk to the level of the bullied.

He fell back on a familiar mantra. If they knock you down three times, then stand up four.

The biggest problem was that almost anyone could have been involved, how would he know who to avoid? How could he find them and retrieve what was his? Come to think of it, even if he did find them he had no idea what he would do then. Confront them? Reason with them? Both pointless. This was it then, he would have to take it on the chin and go home empty handed. Two weeks' work just to give some ancient buffoons a place to rest for a few hours.

He felt utterly lost. He didn't know what to do next. Not in terms of revenge, or what he would do to get the stools back, he simply didn't know what to do right in this moment. Should he stay here, go home, walk, sleep, whittle? The emptiness filled the hole that created it and consumed him. He decided to look for them. Perhaps they were pushed along by some playful animals. He knew that was impossible but he ran with it, scouring the surrounding area for any sign of his futile labour.

Nothing.

He slumped down on a muddy slope and stared into the undergrowth, thinking. Perhaps Bones could help. He was the one person in all of Boardom that he could call a friend. He was like a brother to Cobble but without all that 'I can throw this rock further than you' sibling nonsense he had to endure with Chip. He was a tall, gangly collection of limbs entirely unlike every other member of the tribe. He could have been dropped from the sky for all the likeness he had to anyone else. Cobble often thought that this was the reason they were such good friends. They each made up the entirety of their social circle; it was more of a social colon. They liked it that way though, as any outsider with the smallest pebble of imagination would.

Bones was a willing student. He wasn't bad at creativity, but he wasn't that good either. His skills lay elsewhere and he was often Cobble's shadow as they wandered the terrain, searching for the missing pieces in Cobble's latest creation; a rabbit's leg bone, a half-moon stone or a waxy leaf. Over the moons together they each developed a role of sorts; Cobble leading the way with his inventions and hypothetical musings, and Bones playing the support role, usually foraging for the items on Cobble's lists. He had quietly honed his skills until he was as adept at them as Cobble was at original thought. If you said you wanted a speckled egg from a starling's nest, Bones would have it found, delivered and scrambled before you noticed he was no longer listening.

They had developed a friendship from the outset. Bones had appeared suddenly one morning many years ago. He was still a baby then, but Cobble had been an inquisitive toddler and would play with him when no-one else would. As they grew up together they became inseparable and were the scourge of Moss and her apple stores, among many other things. In all those years Cobble never considered how different Bones looked compared to the rest of the tribe. He was so familiar to him that he may as well have been asked how two mountains differed. They were both pointy and made of rock, anything else was irrelevant. Had he given it some thought he might have said he looked thinner, even at that age, and his nose wasn't quite as flat as those of the rest of the tribe. Cobble was too young to understand that this was odd, it was just a boy to play with. He would join in with his games of Stick-Stack, and was the only one who would play 'Hunter Gatherer' with him. Playing it on his own passed time, in a neutral sort of way, but playing it with a friend made it positively enjoyable. There was never any awkwardness to it, as there often is with adults. Children only see the time immediately in front of them, and are all the more contented for it.

Soon enough they were the only stakeholders in each other's

time.

Cobble set off to find him.

'Bones! Someone has taken the stools and I need your help to find them,' he said, bypassing any polite preamble. 'Now!'

'Right-o!'

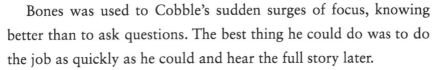

Bones was used to Cobble's sudden surges of focus, knowing better than to ask questions. The best thing he could do was to do the job as quickly as he could and hear the full story later.

They arrived at the clearing and split up. Cobble searched new ground, kicking leaves and half-heartedly peering round trees. His mind was elsewhere as he considered why someone would do this to him. He never crossed anyone in the tribe, it wasn't in his make-up. There weren't any trouble makers either per se, although he had experienced plenty of snide comments and cold shoulders recently. You could chill a bowl of apple juice on his back if you could find a way to balance it. Maybe nobody from the tribe was involved; perhaps there were other people in the area after all.

No-one living in Boardom had ever met another Neanderthal and it was widely assumed that they were the only ones in the universe, although the universe itself was not widely assumed. Cobble wasn't so sure. The problem, he thought, was there was no catalyst for a theoretical debate and so the status quo had become the boundary to their imagination. If there were others in the area then he might be able to join them. The thought gave him a jolt and made his mind race. The tribe had a saying; 'Better the rat you have than the deer you don't.' When it came to the tribe Cobble couldn't have disagreed more. Surely the unknown was better than this. He pushed the thought from his head, determined not to nurture a false hope, and went looking for Bones.

Bones was retracing Cobble's earlier search. If anyone was going to find a trace of the stools it was him. He had moved in zigzags up and down the forest, studying the ground at his feet and the branches at his head. That was his tried and trusted method and usually yielded results.

'Well?' enquired Cobble.

'Nothing, I'm afraid. If an animal had moved them, or if some-one had hidden them, I would have known but there's no sign of them here. They're either high up in a tree, which seems unlikely, or they've been taken away by someone.'

'So,' said Cobble pensively, 'either someone from Boardom has started playing games with us, or...'

He paused, wondering if this would sound crazier out loud than it did in his head.

'...or someone else took them.'

Bones was running after Cobble's train of thought but it was too fast for him.

'Someone else?'

'You know, from another tribe.'

'Are you having another one of your moments Cobble?' said Bones with experience.

'Maybe,' he replied. 'Maybe I am, but what if I'm not? Could you imagine that, Bones? Another tribe for us to join.' There was no stopping him now. 'They would surely be more advanced than this lot. They probably already have benches!'

A thought fluttered into his consciousness, put its slippers on and settled down for the night.

'Bones,' he said, the gravity dripping off his lowered voice.

Bones looked nervous. Oh cripes, where is this going.

'What if… What if they were so much more advanced than us that we would look like the half-witted fools?'

The very idea of it made him want to run in every direction until he found them.

'Do you think I'm crazy Bones?'

'Right now?' He considered his answer carefully. 'Slightly more than normal I would say.'

'Perhaps you're right Bones, perhaps you're right.'

He steadily brought himself back to reality. There was probably no-one else out there, he knew, but the dream was too sweet to ignore.

'Let's go home Bones, the festival will be starting and we deserve some of the food if not the company.'

As they approached the Meeting Patch it was easy for Cobble and Bones to see the festival was in full flow. There was the noise coming from the Song Contest at the Obelisk as Tark belted out his number for the year. There was also a scattering of half eaten food covering the ground, but mostly it was the smell. The earthy waft of meat and roasted nuts fought commendably against the powerful stench of the latrine. They headed to the women's circle, took a selection of meats and settled down near the tribal fire pit away from the crowds at the Obelisk.

Cobble had been quiet on the way home as the logical part of his brain parried back and forth with his imagination.

'There has to be another group out there,' said Imagination.

'No chance, we would have seen signs of them before,' Logic argued.

'Not if they were so clever they could stay hidden when they wanted to be.'

'If they wanted to stay hidden they wouldn't have taken our stools.'

'They would if they had decided to show their hand.'

'But why would they be so subtle? They could just walk up to us and say hello.'

'Not if they were assessing the threat we pose. They would want to know how we would react if they showed themselves.'

'But they would watch us closely before they did anything,' countered Logic.

'Maybe they have been,' offered Imagination.

'Maybe they have,' conceded Logic.

Cobble opened his mouth to paraphrase this to Bones. It stayed open. Bones had been pointing at the fire, he realised. As he turned his gaze he felt his stomach sink. Poking out of the fire was a half-charred leg of a stool. His stool. There was no doubt that someone from Boardom had taken them and used them as firewood. So maybe this was it; no people in the area waiting to swoop him away to a better life, no great adventure into the unknown. He was trapped, destined to live out his days in the stifling stagnation of Boardom.

Maybe he could leave, said the small part of his brain that looked after gambling matters. He could just walk out across the Great Grey Plain and, well, see what happens. It was the embryo of an idea, albeit an appreciably flawed one.

'I need some space to think,' said Cobble, 'I don't know whether to fight for my place here or disappear into the wilderness. I'm not sure I'll ever know.'

With that he was gone, leaving the rabble to their shouting and Bones to his thoughts.

CHAPTER TWO

THE GOLDEN SOLUTION

The Sun had finally risen, slowly but inevitably, like an almost-too-heavy balloon. Two moons had passed since the Rock Festival and Cobble had been working through the night in Green Forest, allowing the full moon to light his tools as he whittled branches into a host of similar shapes. This was more impressive than it sounds. Green Forest was hated by the men of the tribe, full of creatures that seemed allergic to eating meat. Insects bit and squirrels scratched mercilessly at anyone who met them. They had no fear of men and no reason to. The men could no more capture them than lasso the moon. Cobble, though, was content to swap the irritations of the tribesmen for those of the creatures of the forest.

This time he had cracked it, he was sure. Not like the last time he cracked it, or the time before that. This time was different. This time they would listen. This time they would be convinced. If they didn't see its benefit he would leave, he had decided. He would try to persuade Bones to come with him – that would be better, but he would go either way.

He adjusted his boar skin knapsack on his shoulder, by far his most precious possession. More valuable than the tools they carried. Tools can be made with time and effort, but catching a boar was a different kettle of turnips altogether. The absence of any hunting talent in the tribe meant that animal skins were often handed down from generation to generation, providing warm clothing and occasionally a silly hat. If a man died, his son would inherit his clothes. Fashion was a concept that would have been very difficult to explain to the men.

It was the only kind gesture he had ever received from his father that was of any consequence. It was probably a mistake, he thought begrudgingly, as he headed deeper into the forest to where there was a more diverse choice of wood. The dew on the ground was beginning to find its way through his thin tree bark shoes and onto his feet. The realisation that change was coming for him, whatever form it took, made the heavy tools travel a little lighter on his shoulder.

As he walked he let his mind wander, a habit formed long ago and one that greased the wheels of his inventive disposition. It landed on the short-comings of his tribesfolk again, as it often did. They were seasoned veterans in many things, mostly concerning shouting and scratching, sleeping and eating, and drawing on the cave walls. He realised this might be an exhaustive list. It made him shudder. He also wondered what future generations would think if any member of the tribe possessed even a drop of artistic ability. Where the tribe really struggled, he mused, was in areas like hunting, cooking, surviving. Meat was a rare thing since the tribesfolk had neither the talent nor disposition to hunt. Mushrooms, fruit and nuts were the staple diet, foraged by the women folk and orchestrated by Moss and her daughters; Fern, Leaf and Fern – their father had run out of ideas by the time she got to her third daughter – and she was the closest thing the tribe had to a chief cook. There was occasionally a small flock of sheep who were happy to graze in the area during the warmer months and they provided the tribe with the wool they used for bedding. There was a single goat too, Gowie, who gave the tribe their only source of milk. Any meat came from animals who chose to expire within sight of the Meeting Patch. Some men still ate it raw, although their numbers were dwindling.

This was where he should focus his enterprise, he had decided. If he could help to provide the tribe with more animals for meat and clothing then he would surely win the respect of the tribe at last.

His train of thought took another turn.

It had all changed on the night his father and only brother took their drunken one way stagger into the latrine pit. It was the day the tribe's obligations to Cobble ended. Block's deeds were fading into the mists of time, mangled by hyperbole and understatement at the fire pits. His brother Chip had always been the more popular of Block's sons. He was taller, less ugly and, crucially, better at shouting than Cobble. Their fall was dozens of moons ago now and the tribe no longer had to feign interest and awe at his inventions. Gone were the gasps and gesticulations. Gone were the visits to see the latest creation of Cobble the Stout. Gone too was the flattering name, he was now Cobble the Small. Or Wobble, Hobble or any other –obble that came to mind. The pettiness rankled with him more than anything else, perhaps more than the death of his father and brother. There are stages of grief, a way to cope and move on. There are no stages of irritation – it is indelible, a part of your personality. If it irritates you once it will most likely irritate you forever.

He could never have said to have been close to his father, he wasn't good enough at shouting for that. He assumed his father held some version of affection for him, but it seemed to Cobble it would have been a dutiful reaction rather than the easy, natural warmth Block had for Chip.

Cobble walked on through the forest looking for Bones as his thoughts ambled back to his inventions. On one occasion he had designed a sort of knife with three small prongs attached to one end. He showed it to Rankor, the tribe's current leader, explaining that it would help to spear the hot meat in the fire pit, allowing the user to pick up the meat while it was still warm and tender. It had reminded him of a nearby path that split into three at the large oak tree near Stony Bridge. He decided to call it a 'fork'.

'What's wrong with pouring water over the fire, Bobble?' Rankor had said.

He gave up.

Rumble...

It was two days ago now when the most important idea of his life had presented itself for appraisal in his mind. He had been sheltering from a storm under a rocky overhang with Bones as his mind went back and forth between problem and potential solution.

They love to eat meat but getting meat takes effort. Problem.

They are astoundingly lazy. Problem.

They have few tools to catch anything anyway. Problem.

They need a tool to help them hunt. Solution.

They won't hunt because they are lazy. Problem.

They need a tool that requires little effort to use. Solution.

They still won't leave the Meeting Patch anyway. Problem.

They need a tool that requires little effort to use and doesn't require them to leave the Meeting Patch. Solution.

It had taken some time, but the Brownian motion of his synapses had eventually arrived at a gateway to the solution. He had no definitive idea of what it could be, but it was a start. He would create a tool that would help the tribe get more meat without having to muster too much actual effort. Then they would appreciate...

'Ooooow!'

Cobble turned to Bones who was rubbing his leg energetically.

'Ooooowooow!'

A branch had torn away from a tree, landing point first on Bones' thinly padded leg. His limbs were like deerskin stretched over a boulder and gave him no protection from the bumps and scrapes that others wouldn't even notice. A small red patch formed just below his angular knee.

Cobble leapt to his feet. 'Fantastic!'

'Ow! Ow! Ow!' hopped Bones. 'Wait, what? A little sympathy here Cobble! Look at my leg, it's bloody sore! It's bloody and sore!'

'No, no it's not that... it's... yes. Yes! That's it Bones, you wonderfully pointy man!'

'Erm....'

'Exactly!'

'Cobble? You've gone a funny shade of red.'

'Bones,' said Cobble, ignoring the observation and in a suddenly confident and serious tone, 'I have the answer!'

While Cobble spent the cool night whittling, Bones had wandered the forest looking for dung. It wasn't his first choice when it came to passing time in the night but he understood the importance of it. Dung was the key, the bigger the better. Finding dung meant finding an animal, finding an animal meant finding prey, and finding prey meant they could test Cobble's grand plan.

Looking for stools again, he thought, drolly. In any enterprise worth the effort there is always someone in charge of the dung. It usually concerned ways to remove it without anyone noticing, but every so often it required them to collect it.

It was in a clearing not more than a thousand paces from the Meeting Patch. A great steaming mound that would have turned Bones' stomach had it the room to move in his taut frame. Boar dung. If he was prone to lyrical waxing he would have thought about the circle of life, the parallels between Cobble and his father, the symbolic resonance of the boar. He wasn't, however, so he didn't. Instead he simply pointed.

'Poo! Cobble! Poo!'

There was a second gift his father gave him, Cobble realised, this one given involuntarily from the grave. He had struggled to find anything that could be used as string. Plant stalks were too fragile, branches were too sturdy. What he needed was something in the sweet spot between the two. His mind was hinting at something he had seen before, something perfect. He let it drift over his memories.

For once Cobble was glad his father was the boasting type. Whenever the famous story of the boar slaying was retold you could be sure Block would add in some new detail, doubtless conjured from the lonely part of his brain that was home to his imagination. He remembered his father said he tied up the beast with waxy branches from a tree that grew long, four fingered leaves. Cobble hoped that part, at least, was true.

He set his bag down and scouted around, finding one about twenty paces from where he worked. He peeled away the bark, revealing the shiny yellow wood inside. He ran back to his work station and took out his flint. He split the branch, split it again and again and again until he had a small pile of flexible strings that no longer resembled wood as he would describe it. Progress, he thought.

He had tried the boughs of a dozen different trees to find just the right kind of wood for the arm of his new hunting tool. Some were too rigid, some were too flimsy. He needed a strong but supple wood that would bend but never break. None of those he tested had worked. He was close to giving up, sure that the perfect wood didn't exist. He knew if he could find the right wood he could make it. He steeled himself, knowing that if it was easy to do then some-one else would have done it before him. Or would they? The tribe had been lazy for so long it was almost genetic. If it wasn't for Rockball and the Rock Festival they may not have moved at all. He leant against a large oak tree, perfectly still other than the tapping of his index finger against the rugged bark. It always twitched when he was concentrating, not that he had ever noticed. It came from some dark, unseen part of his nervous system and seemed to bypass his consciousness completely.

Tap tap tap. Tap tap tap.

He went through every piece of wood in his mind again. The oak was too strong, the elm was too supple. None of them seemed to have that perfect characteristic he was looking for. He had to find a strong wood that wasn't strong. Impossible. He slumped down a little further into the earth and watched a line of ants crawl down the trunk at his shoulder. They were industrious little creatures, he mused. Always working, always doing, always solving. They carried small leaves down to the floor and across the clearing to their home somewhere in the undergrowth. There was a kink in the line of black dots and he bent over for a closer look. He was curious in the same way a river was wet. It was a part of him he couldn't switch off. Usually it was for a reason but this time it was idle. To Cobble, idle curiosity was the enemy of regression. His tribe wouldn't even understand that, he realised – the irritating ra…

Something stopped his thoughts in their tracks. It was a pale yellowy-orange colour, shiny and very sticky as an unsuspecting ant had quickly discovered, much to its chagrin.

Wilfred was a small ant. Not small like an ant, but small for an ant. He was never drafted into the Working Party, and was very pleased about this. The heavy lifting that the workers suffered day after day was not in his career plan. He was more interested in the world around him; the soil, the sun, the moon. Existence, feelings, curiosity. He was a dreamer.

As with all young ants of a certain age he had to take the Leafing Certificate, a series of physical and mental examinations that would determine the course of the rest of his life. For the physical element, each ant carried a large branch from a fern leaf through the undulating tunnels of the nest. The fastest and strongest were placed in the Worker Party, spending their lives as cogs in the train, moving greenery from Point A to Point B for the good of The Colony. The slowest and weakest were sent to the mental test zones. Here they directed a line of trainee Working Party ants around a series of obstacles, all designed to encourage a problem solving approach and lateral thinking. Wilfred was only moderately better at this than the physical tests. He was dumped into the steering committee, the least skilled of the Colony's careers. His job was to scout ahead of the train and identify hazards to be avoided. He carried a small section of a red acer leaf to warn the oncoming train of the danger. Wilfred loved his job, it allowed his mind to wander, floating from broad existential monologues to the value of dung, and most points in between. I am more than just an ant, he thought to himself. I can make a difference. I can make The Colony happier with stories of heroes, with song and with dance. I can be more than this. I can… I can… I can't move my left legs…

Bugger.

Something was forming in Cobble's mind as he squashed the stricken ant in his calloused fingers. If he couldn't find the right wood, perhaps he could find the right woods. He looked up at the trunk of the tree towards the fat branches. Blobs of the orangey goo were dotted around it. Jumping to his feet, he pressed his finger into the golden solution. The Golden Solution. He ran from tree to tree. More! This is it! Time may have stood still, it was irrelevant. Time no longer mattered to him; whittling took over Cobble the way water takes over a drowning man.

He stood up and studied his work.

He used the bough of an elm tree to make an arc of supple wood, light and malleable, and used the golden liquid to stick it to a smaller arc from a bough of hard oak. He then tied one of his strings to each end – he would have to get Bones to make a better knot, he thought. He grabbed a twig from the floor. It was a little too misshapen but Cobble had no patience left. He had waited his whole life for this moment. This was what he was supposed to create. This was his. His own. It was his Golden Solution.

He held up the wooden bough with his left hand and put the twig in his right. He pulled back the string, held his breath, and...

'Poo!'

'Poo! Cobble! Poo!'

CHAPTER THREE

BOWING TO PRESSURE

The twig fell from the bough, bouncing off Cobble's shoulder and onto the floor.

'Cobble! I've found some, over here, a great pile of it.'

'That's great Bones, just great. Now if you could kindly step off my foot.'

He picked up the twig and studied it.

'What's wrong with this twig Bones?'

Bones took the shift in conversation in his stride. 'Well it seems to be doing a pretty good job of being a twig. There's nothing particularly untwiggy about it. Should it be doing something else?'

Cobble closed his eyes for an impatient moment. Bones wasn't naturally inquisitive, but he tried. He really tried. That was enough for Cobble. He was otherwise surrounded by people who tried really quite hard to avoid trying at all. It was an art that the tribesfolk had mastered as effectively as rain had mastered falling.

'It's a very twiggy twig Bones, I'll give you that. Remember how we spoke about lateral thinking? Connecting the dots? Focusing on the steps between a problem and a solution and solving them as small individual puzzles?'

'Right, right,' Bones conceded. 'So the twig shouldn't... be a twig?' There was a contortion of effort in his eyebrows.

'Correct! So, what should it be?'

Bones fidgeted with his only possession that wasn't clothing; a stone pendant on a leather necklace. There was a triangular shape scratched into it with a zigzag cutting off one corner and stripes scratched along it. He had always had it and had no knowledge of where it had come from. All he knew was that rubbing it helped him to concentrate.

He stroked it as he went through the steps in his head. We have the wooden bough, we have the string. We need something to travel from the bough to the thing we want to eat.

He still didn't understand how this could help. If you have something in your hand and you send it over to the animal you're chasing, all you have achieved is to give them the thing. Unless you had a lot of the things, all in a row at your feet so you could fire them off efficiently. Now he was thinking like Cobble. You could keep hurling them at the animal until they got stuck in a big pile of them. Then you could go and hit it over the head with a rock. It seemed an odd way to do it, but then none of Cobble's ideas made much sense to him. This felt like original thought and he ran with it.

'Well we would need to have a big row of them...'

'A row?'

'A row. To throw at the animal. Of the twigs.' His confidence evaporated, he was never any good at putting his thoughts in order. He preferred action.

He tried again.

'You would need a row of twigs, not just one, to trap the animal in the pile. Of twigs. That you've fired over to it. So you can hit it with a rock.'

'Thanks for trying Bones. You're thinking outside the cave, and that's a start.'

Cobble passed the twig from hand to hand.

'There are three problems that require a solution Bones. Connect the dots. One; it's too light. It would snap at the slightest strain. Two; it isn't straight. It wouldn't fly true. Three; the tip is blunt. It wouldn't hurt a mouse. So what do we do now?'

'We...' He looked like a wolf trying to fit into a badger skin. '... we... we need a heavier twig?'

'Yes... and...' said Cobble. He was doing so well.

'...and it needs to be straight.'

'Yes!'

'What was the third one again?'

Cobble decided Bones had done enough thinking for today. He sent him off into the Green Forest with a list; small straight branches from a hazel tree, thin and waxy branches from an elm, and as many triangular stones as he could find. They would get more stones near the caves, but he only needed a few for now.

Bones poured his items onto the floor. He had done well, enough to make a dozen... a dozen what? If he was to win the tribe over they would need a name. The tribe may not have been good at naming things but it didn't stop them from doing it. Names gave something an identity and an identity means worth. He looked at the pile of branches on the ground. The row of branches.

A row. Arrow. That was it.

His bough and his arrow.

The spring sun was shining high above the trees and neither of them had slept, so Cobble had told Bones to go home and get some rest. He was settled on the forest floor with his chisel and hammer. This was when he felt most content, alone with his tools and a project.

He started with the hazel branches, chipping off the knobbles with his flint and smoothing the shafts. He grazed a rough stone up and down the lengths, making them as uniform as he could. He dipped them in tree sap and stabbed them, dry end first, into the ground. Next he worked on the stones. He found the deepest side of each and worked the opposite corner into as sharp a point as he could manage. Picking up a small granite cylinder from his bag he ground out a depression into the fat end of the stones. He placed each one, divot first, onto the sap soaked end of the sticks, pushing down as hard as he could to allow the two materials to bond. He tied the thin strips of elm in an 'X' shape around the stone and the branch to secure them further, using one of Bones' more complex knots at the bottom and trimming the excess with his flint.

He had managed to make eleven arrows in all. It was hard work, but worth it. He picked a spot near to where Bones had found the pile of dung and tried to steady himself. His hands were shaking as he picked up his bough. He was never nervous, there was never anything to be nervous about, and it was new territory for him. This had to work. He looked at the arrows. Some were better than others and he chose an average one for the inaugural shot. He didn't want to waste a good one, nor be disheartened if one of his poorer efforts failed to work. He put the wooden end of the arrow into the middle of the elm string with his right hand and directed the stone tipped end to the middle of the bough, gripping it lightly with his fingers. It felt natural.

Even as he was in this most anticipated of moments he was evaluating.

I should chisel a small channel into the end so it will sit more steadily in the string, he thought. He pulled back the string, looked down the hazel shaft and waited for his prey... and waited.

Impatience got the better of him and he moved his aim to a tree about five paces to his left. He gave himself one last moment. It felt as though his life would be split into time that had already passed and the time after he fired this first shot, like a young robin preparing to defy all reason and jump out of its nest. He savoured it, then let go.

Thud!

The arrow sunk into the fattest part of the trunk, slightly off from his aim but that didn't matter. It had worked! He was frozen to the ground for a moment, staring.

It surprised him to discover he was now sprinting towards the tree to investigate the result, flailing his arms as he tried to stop himself. He hit the hard wood with a dull thump and fell to the floor.

He took a moment to stare at the forest roof straight ahead of him and go over the last few seconds. He stood up gingerly. There was a dark patch on the rough bark and Cobble realised it was blood. He raised his hand to his forehead, rubbed his finger and thumb together and looked at the red smear. The shards of bark had ripped a small tear just above his left eye and he grimaced at the pain that started to throb in his head.

He looked around for the familiar pale green leaves that helped him with his self-inflicted cuts. Injuries were a constant in his experimental life and he had learned that these leaves eased the pain a little. He picked a few, crushed them in his hands and pressed them against his forehead, adding more to his bag for later.

Time to head home and rest, he decided, pulling the sunken shaft from the tree and gathering up his tools and arrows. It was almost time to convince.

The pale sun was falling when Cobble woke. He rubbed his eyes and ruffled his hair, liberating the sleepy fog from his mind. He crawled to the mouth of his cave and looked out at the Meeting Patch. The men were lazing in the late sun despite the gentle patter of light rain and there were few signs of activity up and down the openings that lined the last few hundred paces of the Long Mountains. Gowie the goat was tied to his post, munching on a stubborn patch of grass and Moss was working at a pile of fruit in her cave nearby, no doubt preparing the evening meal for the slumbering men. He walked over to her.

'Evening, Moss!'

While Cobble could never claim to have any allies in the group besides Bones, Moss was at least a pleasant sort and would listen to him on the few occasions he felt like a conversation.

'Cobble, my young man, 'ow are you today? Still building your strange contraptions?'

'I am Moss, I am. This time I think you'll be impressed.'

'Oh good, yes, I'm sure I will,' she said supportively. 'Do me a favour, would you, and pass me a flint there?' She waved an arm towards the back of her cave without looking up from her work.

He walked over to the pile of flints Moss kept in one corner, looking again at the drawings on the wall. Most of them were crude and ill-defined scratchings but there was one relatively detailed picture of men dancing merrily with Cave Mountain in the background. It clearly depicted a celebration of some kind, although the clues were scant. Cobble always wondered if it was a Rock Festival, since the mountain seemed to be singing with them, or maybe it was to rejoice in the birth of a new tribe member. Each time he saw it he considered again that their ancestors must have been happier than them. He picked up a new flint and walked back to Moss.

'It will help you more than anyone else,' he said

For the first time Moss looked at Cobble with genuine interest.

'Really? 'ow's that?'

'I've found a way to put meat on the fires, so less foraging for you and your girls.'

Moss' expression changed back to familiar disinterest. Another pipe dream, she realised, the poor thing.

'Good for you Cobble, I'm sure the tribe will be fascinated,' she lied.

Moss knew Cobble was wasted here. He had a mind as sharp as slate and the best thing he could do was to get away from the tribe and find a place where his talents would be appreciated, if there was such a place. It had been so long since any of the tribesfolk had ventured over the horizon that she wasn't sure if 'Somewhere Else' even existed. She turned back to her fruit. Best not to worry herself with it, she decided.

'They will be Moss, they will be.'

He wasn't sure if he had said it with genuine confidence, or whether he was just trying to convince himself.

'I'm putting it to the tribe tonight, will you come and support me? I suspect I'll need it.'

Constant rejection turns engineers into salesmen and Cobble was becoming a master of the art. He would put on a show.

Moss hesitated. She wanted to help him, he deserved it, but actually going to the Obelisk and speaking up for him to the group? That counted as more than politeness and she wasn't sure she should do it.

'We'll see.'

Cobble knew that was a no.

'Have you seen Bones?' he said, letting her off the hook.

'Not since yesterday.'

'Thanks.'

He turned and headed for Bones' cave. When he got there he found his friend bundled into a corner, keeping dry and away from the cool breeze. Snores echoed around the stony walls before being abruptly replaced by a grunt.

'Whuh,' mumbled Bones, focusing his sleepy eyes on the offending foot.

'No need to kick me Cobble, you wouldn't have just nudged my shoulder, no?'

'Less of the grumpiness Bones, we have a lot of work to do.'

'You remember we worked through the night, right? What are you planning now?'

'We're putting on a show!'

Rumble...

He watched as Bones moved out of sight in the crumpled folds at the foot of Cave Mountain. He had given him clear instructions. Very clear. Essential. If Bones missed one step it would all have been for nothing. There was no-one he trusted more though, no-one else was even slightly invested in him for a start, but Bones had proved himself, both as a friend and a reliable assistant of sorts. He steeled himself, spun on his heels and headed to the Meeting Patch.

For moons beyond memory the Obelisk had been the place where important decisions were made. Any decision that affected the whole tribe had to be passed here. It was here that the name Boardom was born after Block's heroics. It was here, too, where the temporary ban on Rockball was enacted after it caused a dramatic fall in the number of tribesfolk with unbroken skulls.

The men of the tribe were as stubborn as they were traditional. Change was dangerous. 'Ask a dead butterfly' they would say. The status quo, on the other hand, meant sleeping the warm afternoons away, having their meals prepared for them and enjoying an occasional shouting contest to keep them ticking over. If anyone wanted to threaten this then the tribe made damn sure it was worth it. A Voting Council would be called and the idea would be put to the group. Nobody enjoyed them so they never lasted long. Short, simple pitches were the order of the day and anyone prone to rambling or tangential monologues were cut short and their proposal wouldn't even make it to the vote.

The idea of a voting system was an unlikely anomaly in Boardom. Eldrick the Confused had proposed that the tribe introduce one shortly after the Stony Bridge Massacre, long before any of the current lot was alive. Half of the tribe wanted to put large stepping stones over the river to allow the collection of food from a wider variety of lands, while the other half wanted to keep the natural barrier to better protect the tribe from unseen predators. What started as a tetchy discussion quickly descended into all out violence and by the end more than twenty men had been killed. The next day, Eldrick had bravely tried to explain how voting could prevent such battles, and offered his proposal as the first time it could be used. He reasoned that in future they could vote on whether the bridge should be built, with those in favour placing white stones in a line and those against using black ones. They could test it by voting on whether they should introduce the voting system.

Fortunately for Eldrick the Confused, the tribe had no concept of this self fulfilling prophecy, nor patience for these matters. One of the brighter sparks asked him how they could end the discussion.

'By voting on it,' Eldrick had said.

'And what colour stone do we need to put in to get this to end?' They replied.

'White.'

'Great. Torgad, go and get some white stones,' they had said, and so the Boardom Voting Council was born.

Cobble knew that the tribe would want to vote on his idea. The real problem was in getting that far. Pitches were not a frequent event, you needed motivation for action and that was always in short supply. More often than not proposals would fall at the first hurdle, with too long a speech causing the gathering to gradually retreat to the familiarity of their caves and fire pits. When Angor the Stupid tried to get around this by supplying fermented blackberry juice to the crowd to keep them interested in his request to reduce the number of official rock fights to one per moon, all he achieved was to add one big one to that moon's total.

Cobble had to give them no choice but to pick up the white stones. Words were his enemy, he knew, so he would keep those to a minimum. What he needed was action. He needed to show them how his bough and arrow worked, then they would be convinced.

He had spoken to Rankor and called for a Voting Council. Rankor's broad shoulders had sagged at the suggestion. It was all too much effort, he thought. Why not leave things be? Still, Cobble seemed to have been on the verge of requesting a council his entire life. Maybe this would be worth it. No, probably not he decided. Still, he acquiesced and had gathered the reluctant tribe to the Obelisk.

'Fellow Tribesfolk,' Rankor began. 'Cobble the Small 'ere has requested a meeting of the Voting Council.'

The crowd let out a small, collective sigh. Cobble glanced anxiously at the spot where Bones should have been.

'Please give him your full attention,' he said. 'This could be anything,' he added quietly.

There was grumbling. Boardom's residents were good at grumbling.

Cobble took Rankor's place in front of the Obelisk. He felt the convergence of so many strands of his life knotting in his stomach. Where is Bones? He lifted his chin and took in the gathering in front of him. Anyone looking at the crowd would have struggled to say where Cobble was. They were in small groups, talking amongst themselves and paying no attention to the biggest moment of his life.

He took a deep breath and roared as loud as he could.

'FRIENDS! I HAVE GREAT NEWS!'

That hooked some of them.

'News? Oooooh' some said.

'Friends? Since when is he my friend?' said Plank, one of the more antagonistic youngsters among them.

Most of them didn't notice.

'YOU WILL BE WARM AT NIGHT AND IN THE WINTERS, AND EAT MEAT EVERY DAY WITHOUT NEEDING TO LEAVE THE TRIBELAND!'

That got the stragglers. The salesman. He lowered his voice and raised his arms.

'I have created a tool that will kill an animal at a hundred paces. I am asking for your vote today to authorise me to train a select group of hunters in how to use it so we can feast on meat every day and have warm clothes each winter.'

Repetition was his friend. If you wanted a Boardom man to believe you, all you had to do was shout it loud enough and often enough.

He reached around to the back of the Obelisk and picked up his bough and arrow, the best arrow he had. There was no need for him to bring two. If the first one didn't work it was over, he had to show them it was easy, even if it wasn't. He lifted them above his head so as many of the crowd as possible could see.

He raised his voice again.

'MY BOUGH AND ARROW!' he roared. 'I HAVE MADE HUNTING SIMPLE!' He didn't believe it himself yet so the tribe certainly shouldn't. This has to be perfect, he thought.

He turned to the rocky outcrop as Bones came into view, leading Gowie the Goat to the edge before leaping back into a small crevice.

Well done Bones, my man.

He raised his bough, fitted the arrow, and pulled back on the waxy string.

This was it.

He closed his eyes, then opened them slowly. Focused. He adjusted his aim slightly to account for the breeze then roared as he released his dreams to the sky.

'Bugger' thought Gowie, as he passed his familiar crags in the mountainside.

Thud.

He had done it! He couldn't have wished for it to have gone better. Surely even this crowd would be impressed.

But something felt wrong. Something felt missing.

Silence.

The rowdy tribe were quiet, entirely quiet. He was in trouble.

'He killed Gowie!' came a shout, breaking the spell.

'He killed Gowie!' said another. And another. Repetition really was the way to a Neanderthal's brain.

'How does that 'elp us? Now we ain't got no milk!'

Cobble hadn't thought of that. Perspective is both friend and enemy of the salesman, he thought. He had either underestimated them or overestimated them, it wasn't clear which. As the commotion threatened to spiral out of control Rankor called them to order.

'QUIET!' he shouted, hoping to bring proceedings to an abrupt end. There was slouching to be done, after all. 'All those who think Gobble should be allowed to complete the training use a white stone, all those against, use black. Granite, please get us started.'

Granite walked to the piles and picked up a white stone.

'I like meat more than milk,' he said, placing the first white stone onto the ground.

It was a sort of logic, Cobble thought. Maybe he could pass through the eye of the needle after all? It caught everyone by surprise, him most of all. Had he underestimated their capacity for reasoning too?

Plank was next. He chose a dark stone and mumbled something about pet killing as he placed it next to Granite's white one.

Young Tark walked up to Cobble and looked him straight in the eye.

'Interesting idea, Cobble,' he said, putting down a white stone.

Cobble wasn't sure what surprised him most; the use of his actual name, or that Tark thought his idea was interesting.

One by one they made their choices. It had boiled down to a choice between meat and milk, keeping it simple as always. Cobble was twitching again, his finger tapping his thigh as the piles grew. They were the same length as the last person to cast their vote stepped up. Moss. Could he count on her? It all came down to this and Cobble wondered if Moss really understood the importance of her vote. Of all the tribe she was the one who might vote for Cobble rather than for meat or milk. Surely this was it, surely he was over the line.

She voted black.

He felt the familiar sting of betrayal as she turned away, unable to look in his direction. Moss could never have been considered a loyal ally, but she was still the runner up to Bones. If she didn't believe in him then all was lost.

He had to leave.

CHAPTER FOUR

THE BONES OF A PLAN

Cobble looked around the plain, grey cave at his sparse belongings. He had to travel light, but prepared. He picked up his bough and arrows, chose a few of his more useful tools and placed them in his boarskin bag with his healing leaves. He looked around again. There was a small wooden flask with a complex interlocking lid that he had made one hot summer. It allowed him to work for long hours in Green Forest without having to trek to the river to quench his thirst. He added it to the tools. He looked at his bed, a thin pile of matted wool used by generations before him. He left it where it lay. The spring air was beginning to warm and he planned on finding a new home before the seasons turned cool again. So that was it, his life in a bag. Some tools and a flask. He would travel with potential on his shoulder and little else.

There was an adventure sitting dormant inside him, he was fairly sure, although the details had always seemed hidden behind a solid wall of latent opportunity. The debacle of the Voting Council had only scratched at the face of it, but the wall had crumbled like ashes in the wind.

He took one last look at the small, dark place that had been his home all his life. He waited for a pang of nostalgia, of childhood memories, scenes from the highlight reel of his life but they never came. He wouldn't miss it, he realised. He turned and headed for the bright opening of the cave without looking back.

Moss was where she always was, next to her pile of fruit at her cave. Without acknowledging her he marched towards the fruit and scooped up an armful of pears and apples. There was some dried meat lying on the airing rocks and he took a few strips. He knew she wouldn't stop him, she was clever enough to know what was happening. She owed him, and this was payback. His bag filled more quickly than he would have liked so he grabbed an apple in each hand, raised an arm to take a bite out of one, paused thoughtfully, and lowered it again. He didn't look at her as he left, instead focusing on the last piece of his rudimentary plan.

'Bones?' he called, into the mouth of the cave. 'Bones, I need to speak to you.'

'Cobble, how are you holding up? I'm sorry it didn't work out for you last night.'

'Us, Bones. It didn't work out for us.'

'Right.'

'I'm leaving.'

Bones' expression didn't change.

'I'm going now. Will you come with me Bones? You have always been my friend, and I think I'll need one.'

'Where are you going?'

'I don't know, Bones, but I know where I'm heading. Across the

Great Grey Plain. Nothing has come that way in living memory and I figure that's for one of two reasons; either because it's so vast and inhospitable that nothing can cross it alive, or because there is some place at the other side that is so comfortable, so advanced that there is no reason for anyone to ever leave. I'm betting on it being the latter, but anything is better than this place.'

'I'm tempted Cobble, but it's a big call. Why not stay here and show the tribe your bough and arrow in real action? If you gave them meat regularly they would come around to the idea. It won't be quick, but I'm sure it would work eventually.'

'I've had enough of eventually, Bones, my whole life has been spent waiting for delayed gratification but it never comes. It's time I took control of my own destiny.'

'You sound like Dongor the Strange, Cobble. Life isn't about destiny or star stories, it's about surviving, getting by.'

'No, it's about using your skills. It's about doing more of what you're good at and getting better at what you're not. I'm going Bones, and I want you to come with me, but I'm going either way. Will you come?'

This all sounded very serious to Bones. He wasn't one for deep, meaningful conversations. Simple priorities made for simple lives. Tradition was valued above all else and if you could rely on tradition you needn't use any energy working out your priorities. Boardom's inhabitants were the master builders of the path of least resistance.

'If you're asking me to join you now, right this minute, then I can't,' said Bones, trying his best to see the gravity of the conversation, 'I'm sorry. It's too much.'

'What can I say to persuade you?'

'Nothing. I'll miss you more than you think I will, but I can't just walk out of here, not without a guarantee that I'll live longer than a single moon.'

The best way to respond to a statement you can't counter is to reply to a different one.

'Just remember that life has breadth as well as length. I hope you find something to fill your days. For me, I'm leaving, and I expect this will be the last we see of each other. Good luck Bones, my man, and so long.'

With that he walked away from his only friend and began his new, and very possibly short, life.

The thick patch of apple trees gave way to open grassland as he crossed a small stone wall that marked the boundary of the village to the west. As he watched the new spring grass flailing in the light breeze he wondered why there was such a thing. No strangers were ever seen around here and he felt the boundary could have been marked anywhere without making the slightest difference to anything. Its very existence was a physical reminder of the illogical dynamics of the tribe. His departure was another one.

So this was it, he was finally leaving Boardom behind.

He was so consumed by frustration and the desire to leave that he hadn't taken time to consider what really lay ahead. It was uncharacteristic of him but now that the journey had begun he found the mental space to think about his immediate future. He had a long walk ahead of him, whichever course of action he chose. All his life his imagination had been a positive talent, now it was a curse. He had visions of strange beasts tearing at him as he pawed uselessly at their scaly skin. He pictured himself lying on the infinite grey floor dying of thirst, of hunger, of exhaustion. Maybe Bones was right, better to be suffocating but alive in Boardom than dying alone in a strange land.

No. This was it, all or nothing.

He pressed on.

When he left Boardom the sun was young and pale, but now it was high in the spring sky and he was getting hungry. His willpower hadn't been very willing at first. The hungry part of his brain had put forward that the two apples in his hand would be more easily carried in his belly. The logical part turned away, pretending to pick a piece of fluff from his shoulder. Now he pulled a pear from his bag and took a bite as he walked. There was no point in stopping while he ate, there was a long way to go and nothing else to do. His trail hugged the very base of the Long Mountains to his left, jutting to the right every now and again as the range stretched its toes into the plain. He wondered where he would sleep that night. He was used to spending the night away from the cave, but it was usually in Green Forest under a full moon until the orange glow of morning nudged him homeward. He was always surrounded by his tools on those nights and they could now double as a weapon, his imagination reminded him.

Keep walking.

His thoughts meandered to the tribe. He wondered when they would notice he was gone. Probably not for a few days, if any of them even noticed at all. This was the right decision, it was a gamble, but it was right.

Keep walking.

He found a sheltered spot beside the mountains and set himself for the first night away from his cave. The events of the last few days caught up with him and he fell into a deep sleep, only waking when the sun hit his eyes with a burst. He ate a strip of the meat for breakfast, gathered his things and stood up to start another day on the plain. His muscles argued for him to lie back down again but he ignored them and headed out.

He walked with no clear destination in mind, as he often did, enjoying the way it allowed his mind to dance around different ideas, filing them away for further investigation or dismissing them as unworkable. As a younger man he would analyse the tribe and their patterns but he had exhausted that avenue in no time. There simply wasn't enough depth to them for a mind as curious as his.

He was tired when he reached the narrow gap between two steep crags that he had chosen as his resting place for the second night. He looked around for obvious dangers but found none. He settled himself in a nook and took out a strip of dried meat. His will power had grown over the day; he had done well to ration his food and was pleased with himself. His bag was on his right, towards the open side of the crags. He picked it up and placed it between himself and the rock wall, ostensibly to help prevent a stranger from stealing it, should they stumble across him. He ate the meat quickly and fell asleep, almost without noticing.

Rumble... rumble...

There was a screeching noise coming from high above him, filling his dream and making his limp body flinch. The searing pain that followed was almost real. He woke with a start and bolted himself upright. A giant face filled his vision and he realised he was in trouble. He flailed helplessly, trying to avoid the sharp beak that lashed at his face. Tools, I need my tools, he thought. His bag was at his side and he lunged for it, beating off his feathery assailant with his right arm as he struggled to get a grip on something with his left. He fumbled in his bag but the raw violence of the bird made it impossible. It was like trying to hammer a chisel into wood and eat an apple at the same time, only more important. The vulture's clawing had left Cobble feeling like a rag in a storm and he realised with a dull shock that he was losing.

Two days, he thought, resignedly. Two bloody days. Bones was right, this was crazy. He still wasn't sure it was wrong, but it was definitely crazy.

The first two serious blows he felt came in quick succession. They were also the last. The first was a forceful peck at his skull and the second was his head bouncing off the rock behind him. He fell back onto the hard floor as the full moon closed its eye.

He was in a clearing in what might have been Green Forest, it didn't look like Green Forest but it felt like it. A butterfly landed on his nose and he crossed his eyes to focus on it.

'Hello there,' he said.

'Hi!' said the butterfly.

This seemed perfectly normal.

'Up to much?' asked Cobble.

'Oh you know, just the usual. Flying, sleeping, regretting change, thinking about the big questions in life, building bridges, pushing mountains, eating walls, climbing water, sneezing trees...'

The butterfly continued its peculiar chat. Seems like a nice chap, thought Cobble, as it disappeared into the air.

He watched a mammoth pass above him just below the canopy.

'Morning!' it called.

'Morning!' replied Cobble.

'Lovely day for a swim, don't you think?'

'Yes, yes it is, isn't it?'

Well this is just lovely. He looked down at his arm, which looked exactly like a squirrel.

'Nut?' asked his arm.

'Here you go,' said Cobble, handing him a hazelnut that had appeared in his unsquirrelled hand.

'Thank you,' said the squirrel as he turned back into an arm.

Blackness.

He stirred a little.

He felt a cool breeze on his face and enjoyed it. As he woke from his dream he sat up, or at least that was the plan. He managed to raise his shoulders an inch or so above the ground before a roaring pain shot across his upper body and sent him back to the floor.

Only then did he realise the attack was real. Perhaps not the flying mammoth, but the vulture?... That was excruciatingly real.

He opened his eyes again and took in his surroundings; tall grey walls of stone on either side of him and a blue sky above. That was it. No bag, no food, no tools, no flask. He was finished, maybe not right away but he knew he was done for. Without food and water he wouldn't last more than a couple of days in this barren wilderness. He thought he may lose consciousness with the pain before then in any case. That would be better, he decided morbidly. He lay back and passed out again.

He had no idea how much time had passed, but when he woke again all he knew was thirst. His throat was as dry as the plain and it took control of all his senses. Bones poured a little water from the flask onto his parched lips. Good old Bones, he thought. He could always rely on him, even in his hallucinations. He passed out again.

He had missed a full day when he finally woke from his deep stupor. The pain had eased in his chest and head. It was still strong, but it had definitely eased. He lifted himself onto his elbows and took a deep breath. Stone walls, blue sky, no bag. He had a vague memory of Bones giving him water but that was just one of many strange visions he had experienced. What he would have given to see Bones' head peering over the edge of the small, dry inlet. Just like that one, he thought. Bones had appeared again, climbing down the jagged face of the wall. This was bordering on cruelty, he thought.

'Cobble! You're awake?'

He sounded real, this was either a particularly vivid hallucination, or...

'Bones?'

'You're a lucky man. Well, apart from the grave wounds and all that.'

'Bones?'

'You need water.' He passed him the flask.

Cobble took a large gulp and spat it out energetically over Bones' face.

'Slowly Cobble, small sips. We can't waste it like that.'

'What are you doing here? How are...? When...?'

'Not now Cobble, I'll explain on the way.'

'On the way where?'

'I don't know. Wherever it is we're going.'

'We?'

Cobble tried to piece the conversation together. None of it made any sense. Stick to the basics, he thought. Bones didn't come with me, but he's here now. That'll do for a start.

'I'm going, kind of, erm, that way,' he said, pointing in a direction that was broadly the opposite way to Boardom.

'Right-o!' said Bones, 'you get yourself rested, I have to gather supplies if we're to make it to the other end of this place.' And with that he was gone.

Moss scraped the ashes from the fire pit absent-mindedly. This was her nineteenth Rock Festival; nineteen times she had helped to prepare the mountain of food, nineteen times she had sat in that circle as the men of the tribe stumbled around her, nineteen times she had helped clean up the mess. She had never really pondered what life would be like without her daily chores, mostly because she hadn't considered there might be a choice. That was the thing with Boardom, she thought, nobody ever made choices. There was an occasional Voting Council, but Cobble's had been the first for a long time and no doubt it would be a long time before they had a need to hold another.

Cobble. Bones.

She hoped they were OK. At first there had been the guilt, but each time it appeared it was beaten down by the knowledge that she had done the right thing. It would be hard for them at first, but if anyone could make it work it was Cobble. Even if there was no other settlement out there he could look after himself. His bough and arrow would keep them fed and his wits would keep them alive. Would they return if they were unable to sustain themselves? She wasn't sure. What she was sure about was that Cobble would make the right decisions for them when he needed to, again.

Occasionally she would feel a pang of jealousy. Whatever was happening to them was an adventure, be it for good or for ill, and her life was the very antithesis of adventure. Did she crave something more? Perhaps, she thought, but there was comfort in the routine she had, even if it was mundane and unrewarding. She had enough food, and the chores kept her busy. Was that enough, though? It didn't matter, it was her reality and no amount of wistful consideration could change it. Could anything change it?

She turned her attention back to the ashes and thought no more about it. Again.

CHAPTER FIVE

A DANCE IN THE DARK

Bones had done as good a job as he could with Cobble's recovery. Any cuts were fairly minor and Bones had looked after these with the leaves Cobble had in his bag. He knew from his mumblings that Cobble had only been knocked out. All he could do was to keep dripping water into his mouth to keep thirst at bay. Time would look after the rest.

Once Cobble was able to walk again they had set off, knowing that the sooner they got to the other side of the plain the better their survival chances.

Bones filled in the gaps as they walked along. He started at the beginning, his conversation with Moss the morning after Cobble's departure.

'She came to see me in my cave,' he began. 'She's a good woman, Cobble.'

'Is she, indeed? Whose side are you on Bones?'

'You know she's been the closest thing I have to a mother, she's been good to me all these years when no-one else bothered. She came to see if I was OK, she knew you had left.'

'Of course she did, she may as well have packed my bag for me!' said Cobble, impatience bubbling in his voice. 'She voted against me at the Voting Council.'

'No she didn't'

'You've been in the sun too long Bones, your memory is bending already'

'She didn't vote against you, she voted against your proposal.'

'Same thing Bones, same thing.'

'She voted for you, Cobble.'

'I'm not like the rest of the tribe, Bones, repeating the same thing doesn't make me believe it.'

I'm no good at this, thought Bones. He removed all subtlety from his speech.

'She voted black because she knew it would force you to leave. She knows you're better than Boardom. She helped you, Cobble.'

Cobble searched for the flaw in Bones' story. He searched again. It would better explain why she let him take so much of the food. Perhaps he was right.

'OK, but how did you find me? Why did you leave?'

'I figured if Moss was right about you then it might apply to me too. My skills are best used when I'm helping you with your plans, so I decided to follow you. I knew I was quicker than you, I can walk in straight lines for a start and I knew you'd be meandering along, lost in your thoughts. I didn't prepare for the journey as well as you did, so when I saw the vulture swooping down I thought I might steal some of his meal.'

'So what happened to the bird?'

'I hit it with a rock.'

'Ah.'

There's a time and a place for every approach, thought Cobble.

'I found your healing leaves and used them on your cuts. When

I ran out I went looking for more. It sounds like I picked the wrong ones though, judging by your talking squirrel.'

'Well I'm glad you came when you did Bones, seems I owe you one.'

'Two, actually. I had to carry your things each time I left the camp.'

'Two it is.'

They had been draining their resources together for three days now. Bones had tried to forage and they had been eating relatively well. Unfortunately it was relative to a starving dog and they were feeling the effects. Water was the biggest problem, the flask was long since empty and their only source was in the fruit that dried out all too quickly in the strong sun. The meat had only lasted two days and they were down to their last apple.

'We need to get out of here,' said Cobble.

Bones walked to the foot of the mountains and scampered up the incline. He had been able to see far down the plain while foraging up the mountain side on his first day and this time he was hoping to finally see the end of the vast land. He reached a flat section at about the height of ten men and looked out to the horizon. They had been travelling for so long that it surprised him to find nothing but flat, grey, parched earth right up to his extended horizon. He headed back down to where Cobble was waiting on the plain, choosing his footings more gingerly than on the way up. He picked a different route down, one with less sheer drops, and found he was far ahead of Cobble by the time his feet were flat on ground level. He turned to call over to him but something stopped him. There was a darkness in the mountainside that caught his eye. It wasn't the almost-black of shadow, it was more like an absolute black, as if the darkest part of the mountain's roots had popped up for a bit of fresh air. He crept closer. There was a natural entrance under a dark grey archway.

'Cobble!' he called. 'Here!'

Bones' attention was elsewhere as Cobble reached him. He swung his gaze slowly from Bones to the blackness and back to Bones. The expression on his friend's face was all he needed to see and knew instantly they had to go in there. They were out of options.

'Let's take a rest before we do anything Bones.'

'No.'

He didn't expect that.

'If we spend too much time thinking about it we won't go in. We'll keep on walking the plain until we run out of food, water and options. The list of things I'd choose over entering that place is a staggering length but dying isn't on it.'

'Well then what are we waiting for?'

They took the few paces up to the entrance. The darkness was like a sinister bear, reaching out to hug them. They inched towards it. Instinctively, they locked their arms together and stepped into the void.

There was a crunch under Cobble's foot that stopped them dead. They had ventured just two steps into the entrance and already they were anxious. Bones kicked the remnants into the light, revealing a pure white bone.

'What do you make of that, Bones?'

'Could be from a wolf, or perhaps a boar. Difficult to say, but I don't like those marks on it either way.'

Cobble crouched down for a closer look. There were three grooves in the bone that could only have been made by another animal.

'It looks as though whatever it was met an untimely end,' said Cobble. 'Do you think it was a creature from inside the mountain that made them?'

'I do now, thanks,' said Bones, trying to hide the irritation in his voice. 'Let's not dwell on it though, eh?'

'We should have a plan in case something happens in there,' said Cobble.

'No we shouldn't, we should see if it leads to the other side as quickly as possible,' countered Bones.

He couldn't argue with that. 'Let's go then.'

If the blackness had been alive it would have felt hard done by at being compared to black. 'There should be a new colour named after me', it would have thought. It would also have wondered why the two strangers passing through were so jumpy.

Cobble brushed against the wall of the tunnel, almost frightening his meagre dinner from him as he leapt and banged his head on the ceiling.

'Ooooowoooow!'

'Shhhhhhh!'

'Easier said than done Bones,' said Cobble, 'there could be anything in here, waiting to jump out at us.'

'Really, do you think so?' said Bones 'Thanks for enlightening my imagination again.'

They shuffled slowly along the tunnel, using one arm to keep each other steady and the other to feel their way along the wall.

Something small crawled up Bones' leg and he kicked out instinctively, hitting Cobble's ankle and sending his friend hopping forwards into the void.

'Sorry Cobble!' he called.

Nothing.

'Cobble? Cobble!'

Nothing.

He flattened his hands to the wall and nudged along the tunnel.

'Cobble?' he called, louder this time.

Nothing.

He started to worry. Had he walked past him? Could he have fallen into the depths of the mountain? Bones' imagination was usually stunted but it had cancelled all other plans for the day and was working overtime on the darkness. The three clawed beast changed from a theory to an absolute reality. That was it, no question. The mysterious creature had Cobble and Bones had to save him. Again.

A sudden howling noise came from a little way ahead, sending him stumbling backwards, followed a few seconds later by a dull thump. He scrabbled to his feet and sprinted forwards in the pitch dark. He stopped himself just as quickly, tumbling to the floor as he did so, as it dawned on him that the thump had come from far below. There was a crevasse in here, he realised with a jolt.

'Cobble!' he roared. 'Cobble!'

'I assume you've gone quite pale,' said Cobble. 'Bones? That is you, right?'

'Cobble? But... the noise...' he stammered.

'I know what made those marks, Bones. Well, I don't know what it was precisely, but it's now at the bottom of the cliff that I assume we're standing at the edge of.'

Bones tried to process the last few seconds. 'What happened?'

'Well you gave me a good kicking for a start – that's one less I owe you by the way – and I lost my balance as I hopped forward. I fell on whatever it was as it was lunging for me and it bounced off me and down the cliff. It was very heroic, Bones, in case anyone asks.'

'Well that's good, right?'

'It is if there is only one of them, yes,' said Cobble with false confidence. 'Let's not wait to find out though. Here, hold my hand, we need to find our way past this cliff face.'

He found protruding pieces of rock on the wall to grip on to as they edged carefully along until they could feel the floor widening below them. From here on they crept slowly, conscious that the surprises may not have finished coming.

It felt like they had been walking for hours when there was a change in the infinite darkness. There was a gradual greying of the walls and they were higher here than where they entered. They moved along more quickly now and before long the opening at the other end of the mountain came into view. They passed through it and covered their eyes as they adjusted to the bright sunshine. They walked for a few more steps to get out of the grip of the mountain, then hopped down a small drop until they felt grass beneath their feet for the first time in days. They lay down and breathed in the crisp fresh air.

'Bones?'

'Yes.'

'Did you notice anything?'

'What do you mean?'

'Did you notice what just happened?'

Bones was lost again.

'We just walked through a mountain,' said Cobble.

'So it seems.'

'And nothing happened to us. Well, nothing we have any lasting evidence of at least. We just walked straight through it.'

'Yes, it does seem rather odd when you put it like that. There was a mysterious creature though.'

'If we ever make it to another tribe we should say there was an underground sea and we had to battle for our lives with a giant... mammoth... yes, and his army of... smaller mammoths, right?'

'Right-o Cobble,' said Bones supportively. 'How did we kill the mammoth? Just in case I'm asked.'

'We... I fired an arrow in the dark and it went right through his eye. How about that?'

'Sounds plausible. How would we know it went through his eye though, and what about the little mammoths?'

'Details, Bones, details. We'll have plenty of time to work that out before the time comes.'

'Quite,' said Bones, in the tolerant tone of a man who knows he's the only one in the conversation who has realised it's hypothetical.

They took in their surroundings for the first time. After the barren wilderness of the Great Grey Plain the first thing that hit them was the colour. The lush green grass seemed more vivid than any they had seen before. There was a lonely conifer to their left and the gentle splashing of a stream to their right. It was the first noise of note they had heard in days. Bones had grabbed the flask and was filling it before Cobble's brain had finished enjoying the grass. They sat under a large bush and drank until they felt sick.

'I'm going to find us some food,' said Bones, and was gone.

Cobble stared at the horizon and wondered what lay ahead for them. Surely no-one from his tribe had ever ventured this far before. This was new territory in every sense of the word. Until now he had just thought of getting away, far away, from Boardom. Now he had to make real decisions. To his left were green fields all the way to the sky, punctuated by clusters of dark green bushes. It probably ran all the way to the Giant Sea, he realised. He wasn't going to take a step nearer to that place if he could help it. A long way ahead of him he could make out a series of green hills that seemed to go on forever. To their left was Unfinished Mountain, the only named place in all the world that couldn't be seen from Boardom. He would ask Bones to climb back up the mountainside for a better view. There was a forest that appeared at the horizon and travelled down on his right side, thinning out as they reached the slope of the mountains. It was as if the trees had been trying to walk over the peaks, gradually giving up as the incline increased. There was only one way to go, Cobble realised with relief. One less decision, we go forwards to the hills.

Bones came back with a selection of fruits neither of them had seen before. Conical red ones with small yellow seeds, round blue ones that looked like the stone marbles children played with at the fire pits at home, and pale green, hairy berries that they decided would be their least favourite of the three. They sampled them all, filling their stomachs for the first time since they started out.

'This is the life, eh Bones? Plenty of food and water and a nice view.'

'I could get used to it.'

'Before we make any decisions would you scramble up the mountain a little and see if there is anything past those hills? If we head that way I'd like us to know what lies beyond.'

He turned to the space were Bones had been, then turned further to see his friend scampering up the grey slope. Good man, he thought.

Bones was back before Cobble's daydreaming had gone very far.

'That forest drops into a valley past the hills, I'd say it's a couple of days' walk away,' said Bones as he sat back down. 'It seems to hook around to the left, cutting off the hills.'

'Then it's settled. We'll rest here and head for the hills in the morning. We can sleep in the open for one night and should reach the forest in time to find a good place to see out tomorrow night.'

CHAPTER SIX

TURNING THE TABLES

As time passed since Cobble's departure, Moss found herself thinking more and more about his decision. The guilt had subsided and she had become enthralled by her visions of the adventures he was doubtless experiencing. During her idle time she created vivid imagery of him in her mind, often surrounded by luscious fruit and roasted meat in a warm oasis of her mind's making. She wanted desperately to believe it was true, perhaps to ease the guilt that lurked quietly in the background, and the idea of it slowly travelled along the path from fiction to fact.

In time, this preoccupation had an unexpected result. It had created a doorway to an idea and Moss' neglected imagination burst through it. The trouble was that nobody had done anything similar to Cobble's grand exit. He was a trailblazer of sorts and Moss was anything but that, she was a grand slave to routine and tradition. What would she do, anyway? She couldn't just up sticks and leave as he had done, there were the children to consider after all. The more she considered her options the more she understood that she was trapped. Since she couldn't leave she would just have to find a way to make her life more exciting where she was, but how? A woman's place was at the caves and nothing was going to change that.

She wavered back and forth, from grand revolutionary ideas to small gestures of defiance, but couldn't picture any of them gaining any traction in this stagnant place. One person couldn't change the world. Cobble was able to change his world, and Bones' too she supposed, but this society had a way of staying the same against all logic. If someone of Cobble's ingenuity couldn't break the spell then no one person could. No one person. Could more than one person make a difference? Moss had taken another step down a road of possibilities. Who would help her? None of the men, that was certain. The women? Most of them were as set in their ways as the men, but not all. She could speak to one of the more forward thinking women and put it to them. Plum was probably the best barometer for her thoughts. She gave off a subtle aura of mischievousness that might just be pliable towards such radical action.

It was at about this point that Moss realised she had no idea what they could actually do. What was she pitching to her? That they needed to change the system? All well and good, she thought, but what if she asked her for specifics? One step at a time. She walked down to the stream where Plum was cleaning some of the men's clothes.

'Hi Plum.'

'Hi Moss, how're you?' said Plum

'I'm...' she considered her answer for a moment, 'I'm hopeful!'

Plum looked up from her washing. 'Hopeful, indeed? That sounds... interesting.'

'Maybe it is, and maybe it ain't. I need to say this out loud to hear how it sounds and you're the best person to say it to, I shouldn't wonder.'

'Are you pregnant again, missus? What have I told you about, you know...' she said with a wink and a gentle elbow.

'No, no. It's nothing like that Plum. In fact, it's almost the opposite.'

'There's an opposite?'

'Listen,' said Moss, ignoring the tangent, 'I've been thinking about Cobble and his disappearance.'

'Ah yes, Cobble. I reckon I remember him. He was a nice young man, if a little peculiar, wasn't he? Short fellow, right?'

'Yes. Well, yes and no. He was a nice man, and short. I'm beginning to wonder, though, if he weren't peculiar at all, if you get my meaning. I think maybe we're the peculiar ones.'

'Blimey Moss! Who have you been talking to?' said Plum.

'Nobody, that's the whole reason I'm here!' she said, with a liberal dash of impatience. 'What if he was the sensible one and we're the fools for stayin' in this punishing place.'

'What if he was the sensible one? Moss, he wandered off on his own into the wild. He's already a wolf's dinner as likely as not.'

Moss didn't have an argument for that, her arsenal was made up of a big pile of 'ifs' and she needed something more substantial if she was to make a difference.

'What I'm trying to say, Plum, is that we do all the work here while the men lounge around all day. We may not be able to have great adventures like Cobble or Bones but we can at least make our lives more enjoyable.'

'But this is how things are, Moss, this is how it is supposed to be. It ain't going to do no-one no good dreaming like that.'

'Says who?' said Moss.

There was a pregnant pause and Moss smiled inside at the subtle irony.

'Well, nobody says it exactly, it just is,' said Plum weakly.

'Exactly! We can make a different life for ourselves right 'ere, without going on some great escapade.'

'How?' said Plum, letting the word hang in the air.

'Well,' said Moss 'that's where I need your 'elp. I ain't really thought this through to the end if I'm honest, it's more of a vague vision at the moment. I was hoping you would 'elp me gather some of the women to a meeting so we could come up with a plan of action.'

'This all sounds very subversive, are you sure this is a path you want to go down? It might make things worse.'

'I'm sure, Plum, but I need your help.'

'Good,' said Plum, 'I've been waiting for you to ask me for a long time. We meet at Stonybridge each quarter moon.'

CHAPTER SEVEN

SETTING SUN

At first light they were up, Bones carrying the full bag of tools and vittles and Cobble carrying his bough and arrows. They had walked unhurriedly for the whole of the previous day, a good night's rest and their full bellies allowing them to minimise their breaks, and they had slept soundly in the open on the second night, despite the lack of shelter. The sun had been brazen the day before as they began their crossing of the newly named Greenfields but was now valiantly fighting a losing battle with some relentlessly encroaching rain clouds. The breeze had gathered up its bulk and begun to throw itself around with aggression. They had no cover with them and were soaked through before they had settled into their stride. Cobble made a mental note to investigate how to make a portable rain shelter.

By the time they reached the first gentle slope of the hills they were cold and exhausted. Each step was a slump and they craved the shelter of the forest, now no more than a thousand paces away.

Cobble found himself hoping more and more that they would meet another tribe, if one even existed. He wanted to find more like-minded people to settle down with and live a happy, productive life. Perhaps even find a woman to keep him and give him little Cobbles to teach in the ways of an engineer. Maybe just this little adventure was enough for the story he wanted. There was the vulture, that was a good one. He could exaggerate his injuries a bit there, and the mammoth army in the tunnel might seal it. A part of him wished something treacherous really did happen in the mountain. What were the chances that they would pass right through a mountain with nothing critical happening to them? Typical, he thought.

'Let's rest on the edge of the forest for the night, the sky is darkening again and I don't fancy going into that woods without seeing it in the sun first.'

Rumble... rumble...

The first offering of trees showed themselves in the morning sun as they climbed the last sodden hill. It didn't seem half as threatening anymore, Cobble thought damply. What he couldn't see was the lower half of his right leg as it went through the sodden green floor and into the hill, quickly followed by the rest of his rather surprised body.

Bones hopped backwards as Cobble fell and was only fractionally less surprised to notice he too was disappearing.

Scrub was a responsible badger, not like those young ones. They think they can cut corners and do a half-baked job on Patrol. Life was too easy these days, he often thought to himself, what we need is a good scare to focus the minds of those softies. His Patrol partner today was Warble, a perfect example of a young upstart. He had already tried to take a break and they had only been on shift for an hour. Bloody cubs.

The Patrol had been a part of the cete's daily life since the Great Rat Attack. The passage of time had worn away at the actual story until it was overtaken by the idea of it. It was bad, that was all anyone knew for certain, and should be prevented at all costs. A Patrol was on duty at all times, criss-crossing around the sett checking for undefined dangers. No-one had ever actually found anything noteworthy during a Patrol, of course, but that wasn't the point.

They had reached one end of the maze, a large chamber that served no clear purpose.

'Do keep up Warble! You're not in the play chamber now young cub, this is adult work.'

Warble hesitated for a couple of disrespectful seconds before trudging over to him, dragging his feet on the floor of the soil tunnel.

'Come on! That's Section One done, we'll head back through to the previous chamber. You can have a break then, and not before. Come on!'

'Yessir!' said Warble with a healthy dollop of insubordination.

'I'm not waiting for you any more, you damn slacker, I'll wait for you at the tunnel.'

Scrub marched back out of the chamber and into the tunnel at the far side.

'I don't even know why we do these stupid Patrols,' Warble muttered to himself, 'another pointless relic from the past. When I'm in charge the first thing I'll do is…'

His ramblings were interrupted by a large leg stamping heavily on his back, followed swiftly by the rest of Cobble.

If Warble had been given the opportunity to look for a bright side he may have noticed that he expired just in time to prevent him hearing the crunches and squishes of his former body as it did so.

Bones thumped hard onto the floor next to Cobble and his recently deceased cushion. They were surrounded by hard, compacted soil, brightened up by the sunlight that their impromptu visit had allowed into the hole. There was a narrow tunnel ahead of them and they could hear scuffling noises coming from it, getting quieter as they listened.

'Are you OK, Bones?' said Cobble as he rolled off the former badger.

'I'd be better if I'd had the soft landing.'

'Fair point, Bones. It seems I may have found our dinner at least.'

'Maybe we should start at finding a way out first though, eh?'

They studied their surroundings for the first time. The drop was higher than two men and the walls had been smoothed and hardened by the passage of time and badgers. The only other break in the wall was the tunnel at the far side.

'Stand on this, Bones,' said Cobble, locking his fingers together to make a step.

Bones put his right foot into the cradle and hauled himself up, reaching up towards the sky and failing to reach the lip as he did so.

'Throw me upwards as hard as you can, Cobble,' he said.

Cobble took a deep breath and thrust Bones' foot as high as he could but they were still more than a full arm's length short. They tried half a dozen times before giving up.

'We need some of your sideways thinking, Cobble,' said Bones. 'There must be some way out.'

Cobble looked about him. There was nothing they could use. None of his tools would have helped them, the hardened walls were unyielding and refused to allow a flint or arrow to chisel any steps into it and his only other tools were blunt. He looked at the badger and pondered. That would raise them up a bit, he supposed.

'Here, let's try this.'

He dragged it across to the wall and stood on it. His feet sunk further than he would have liked and he tried to push the mental picture from his mind. Bones put his foot into Cobble's hands again and leapt for the hole's edge. As he did so, Cobble's feet sunk further still into the stricken animal, disturbing his balance and sending them tumbling back to the cavern floor.

'Well that was disgusting and fruitless,' said Cobble, 'like the raw meat dinners the old men eat' he added, trying to lift the tension with a joke.

'There's only one thing we can do,' said Bones, ignoring the effort. 'We have to go into the tunnel.'

They inspected it more closely now, peering into the gloom. It was narrower than at first glance and too tight for Cobble, they realised. There was only one option left to them.

'Don't worry about meeting any more badgers, Bones,' said Cobble counter-productively. 'Just keep heading up until you reach their exit, then find a sturdy branch and come back to our opening to haul me up.'

'Right-o!' said Bones. 'Don't go anywhere now, do you hear?' he added, with more light-heartedness than he felt, and with that he was gone.

It was easy going at first for someone of Bones' physique. He crawled along on his elbows for a time before he reached a fork in the tunnels. One direction sloped gently downwards and the other was flat but narrow. He chose the flat one, hoping it would rise to the threshold before his heart rate did. As the tunnel shrunk it constricted his arms until they were pressed up against his body and each heft of his elbows only moved him an inch or two at a time. He was used to searching in unusual places for Cobble's creations but nothing like this, and the thought that he might become wedged was beginning to creep into his mind. He had no choice but to keep inching forward in the hope that the ground would release its grip before it locked him irreversibly.

Inch.

Inch.

He felt a layer of air between his forearm and torso and realised he had made it through for now. It was almost completely dark and for a moment Bones was back in the mountain again. Another pessimistic saying from Boardom crossed his mind; 'Out of the bear's mouth into the fire pit'. If he and Cobble ever made it to another tribe he would make sure they had some positive sayings in their collection, he decided.

He could now crawl at a good pace, although the tunnel was undulating as he advanced. It was difficult for him to work out whether he was getting closer to the surface or further away. He pressed on and hoped for some sign he was heading in the right direction.

As Scrub reached the fork he heard the two loud thumps and wondered what mischief Warble was up to now. Damn cubs, he thought. He used the fork to turn himself around and headed back to the cavern. He had only travelled a short way when strange deep noises came down the tunnel and made his ears prick. They were unfamiliar to him and that meant danger, he should tell the rest of the cete right away. The Patrol has done its work, he thought smugly as he thundered through the maze. This will show them!

He reached the main room of the sett and called out. In moments he was surrounded by large male adults with confused looks on their faces. He described what he had heard and suggested, as the Duty Patrol Badger and therefore the ranking officer, that they should all march to face whatever had intruded into their peaceful home.

A clamour sounded ahead of Bones, similar to the noise they heard in the tunnel when they first dropped into the hill, and he wondered if it was another badger or something more sinister he should be really worried about. As his imagination put forward suggestions for him there was a sudden drop in the floor and he felt a widening of the walls. The darkness had sequestered his vision but it felt as though he was in a fairly large opening.

It was a very large opening as it happened, large enough to fit a dozen primed badgers.

'What is that?' said Morg, one of the hastier members of the cete.

'Shhhhh…' said Scrub.

'I was only saying…' said Morg, ploughing on regardless.

'It might be the last thing you ever say if you don't shut up!' said Scrub tetchily.

To Bones, they sounded like a room full of lizards with bad coughs. He had no idea how he might get past them safely, so he decided to take the only option available to him. If they were the badgers who lived here then he could guess two things about them; they were smaller than him and they could see better than he could in the darkness.

'He crawled out into the space and raised himself up to a crouch.

'Bloody hell!' said four of the badgers at once.

'Erm, everybody… I think maybe we should head back to base,' said Scrub. 'What do you think? Hello?… Hello?…'

Scrub looked around and found he was alone.

'Bunch of cowards,' he said aloud to himself as he charged after them to the safety of the base.

There was a loud scuffling to Bones' left followed by one last growl. Silence.

Bones was out of his comfort zone in every sense. Cobble had always tried to teach him to think creatively but he had never quite got the hang of it. To Bones, getting his thoughts in a straight line was hard enough, getting them to move about until they solved a puzzle was all but impossible. It was like trying to teach fire to play musical rocks.

Step by step, Cobble had said. Boil the situation down to a series of small puzzles that need to be solved. He steadied himself and studied the basics of his situation. He was lost in a dark underground maze and needed to get out. He needed to find a way out. The creatures fled when they saw him so they must have been scared. If they were scared they would go to a safe place, most likely the furthest place from the surface. If he followed them he will more than likely be further from the exit and they might attack him.

He felt like he had solved the first puzzle. Don't follow them. Good.

Next he needed to know where he should go. Not down their tunnel and not back to where he came from. He could go back to the fork in the path but he wasn't sure he would make it through the tight channels again. Even if he could he wouldn't have space to turn around and that meant going all the way back to Cobble. If they were to make it out of here there had to be another tunnel leading out from this chamber.

He fumbled along the walls, feeling his way from the floor to the ceiling for any sign of a hole. He guessed he was almost back to where he started when his arm found thin air in the centre of the wall. He felt around the edges and was relieved to find it was wide enough for him to slide into. He pulled himself up and started crawling. The ground was rising distinctly and before long he felt sure he was near the surface. He pushed at the ceiling every so often, hoping for a split in the ground above him but finding none. The tunnel turned to his right and his heart sank as he felt a dead end in front of him. Not quite a dead end though. It wasn't a vertical wall, just a very steep section. He clambered up until he reached a blockade of soft earth. As he burrowed through it the walls of the tunnel began to lighten and before long there was a speck of orange sky. He scrabbled furiously, pulling himself out of the depths to lie on his back as he sucked in the crisp air.

He had done it! A rush of satisfaction ran through his body and he finally understood why Cobble was so dedicated to his work. He had solved a puzzle on his own. He looked at the sky above him. The day hadn't waited for them and they still had to find a place to rest for the night. He stood up and headed to the very edge of the forest to find something to rescue Cobble from the hill.

CHAPTER EIGHT

WITH A HISS AND A WINK

'Will this one do?' Bones called into the hole as he lowered the hefty branch. Bones felt it take the weight and heaved it upwards. Cobble's head poked out of the hole and he lifted himself over the lip, dragging the badger with him as he slumped to the floor beside Bones.

'You took your time!'

'You're welcome.'

In the end they made camp near a small stream a few yards into the forest. It was a welcoming place after the trials of the badger sett and Cobble had made a small fire to warm them. He began to prepare the meat while Bones foraged for something to flavour it. He sliced open the belly of the badger with his flint and emptied the insides, putting them to one side for later. He was skinning the animal when something hooked his thoughts. He turned back to the innards and stared at them, then picked up a long, wet section. He stared some more. Using his flint he chopped a length of the intestine and studied it. This could work, he thought to himself.

Bones returned to their camp with an armful of provisions; leaves to flavour the meat and mushrooms and nuts to add some texture to their dry meal.

'No spots, Cobble, just like you said.'

'Great,' said Cobble distractedly.

'Everything OK?'

'Yes, yes. Sorry. I have an idea, something to make our bough more effective. This badger's guts may make the perfect string for the bough. It stretches a little but not too much. If we dry it out I think it will be perfect.'

'Well it sounds like you think it'll work,' said Bones, choosing his words carefully.

'I could wrap the bough in soft, thin branches to give a better grip for my hands too,' thought Cobble aloud.

Cobble laid out sections of the guts on the ground in the hope they would dry enough overnight and turned his attention back to the skewered meat. The badger was tough but filling and their stomachs were as grateful as they had been in days. When they had finished they slouched against a large root and watched the gentle swaying of the branches above them.

'Cobble?' said Bones.

'Yes?'

'What's our plan? I mean, when do we stop moving? We can't just keep wandering day after day.'

'You're right, Bones. We need a plan. We're already a long way from home and all we've met along the way are a few beasts. There must be another tribe out here, I'm sure of it, but if we don't find one soon we'll have to make our own.'

'I'm not sure that's a solid long term strategy, Cobble.'

'I'm not even sure it's a good short term one,' conceded Cobble, 'but there doesn't seem to be much we can do about it. Let's say we get through this forest and keep going for another few days. If we don't meet anyone we'll find a nice cave and settle down and let them come to us.'

'Right-o. When no-one shows up, what then?'

'If, Bones, if.'

Bones knew what he had signed up for when he left Boardom, but the reality of it was starting to bite. They needed to stop, or find someone, before their food supplies ran out. The badger was a lucky kill and they hadn't found anything else worth hunting since they left Boardom. Hopefully the forest would provide them with enough to get through it and maybe even a day or two after, but then they would be struggling. Having no destination in mind made it all the more difficult. Journeys always seem longer when you can't picture the end, thought Bones.

The pine needles made a comfortable enough bed and they slept heavily until the pale sun sliced through the trunks and stirred them. Cobble was already up and about when Bones finally woke. While his friend slept Cobble had been busying himself with the grisly update to his bough.

The badger's insides had dried just as he had hoped and he made quick work of tying one to his bough, testing it with a strong pull. It felt like a new weapon altogether and it comforted him to know that he could make a new one wherever there was an animal to supply him.

They packed up their things and set off. They had chosen to follow the stream into the heart of the forest, assuming that if anyone lived here then they would surely settle near the water. It was slow but pleasant going as they picked their way through the increasingly stony terrain and they felt their mood lighten as they went.

'What will we do if we meet another tribe?' said Bones.

'I think we start with 'hello', what do you think?'

'Hello is a good start, I suppose. Did you have anything more substantial in mind?'

'Well I guess we'll have to earn their trust, show them our value and persuade them to let us join their tribe.'

'You sound like you just made that up, Cobble.'

'I did. I honestly haven't given it much thought.'

This surprised Bones. He always assumed Cobble had a grand master plan, one that would see them through to some contented end. To find out Cobble was improvising as much as he was worried him.

'We should have a real plan,' said Bones, 'and you're the plan man in this operation so you should get thinking.'

Cobble wasn't used to Bones being so forthright. He was usually as undemanding as a stick in a stream, happy to go along with whatever Cobble asked of him. He felt an increased sense of obligation to end their journey as soon as he could. Disappointingly, all this achieved was to put into sharp focus the distinct absence of an end game for them.

They walked on along the stream, much quieter than before, each lost in their own thoughts. Cobble was concentrating, trying to conjure a worthwhile plan while Bones spent the time hoping that was precisely what he was doing. Neither noticed that the forest was strangely quiet and the trees were becoming more densely packed.

They reached a hollow among some steep roots in the forest floor and set themselves down for the evening. Only then did they really take in their changed surroundings.

'We must be close to the halfway point, look how closely packed the trees are here,' said Cobble, bursting the silence.

'It's eerily quiet too,' said Bones.

'We shouldn't stay here long, it's giving me the heebie-jeebies. If we're about halfway through now then we should make it to the other side by tomorrow night. Let's wake early if we can and walk a bit quicker tomorrow.'

There was no argument from Bones. They had their meal of badger meat, nuts and mushrooms and made themselves comfortable in the hollow. The sooner they slept the earlier they'd wake they reasoned, but as they drifted into sleep there came a hissing noise from high up in the trees to their left. They opened their eyes sharply and stared at each other.

'Can snakes climb trees?' whispered Bones.

'It's not a question I've mulled over too often I have to say, Bones, but I assume so.'

'It didn't sound like a bird, or anything else you'd expect in a tree. It must have been a snake. I wonder what it tastes like?'

'That's probably a discussion for another time. Let's concentrate on the immediate peril here, eh?'

'Right-o! So what's the plan?'

'Give me a second, Bones, I was asleep ten seconds ago!' said Cobble tetchily, 'let's wait to hear if it happens again.'

'Brilliant, Cobble. I like the simplicity,' said Bones with a wink.

There was another hiss, this time lower down and to the right.

'What was the next part of your plan again?' said Bones.

'I quite like the idea of hiding, how about you?'

'Hiding is good, let's do that.'

They lay as flat as they could, covering their bodies with forest detritus. Only their heads and shoulders were visible and they were deep into the back of the hollow. They hoped that was enough but both of them knew that their scent was likely to betray them to the tree-snakes. The hissing continued, from all around them now, and was getting louder – or closer, it was hard to tell – until they felt as though they would be trapped like seeds in a pod until daylight, if they were lucky. Neither dared to move for fear that the snakes would flash at them and sink their stinging teeth into their half hidden bodies.

As it turns out, they needn't have worried about snakes at all.

A large shadow fell from the nearest tree and landed, half crouched and pointing a short wooden spear at their faces.

'Not snakes then,' said Bones.

CHAPTER NINE

A MEETING OF MEN

There were six of them. Bones and Cobble were white with fear as they were frogmarched along the stream's edge and deeper into the forest. The bough and arrow looked menacing in the hands of someone else and it struck Cobble how important it was to them. They could hear their captors talking in strange tones as they walked.

'He's a funny looking chap, what?'

'Quite so Pingo, quite so.'

'I say Tarpin! Look at his nose, it's so big. And what on earth is happening with those eyebrows?'

'I'd say he's one of those Hairmen Old Bungo was always on about. Seems he may not have been as cuckoo as we all thought, what?'

'Indeed.'

'The other one isn't quite as... round.'

'No, he looks almost normal doesn't he? His nose is, well, a standard looking nose. I wonder if he's one of us? I don't recognise him though, do you?'

'He has too much hair to be one of us, Pingo, but he certainly doesn't look exactly like a Hairman either. Tiff will simply adore this.'

They had been walking for about a thousand paces or so when they reached the village in the clearing. It was vaguely square with the largest oak tree either of them had ever seen in one corner. There was a fire pit in the middle, although it wasn't alight. A tall, muscular man with purple colouring smeared around his thin nose and a crown of twigs on his head stood to attention in front of them. He was bald from top to bottom and had a look in his eye that may have been menace, or perhaps he was just concentrating, it was difficult to decode. It occurred to the captives that this was an odd group of people. Quite apart from their strange appearance, they looked as threatening as a pack of wolves in a cave but their tone was of a different style altogether. If all you could do was hear them they would seem like a mild mannered bunch, a bit peculiar perhaps, but harmless. The combination was disturbing and they didn't know how to react.

'Ho! Tiff!' called Pingo, setting his captives' things on the floor. 'Take a look at these chaps.'

'Whatto!' said Tiff, raising a long, tanned palm to the newcomers. 'Welcome to Nutty Woods! Please, sit.'

Cobble and Bones exchanged glances. Very different glances. Bones didn't know whether to be afraid or comforted and the look he gave was equally confused. Cobble, on the other hand, was sure. His eyes had moved beyond glinting and were hurtling towards exhilaration. This was it! There were more people out here. Granted, they were funny looking but they were broadly the same and they spoke a version of Boardom's language. He strode forward and took a seat in the Square that seemed to serve as the village meeting place.

'Gentlemen, you are strange looking folk. Where do you call home?' said Tiff in a friendly tone 'And how did you get that cut on your head?' he added, pointing to the mark above Cobble's eye.

Cobble touched the cut with his hand. So much had happened since then he had all but forgotten about it. 'My name is Cobble the… Maker, and this is my friend Bones. We have travelled a long way from our old home in search of somewhere new,' he said, with more formality than he intended. 'Our tribe lives in Boardom across the mountains to the north.'

'Marvellous! How thrilling! Please, tell all of us your story, from the beginning if you will,' said Tiff, waving the rest of the group to sit.

As he ordered his thoughts Cobble realised for the first time that they were almost certainly no longer in danger, nor in a rush, so he started from the earliest point he could remember. He described the Boardom tribe in fine, unflattering detail and explained his motivation to leave.

'Well this is fantastic,' said Balcor, a tall specimen with a spear slung permanently over his shoulder.

'I say, we haven't even got to the good bit I expect,' said Pingo.

'Yes, quite a story,' agreed a third man 'but just a story all the same. What's the real truth behind them? That's what I want to know.'

'Come now, Jutt, we can do without your cantankerous talk for just a few minutes. We haven't had entertainment like this since Fettle split open that wasps' nest at the waterfall.'

'That wasn't entertaining for all of us,' said Fettle.

'Gentlemen, gentleman!' said Tiff, raising both arms to diffuse the tension. 'Cobble here was just building up to grand climax I'm sure. Cobble, please.'

Cobble continued, across the Great Grey Plain and through the mountains to the badger sett until he had arrived at the hollow in the forest where Pingo and Tarpin had escorted them to Nutty Woods.

'So that's how we got here,' he concluded. 'I hope it was of interest to you.'

'Well, well Cobble! It is more interesting than you might imagine, young... man? Yes, my apologies. Young man,' said Tiff with awkward interest. 'I will tell you our tale soon enough, but first let us eat. Fettle, bring out some food for our guests.'

Fettle scurried off in search of food, returning every so often with handfuls of nuts and leaves. He laid them on the ground in the centre of the group.

'We are particularly lucky here,' said Tiff. 'We have more food than we have had in many moons. It's just nuts and leaves I'm afraid, but the supply is endless.'

'Is this all you have?' said Bones before his brain had authorised it. 'I mean, is it always just nuts and leaves? You must have meat once in a while?'

A raucous laughter filled the clearing.

'Meat? Oh I say these guys are a hoot!' said Balcor.

'But surely you must hunt every so often? I mean, look at you! You're all huge. You could hunt anything you fancied. I'd say you could take down a mammoth if you put your minds to it' said Bones, ploughing on. 'You must have caught something to have been able to make a home here.'

'Aha!' said Tiff. 'That, I think, is too far into our story. Please, allow me to begin our tale.'

'Oh fabulous, I love a good yarn,' said Tarpin.

The group settled down as Tiff began. He spoke with the style of one who was used to telling a story and his audience was happy to listen.

'Our home is far away from here, to the south where the sun glows more warmly and the cherry blossom trees grow aplenty. There were many more of us when we lived there, hundreds in fact. We lived in comfort and our numbers were always rising. As we grew it became harder to find enough food and it began to cost us dearly. Our hunters had to travel further afield to find meat for us and one by one they stopped returning. We don't know whether they found another village and abandoned us, or they succumbed to unknown perils in strange lands. All we knew was that our ability to feed ourselves was waning. We had drained our lands of food and our small stream was beginning to dry.'

A pair of jet black miner birds glided down from a nearby sycamore tree and landed next to Tiff. One of them pecked at an egg sized stone.

'Whoa there matey!' said Spike, as wiry and wily a miner bird as has ever been. 'That'd be a stone you're trying to crack. The only thing that'll break if you keep that up is your own beak.'

'But it's an egg, Spike. Look, it's egg shaped,' said Budge with what constituted a sound logic to him. Between them they evened out to average intelligence.

'Why don't you have a go at that man's head then? That's egg shaped'

Budge snapped his neck around to look at the man, then back to Spike. He tilted his head and gave a curious look. 'Because it's a man's head, Spike, not an egg.' There was that logic again.

'Never mind, Budge.'

'When our numbers were down to just a hundred we had no choice but to leave in search of a better place to spend our days. Our first great mistake was to assume there were better lands. The last hundred of us packed up as much as we could and headed north and west, away from our home, and soon found the land to be cold, dry and barren. We had precious little food and fewer means to find any. We found no water and the size of our group was falling as we moved but we carried on, hoping to find a paradise in the dust. The days were hard, and the nights were cold. The price of the rich memories of Cherry Woods was the knowledge of the barren future it brought us. The weaker members fell by the wayside one by one and it seemed to those of us who had survived this far that we were doomed. In time we shrank to those you see here, a band of ten men and two ladies, and old Lorro too of course. Those infernal snakes got the better of her within a week of our arrival.'

'So there are snakes here?' interrupted Cobble. 'We thought we heard some in the trees but then you showed yourselves and we assumed the hissing was you.'

'Ah, yes. You see, we were sort of hiding from them. Ever since poor Lorro was killed we've tried to find a way to stop them but

I'm afraid we haven't been very good at it. The best approach we've found is to climb the trees when they come into our camp, but that only works for so long and we have to jump down as they climb up. It would appear you happened to be resting at the base of the tree that old Balcor here had climbed. Funny how things go, what?'

'Lorro! Lorro!' squawked Budge.

'Lorro! Lorro!' squawked Spike.

The group turned as one to the birds. None of them had ever seen, or heard, a miner bird before and it came as something of a surprise to hear them speak their language. It was made all the more remarkable since the concept of magic had not yet been discussed by anyone in all of history. After countless millennia without it, this rag-tag group of underachievers managed to create it and ignore it all by themselves in a moment.

'Did those birds just say 'Lorro'?' said a hesitant Balcor.

'...' said everyone else simultaneously.

'Surely you've caught some though?' said Bones, ignoring both revelations at the same time.

Tiff gathered himself, choosing to ignore the strange birds in the hope that his brain wouldn't have to rationalise it any time soon.

'When the green tops of the forest first showed themselves we were weak and frail but the hope gave us renewed impetus and we forged on. After so many moons without a home we had finally found somewhere to settle and survive. We found water and leaves to see us through the first night and soon learned how to forage for nuts. We were rather poor at hunting at the best of times and those snakes are such slippery devils. We gave up after a few moons and focused on getting as many nuts into storage as we could. We post guards at all times in case the snakes come into the village and that seems to be working. The nuts are rather good really, once you get used to them.'

Cobble and Bones soaked up the story. As Tiff unwound his tale they realised how much they had missed the company of others, and how lucky they were to find people so different to them and yet seemingly friendly. It was too early to feel as though they had found a new home, but the signs were good.

'So that is how we came to be here, in Nutty Woods. In a nutshell, so to speak,' said Tiff, finishing his synopsis.

'What are ladies?' said Bones.

'Interesting,' said Tiff. 'I believe you call them women. We like to be a little more... respectful here.'

'It sounds like you've been through a lot,' said Cobble, 'but I still don't understand why you won't hunt. There must be a bounty of animals here, not just the snakes.'

'Ah!' said Tiff, with an embarrassed voice. 'Yes, well, we never quite... you know?... got around to it, what with everything that's been going on.'

'Never got around to it?' said Bones, like an incredulous parrot. 'Never got around to it? How long have you been living here?'

'Oh, I'd say about two or three years,' said Tiff.

Bones steeled his patience and spoke slowly. 'So why have you never "got around to it"?'

'Well, you see, erm...' said Tiff.

'It's because we can't!' blurted Jutt. 'That's the damn problem with this crew. No practical ability.'

'Come now Jutt, please. Let's not get ahead of ourselves here,' said Tiff.

'Well it's true, none of us have the slightest notion how to hunt.

We've been eating like rabbits for years and not one of us has made any progress with our Tasks.'

'OK, OK,' said Tiff, 'Cobble, Bones, please let me explain. Our small group means that our talents have become very specific. Frankly, we are really quite excellent at knowing what we're not good at. Examples flood out of us like leaves in the wind. Where we struggle is with, well, making things. To be honest with you we are dreadful at it, quite dreadful. We have tried, we really have. We even gave ourselves Tasks to complete; building shelters, hunting animals, making warm clothing and so on. We have all been able to pinpoint what we need to learn, we just can't make the damn things, pardon my language. When Fettle smashed open the wasps' nest he was trying to find a way to make a water holder. It's rather sad, I suppose.'

Cobble and Bones looked at each other.

'So, let me get this straight,' said Cobble, 'You know what you need to survive but you can't turn your ideas into reality. Is that about right?'

'Quite so, Cobble,' said Tiff.

'Quite so! Quite so!' Squawked Spike.

'Lorro! Lorro!' Squawked Budge.

'...'

'It seems we may be able to help each other,' said Bones. 'Cobble here is a master at the very thing you're lacking. If you tell him what you need I'm sure he can make it for you.'

'That all sounds very convenient,' said Jutt. 'We capture you and you can suddenly solve all of our problems. I suppose it involves you being given your strange contraption back too, what?'

'It's not sudden, Jutt. We've always been able to solve your problems. We just hadn't met yet. Would you like proof?' said Cobble, determined not to let this opportunity at a new life pass him by.

'Of course we would!' said Jutt with hostility.

'Please, Jutt, now is not the time for one of your belligerent performances,' said Tiff, raising a hand. 'Please, Cobble, show us something that might help us.'

'If you will allow me to gather my things I will show you how you can hunt again. It will change your lives.' He was selling again.

'Aha!' said Jutt. 'You would like us to give you your things back so you can show us how to kill something. Tiff, you can hear this too, right? We may not be very good at making things but that doesn't mean we're dim-witted.'

Cobble wondered whether the real power here was with Jutt. It seemed to him that the others craved a simple life, and one likely to involve the humouring of Jutt and his resentment. Speculation gives a chance at success, he thought. Leaving Boardom was a risk and he will have to risk more before their lives could settle into a new normality. He acted on his instinct.

'Then let me prove to you beyond doubt that we can help you, that we want to help you. If we convince you of our intentions then in return we can join your company and make a new home for us here. What do you say?'

Tiff stood up, turning first to Jutt. 'I insist you keep your tongue still, Jutt. We are slowly expiring here, what do we have to lose?' He turned to Cobble, 'Let's see what you have to offer us, young man.' He gestured to Fettle to pass over the bag and bough.

'Thank you,' said Cobble, 'you won't regret it.' I might though, he added to himself.

'So we're just going to ignore the talking birds then, are we?'

said Tarpin.

'Bones, please stand by that tree there,' he said, pointing at the large oak, 'with your back straight up against the bark if you would.'

'I'll take that as a yes,' said Tarpin.

Bones gave him a curious look, but he was well used to Cobble and his zigzag thinking. He knew better than to question it and possibly wouldn't have understood the answer anyway. He positioned himself against the tree and waited to discover what was in store.

Cobble picked up a large round mushroom from their bag and placed it on top of Bones' concerned head. He stood on the opposite side of the Square and fitted an arrow to his bough, lowering his head to get a better aim.

Doubt entered his mind like a fire in a forest. He knew he wasn't a good enough aim yet to guarantee hitting his target and this time everything was at stake. If he missed then the people of Nutty Woods were unlikely to take them in, especially since they were struggling to feed themselves as it was. He could easily hit Bones, too. What then? The very thought of it was terrifying. As his mind accelerated towards uncertainty there was a blur of movement in the corner of his eye. With simple instinct he spun on his heels and fired his arrow towards it. The village folk dived to the floor as one as they realised Jutt was right.

There was a dull thump as the arrow slammed unseen into an unfortunate ferret.

'Grab him, you fools!' roared Jutt. 'I bloody well told you!'

Two large arms locked onto Cobble and held him fast as he struggled.

'Wait! Wait!' called Cobble. 'Look!'

'I'm awfully sorry,' said Tiff, 'but it seems to me you can't be trusted. It pains me to say it but Jutt was right. We won't harm you, of course, but we will be keeping your things as I'm sure you can understand. We have enough trouble without inviting a wolf into our home.'

Bones watched his new home evaporating in front of him. Solve the puzzles, he implored himself. Step by step. Think, Bones!

He slipped around the oak, hiding from view. He quietly picked his way from tree to tree until he was standing over the recently stricken ferret. He picked it up and strode into the commotion.

'Gentlemen!' he called out. 'Please, look!'

Bones' arms were holding the dripping animal high above his head. 'I believe this is sufficient proof.'

The inhabitants of Nutty Woods looked like stunned survivors of an earthquake.

'I say!' said Pingo, breaking the spell. 'It seems we may have found our missing link. Cobble here is a making man!'

'Making man!' Squawked the two birds together.

CHAPTER TEN

A DIFFERENT PATH

They huddled together in the half light, each woman stealing warmth from the next. This was the fourth 'Subversive Women Of Boardom' meeting since Plum's extraordinary revelation to Moss at the stream and they were nearly ready. They had met daily, now that there was some substance to their discussions.

Plum had explained to the newcomers that the disillusion within the womenfolk had begun long ago, but their SWOB movement was painfully slow at building momentum, like trying to start a landslide with a grain of sand. It was too perilous to openly recruit to their cause so they had no choice but to wait for people to come to them. All they could do was try and accelerate the process. They had done their best to cultivate a sense of frustration with the existing structure, with silent whispers that spoke of the possibilities change could bring. They executed small but frequent missions, often as trivial as blaming one of the men for the spillage of a water pot, or the snapping of a stirring stick. Subtlety was an excruciatingly slow way of going about it but was critical to their success, and ultimately effective. They had completed their first large scale mission earlier that moon. Plum had identified Cobble as a like-minded spirit and suggested they openly recruit him. The group had decided against it, worried it might scare him away. Instead, they kept to their strengths and stayed in the shadows, literally in this case. Six of them had watched him from the trees for two weeks as he turned his hand to the stools and bench. Any guilt they may have felt was conquered by the importance of their work; no revolution ever succeeded without the oppressed behaving like the elite. While Cobble dragged the bench back to the Meeting Patch they dropped down, grabbed the stools and made a circuitous route home, turning away from Boardom before heading back by the shore of the Giant Sea.

Plum had felt a small pocket of guilt rise up as she smashed the stools in her cave but swiftly pushed it back down, knowing it was worth it if their plan worked. They had each taken a few of the wooden legs, laying them in the fires around the Meeting Patch and hoping they would deliver the reaction they wanted.

They were half right.

Cobble had finally broken, and unwittingly taken the first real action for their cause. It had surprised even the most sceptical of the group to see how close their scheming had come to failure, but he had been defeated, and had left the confines of the tribe at last. It gave them the biggest recruitment spike since they formed their seditious union so long ago.

They steered all the talk among the unrecruited women to the mistreatment of Cobble, with Plum as the primary catalyst. People began to speak more openly about it and the existing members were able to enlist more brazenly than before. Plum was the ideal recruiter-general and wasted no time in bumping the numbers.

'What do you make of poor little Cobble having to disappear to save his skin?' Plum had said, heavy with spin. 'Wasn't that just the strangest thing?'

'Oh yes,' agreed Pippy, 'very strange and no mistake.'

'Just think what we could have done with his bough and arrow. We would have some time to ourselves by now instead of foraging and cleaning all day, can you imagine that?'

'I hadn't thought of it like that I hadn't, Plum. I s'pose you're right.'

'We should do something about it really, shouldn't we?'

'Oh yeah, absolutely,' Pippy had said sycophantically.

'Why don't you try and think of a plan while I gather us women together? Let's say we'll meet at Stonybridge at the next quarter moon.'

'Oh, well. Yes, yes, alright, Plum,' Pippy had said, a little dubiously.

That was enough to snare her, Plum knew. One benefit that came from the dearth of original thought in Boardom was that you could generally rely on people to agree with your opinion, if you said it confidently enough.

So it continued. One by one the women of the tribe joined together to form the SWOBs and an all out rebellion. In secret, naturally, they were still new to this whole courage idea after all.

The final part of their plan was their great crescendo. They had needed numbers for it to succeed but now they had them and it was time to start making real preparations. They met more often, daily when they could manage it. They worked at their chores by day and their revolution by night. The whole enterprise was a gamble and they had decided to carry that sentiment through to their final plan. They took their inspiration from Cobble, choosing to leave

Boardom in the hope of finding a new and better life elsewhere. It was far less straightforward for them as it was for him, though, and they knew that they had to plan it meticulously.

'Our first challenge is to work out how to get out of 'ere. We can't just up sticks and walk off,' said Faun. 'We'd be hauled back to the storage caves before the last of us had straightened our backs.'

'Couldn't we just, you know, put less turnips in their soup so they have to go off and hunt?' said Sarka. 'That's what we was doing when we had that bad weather and most of the turnips went rotten.'

'It's what we were doing, Sarka, not was. In fact, it's what we did, not what we were doing,' said Plum, 'and it's fewer, not le... oh forget it.'

There were some things even a revolutionary couldn't change and poor grammar was one of them.

'It's impossible,' said Flow. 'The men never leave, they don't, and they're always looking for something from us.'

'Let's break it down,' said Moss, 'we can't be seen leaving so we'll have to find a way to get the men away from their fire pits. That way they won't be able to see us and they won't be able to ask us for anything neither.'

'There's no bloomin' chance of that,' said Sarka 'You might as well ask the Heather Hills to dance a jig.'

'Then let's get creative,' said Plum. 'What do they all love so much that it would cause 'em to move?'

The silence was overwhelming.

Flow cleared her throat timidly. 'We could maybe, you know, tell them we had prepared, say, a feast for them in... erm... Green Forest?' she offered.

'That, little Flow, is a tremendous idea!' said Moss.

'Nice idea,' said Faun, in the tone of one who was about to shoot fatal holes in it, 'but as soon as they realised it was a lie they'd be back, and they'd demand answers. It wouldn't give us enough time.'

'Then we turn the lie into a truth,' countered Plum.

The idea of the feast had crystallised their resolve and Plum had allocated a role in the preparations to each of them; some looked after the organisation of the feast, while others concerned themselves with the journey. Moss was the chief cook in Boardom and so was put in charge of the feast. She sent groups of women into the forest with instructions on what food to gather, and how much. There was no such thing as too much food at the best of times, but it was vital that the stores didn't run out this time. Not only did they have to keep the men fed for a full day, they also needed to harvest food for the journey and so most of the women were made busy with this part of the conspiracy. To some she gave the task of preparing the feasting area. Cobble's clearing would have been ideal, had it been further away from the village, so they had settled on another, much further away. The new bench was moved in and the fire pits dug. Things were going well.

At least, that's what she thought. Their lack of experience in large scale escapes meant that key aspects were missed. They forgot about water, for one. It was quite an important oversight, all things considered, but at least they would have berry bushes to plunder as they went. Maybe. They also hadn't considered how they would keep warm at night. Still, they were trying and that was the main thing.

Plum led the expeditionary planning. She was a natural plotter and spent most of her time scheming to upset the prevailing hierarchy. That was the problem with revolutionaries, they were always up to something mischievous. If she ever made it to the top of the social pile she would probably cultivate an uprising against her and have herself confined to caves on short rations.

She had no way of knowing which direction Cobble had taken and dismissed the idea of trying to follow him, hoping instead that their paths crossed by chance, if he was still alive. The quandary, as she saw it, was to know which way they should go. Travelling in an arbitrary direction meant meeting an arbitrary fate and so she had put her mind to conjuring an elegant solution. A pair of scouts would travel quickly for a day in different directions, then return to report back to the group. They could then make a reasoned decision as to which direction they would go the following morning. This process could be repeated, using different scouts each time, to find their way to a place where they could settle down. It also allowed for a day's rest between each march. There were two babies to consider, too. Flora was the most adept at making the basic clothing they wore during the winter, so she was put to making two slings and each woman would take their turn carrying.

They were nearly there. The feast was two days away and the first scouting parties would leave tomorrow.

Plum shaded her eyes from the returning sun as she searched along the feet of the mountains and around to the horizon for a sign. It had rained for most of the day and she wondered how their scouts had fared in the inclement weather. She had been as still as rock since lunch and her right leg had started to tingle. She stood up awkwardly and slowly extended her limbs. Time has a way of distorting itself when there is nothing else to distract it and she wondered if she would ever lay her eyes on the specks she was waiting for.

When the first people settled in Boardom, long before it was given a name, they had tried to measure time more accurately so they would know how long their fermented blackberries should spend on the fire before they were ready. Some watched the bubbling mass as it boiled, while others passed the time playing a quick bash of Rockball. The subsequent discussion about whether the blackberries had boiled for long enough soon descended into an all out brawl, with one man breaking an arm and another losing a sizable portion of his dignity. Time itself wasn't the problem, they deduced. It tended to pass at a more or less uniform pace in their experience. The problem was perspective and, more specifically, what else you were doing while it happened to you, and so their leader ruled that as many jobs as possible should be done while also doing something else. Their next leap of logic was to discover that time passed like the wind if you were sleeping and this, in turn led to the Great Naked Winter after their clothes were washed downstream when Anselm the Despised took a nap while cleaning them.

Everything was ready. Or at least, it was as ready as the women thought they needed to be. They had never done anything remotely like this before so they were making a lot of it up as they went along. Moss had announced to the men that there would be a grand feast to honour their admirable and steadfast leadership of Boardom – the flattery was Plum's idea – and the return of the first scouts was already overdue. Plum had chosen Faun and Pippy for the opening reconnaissance. This would be the only venture where speed was imperative and it was assumed they were the swiftest and strongest, although nobody had ever had reason to measure such things. They had decided to march in different directions for a full day before spending the night where they found themselves, returning with their reports the following day. They had to ensure the convoy covered as much ground as possible on the first day and it would be hard going for the less mobile women when they finally left, but they could rest more as the land widened between themselves and Boardom. The men would be paraded to the clearing at first light and showered with compliments. The women would then leave them to their feast and retreat to the village, ostensibly to work on their daily chores. They would gather up their things and make off in the direction the scouts advised.

Pippy and Faun were to hug the base of the mountains before splitting, minimising their chances of being spotted and this was where Plum focussed her gaze. She squinted into the sun and saw what might have been a speck a little way out from the rocks. She rubbed her eyes and looked again. Definitely a speck, she thought, as she waited for it to transform. In a few minutes she could make out the distinct figure of Faun and it was all she could do to not run out to meet her. Instead, she scrambled down from her vantage point and scurried to the storage caves.

'Evening, Plum!' said Faun nonchalantly as she walked into the cave. 'Been busy?'

'Faun! You have no idea how glad I am to see you!' said Plum, struggling to contain her apprehension. 'Tell me everything.'

CHAPTER ELEVEN

FEAST AND FAMINE

'There ain't nothing but grasslands for miles,' said Faun. 'The odd splash of bushes here an' there but nothin' worth the journey. The first water I saw was when I finally came round to the Giant Sea and it was a struggle even for one person to make it through one night, I'm sorry.'

Plum was devastated.

'Then we must hope that Pippy has better news.'

'She does!' said Pippy, sweeping into the cave. 'There is a forest in a deep valley, probably three or four days' walk from here. I couldn't reach it but I climbed a good bit up the mountains and could see a dark stripe of treetops. There was a small stream that ran down from the range and out towards Unfinished Mountain. I'm sure there'll be a natural shelter there once we reach it. In the meantime we can stick to the range and find some cover there before heading out over the grasslands. It's perfect, Plum!'

'Do you think we could all make it far enough away in a single day?'

'If we left early I reckon we could. It'll be a long day I shouldn't wonder, but it's been a long life for us too and I for one would relish the chance to scarper to a new one.'

'Then it's settled,' said Plum. 'As soon as the men have been herded to the feast we'll make our move. We'll march in pairs, with the slowest at the front so they don't fall behind and the strongest at the back so they can see everything.'

What bags they had were packed with food, mostly fruit to keep their thirst quenched, and the younger members of the train were hoisted onto backs. This was it, thought Plum, it's happening. The men had been escorted far into Green Forest and with any luck they wouldn't return until the sun was hiding and the women were out of sight.

There was little in the way of ceremony as they took their first steps away from Boardom and towards their new life. The ease with which the women had embraced her revolution had surprised Plum and she found herself wondering how it had taken so long in the end. She took a roll call before they moved off.

'Moss, Pippy, Faun?'

"ere, 'ere, 'ere.'

'Sarka, Flora, Keera?'

'All 'ere.'

'Flow, Meed, Daffy?'

'All present and correct, missus.'

'The two babies?'

Pippy made a crying noise 'Both 'ere!'

'Fern?'

'Which one?' said one of the Ferns. 'I'm here, but I can't see

Fern.'

'She meant me,' said the other Fern from behind Moss.

'Leaf?'

'"ere.' came a squeaky voice.

'Then we're ready. Pair up and let's go.'

Plum was walking with Daffy, a short, plump woman with small hands and a sullen disposition.

'So we're finally on our way then, eh?'

'Looks that way.' said Daffy with customary succinctness.

Plum put a catalyst into the conversation. 'Do you think we've made the right decision?'

'Time will tell.'

Of course it would.

'Do you think you'll be OK to make it to the first night stop?' said Plum, desperate to find some traction. 'It's like nothing any of us have done before, it's going to be a hard day.'

'I'll be fine.'

Plum conceded defeat and explored her thoughts for a more stimulating discussion.

Moss was travelling with Meed, a tall woman with a mop of thick, matted hair. She was the life and soul of the group, reliably humorous and rarely serious. If there was a punch line hanging in the air you could be sure she would grab it with both hands and shower it over everyone. Her anecdotes seemed to be pulled from an eternal well of material and were a constant source of entertainment and she had the kind of memory that was always reminded of a story while others were telling theirs.

'This little procession reminds me of that snowstorm when we were children,' said Meed.

'Does it?' said Moss, wondering what the connection was but keen to hear the tale. 'Why?'

'Do you remember a gang of us walked all the way to the Heather Hills and clambered up through hip high snow? We took lily pads from the Giant Sea so we could whoosh down the hillside over and over again. Flora was so scared she turned and ran all the way back to the Obelisk.'

'That's right! I remember some thoughtless oaf pushed me from the top too and I ended up in a freezing bundle at the bottom of the hill.'

'Don't call me a thoughtless oaf,' said Meed, 'I put a lot of thought into that, as it happens.'

'So it was you! I should have known,' said Moss with a playful nudge of Meed's shoulder.

'You didn't seem to mind it at the time, you had a grin on your face the size of Cave Mountain!'

'That's true enough,' said Moss. 'They were good times, eh? Before the womanly chores of the village were given to us. Here's hoping we can enjoy life as much again now, wherever we end up.'

Meed countered the serious tone in her usual way.

'If it's cold enough to snow in our new home, I'm turning back to boil turnips!'

Rumble... rumble...

Moss shaded her eyes with her hand as she turned to Pippy.

'I'm not sure we've prepared well enough. I reckon we ain't got enough food for starters and the babies need something to drink more than berry juice.'

'We did as much as we could've in the time, ain't no point moaning about it now. What's done is done' said Pippy.

'It's a worry though and no mistake. Where do you think this will take us?' said Moss.

'I reckon it'll be tough at first but once we settle down we'll be 'appier than we've ever been. Perhaps we'll find another tribe to join, one where the men are more pleasant and less demanding.'

'That'd be nice,' said Moss 'but I reckon they're all the same. No 'arm in trying though, eh? I dare say we'll find somewhere comfortable for the time being. If there are men out there worth joining up with then they'll be the type to go exploring, likely as not. They can come to us for a change.'

'Maybe you're right Moss. What I'm focused on is the chance we'll get some time to ourselves once in a while. Can you imagine just lying back staring at the birds?'

'Honestly, no. I can't imagine having time to myself at all. Maybe I'll take up walking, it must be bleedin' lovely to go walking in an area you don't recognise. Everything would be new, everything would be a surprise.'

Moss' gaze paused as she considered the possibilities.

'Let's pick up the pace,' she said, lengthening her gait, 'This is our only chance.'

They had spent the night huddled tightly against the Long Mountains. Shelter was minimal but they were too exhausted to care. They slept soundly and woke later than they would have liked, but they had achieved their first goal at least. They were further away from the grip of Boardom than they had ever been and it lifted their spirits, as well as their heavy legs, as they set off for another day's walk. Plum spent the day moving up and down the line, stopping here and there to talk to each of the women. It was partly to keep the group focused on the distance they were covering but mainly to get away from Daffy and her dull company.

The sun was starting to set again and she still had to find a place for them to spend the night. She called over to Moss and they made their way to the front, scanning the landscape for a suitable resting place. The group were making their way along the green plains, keeping the edge of the mountain range to their right. The only other significant feature was the ever present sight of Unfinished Mountain far off to the left.

'See that line of rock poking out from the mountains?' said Moss, pointing towards the horizon straight ahead of them. 'That's the first place I've seen in a while that might do as a shelter for tonight, what d'you reckon?'

'I think I'd have to be pretty desperate to use that as a night stop,' said Plum, 'but that's exactly what we are and I ain't seen a single cave all day. If the other side of it stretches into the mountain a little way then we should use it.'

'I would have liked to get further today,' said Moss 'but we should be grateful for the ground we have covered. I can't see the men making it this far, even if they left soon after us – which I doubt.'

'You're right. Let's use that if there is room for us all to shelter. If there isn't then we'll have to keep going. Better to find a good spot tired than a poor spot with energy to spare.'

Plum stretched her neck as they approached the jutting rock, hoping to see a large inlet to shelter in. Her legs were aching and she struggled to convince herself that the others would make it any further than this today. The young ones had been passed around the whole group but gradually the older members had to be left out of the sequence. By now there were only three of them left who could carry the burdens and they had to take it in turns, one by one, to have a break. She sped up to take a look.

As she got closer she waited for her line of sight to be filled with cold grey rock but it never came. She stepped over the lowest point in the stone and saw to her right a deep, dark cut in the mountainside, almost a hundred paces deep. She stepped into the space, studying the area that would be their home for the night. For the most part it was unremarkable, cold grey rock that rose up from the floor towards the sky and the occasional detritus from ancient storms. In parts it protruded into the space, sometimes providing a natural shelter and sometimes a peril for unattentive heads. As she reached the dead end she could make out a dark brown patch that stood out from the monochrome scene like antlers on a duck. She would have said it was huddled into its corner, if it did indeed have the ability to move.

It gave off an aura of latent mobility, that was for sure, putting her on edge and shortening her stride. She looked around for something to prod it with, preferably something very long. She retreated a little way towards the exit and found a broken branch trapped between a boulder and the rock face. She picked it up and tip-toed back towards the dead end of the inlet, her gaze locked on to the stationery smudge. It still hadn't moved, perhaps it was just blown here. That made sense to the part of her brain in charge of reassurance, there was no way someone could survive out here on their own. Unfortunately, the part of her brain in charge of health and safety pointed out that it may be part way through a journey, one that may involve hitting as many people as possible quite hard on the head. She held the branch a little tighter and crept on.

If she extended her arm as far as it would go, and held the very last part of the branch that gave a meaningful grip, she could almost flick the nearest fold of the smudge. It was now clear to her that the brown was an animal skin, although it had long since ceased to be attached to its symbiotic owner. She took another small step, stretched out the branch that was at least three times shorter than she would have liked, and gave a gentle swish into thin air.

Reluctant bravery is a universal behaviour that exists in all living things and almost always involves spiders. If a man wanted to flick one from his dinner you could be sure that the first attempt would be a subconsciously deliberate miss. The act of fooling oneself is then free to make way for impatience, who usually swats the spider and half of the dinner into the face of a girl you were desperately trying to look cool in front of.

Plum took another swipe, this time moving a tiny part of the brown bundle, and leapt backwards.

Nothing.

Her impatience had now had enough. She stepped forward and poked whatever it was firmly in its centre.

A hoarse shout came from the bundle, followed by a guttural clearing of a throat, frightening Plum backwards.

'Hey! Get out of my... wherever I am!' said the bundle.

The folds moved, revealing what was almost certainly the head of a man, although further inspection would be required to be absolutely sure. At first glance it was just hair, one great big clump of matted filth. It also seemed to act as a storage facility of sorts judging by the remnants of food on display.

'Hello,' said Plum to the hair.

'Who are you and what are you playing at disturbing my morning nap?'

'It's the evening, as it happens,' said Plum.

'No it's not, and I should know. I had my long sleep earlier, then I had my breakfast and took my nap. So there you have it, it's my morning nap you've disturbed.'

There was a sort of logic to his point. Dodd lived on his own timeline and any outside factors were purely aesthetic. Over the years both his routine and his outlook had gradually shifted, in tandem with his isolation. Now his uncalibrated point of view was all he had to go on. If he decided that the sun was green then, in the absence of anyone to tell him otherwise, it was undeniably green.

Plum thought it best to change the subject.

'Right, well, yes,' she said, unsure where to go from here. 'There are a few of my tribe on their way, do you mind if we use your... home... to shelter for the night?'

'How many of you are there? I don't like crowds so much.'

'There are thirteen of us, fifteen if you count the babies.'

'Babies? So there are men with you?'

'No, we've left them behind.'

'Sarcasm isn't pretty on a woman,' said Dodd with sincerity.

'I wasn't being sarcastic. We really have left them behind, is that so surprising?'

'Yes.'

'Well, yes, I suppose it is a bit unusual,' Plum conceded.

Hearing someone who had a different perspective of their decision for the first time was more illuminating than she would have expected. Unusual doesn't mean wrong though, she assured herself.

'Where have you come from?' said Dodd.

She wondered whether she should reveal such a key piece of information to this stranger. She didn't yet know if he could be trusted, despite it being clear he hadn't been part of a tribe for a long time, if at all. She decided to keep their origins secret for now.

'We're from a place called Greasy Bee,' she said, using the first words that popped into her mind and wishing she had thought of something better.

'Greasy Bee? Is that so? And where did that name come from?' asked Dodd with faux mildness.

'Well, as I understand it,' said Plum, fumbling in vain through her catalogue of stories, 'there was a beehive near the, erm, cooking fire pit, and one day it fell onto... a goat that was cooking there. It covered the hive in grease and gave the village its name.'

'I see,' said Dodd. 'Strange that a beehive would do that, I would have thought a wasps' nest would be more prone to falling than a beehive. Are you sure you're not from Greasy Wasp?'

This man was more astute than his appearance would suggest. Plum knew she had been rumbled but it was too late to backtrack now.

'Don't ask me, I didn't name the place. You know what stories are like, they change more often than the wind.'

'That's true enough,' said Dodd. 'By tomorrow you'll be telling me you're from a place called Boardom and you've escaped to follow a pair of young men into the wilderness.'

Plum walked back to the women and took one of the babies from Faun.

'There's a stranger in there' she said, pointing back to the shelter and raising her voice for them all to hear. 'He seems to know where we've come from, and has guessed at least part of where we're heading. I don't know why or how, but I don't see any other option for us but to settle there for the night, with or without him.'

'How does he know we're from Boardom?' said Pippy. 'No-one saw us leave and no-one has even visited Boardom in all our lifetimes, as far as I know.'

'I'm as mystified as you are, but there will be plenty of time for questions before we get some much needed sleep. Come on, let's get out of sight.'

'You're back,' said Dodd as they reached the far end of his shelter, 'and by the looks on your faces you've brought plenty of questions with you. Please, take the weight off your feet.' He motioned for them to sit down and settled himself a little more comfortably in his corner.

'Let's start with your name,' said Moss.

'I haven't used it for a long time, but I believe I was called... Dodd. Yes, that was it. Dodd.' He seemed to mull over the word as he said it and it fell from his mouth like an unfamiliar pebble.

'Well, Dodd, you ain't wrong 'bout us 'avin' questions,' said Flow in her thick Boardom accent, managing to drop almost as many letters as she kept. 'You can start with why you think we're from a place called... what was it again, Plum? Borndog?'

'Boardom,' said Plum flatly, playing along despite Flow's transparent attempt at innocence.

'Right, Boardom. Well, Dodd?'

'You get straight to the point don't you? Don't you want to know who I am first?'

'Tell us in whichever order you prefer,' said Moss diplomatically. 'We have all night.'

'Then I think I'll start with who I am. It will be nice to tell my tale again, it's been so long since I had anyone to talk to and you seem like a good audience, if a little on the sharp side.' He spoke with a softness that wasn't there when he was on his own with Plum. 'I'm a little out of practice I'm afraid, so this may be a very short version or a very long one. It seems my sense of time is now a fraction unorthodox.'

Keera and Sarka settled the babies down while Meed and Moss passed some fruit around. Dodd stared at the plump pears with something approaching desperation. The look was enough and Meed passed one to him.

'Sorry,' said Dodd, apologising before he had even finished snatching it from her hand, 'and thank you.' He took three bites before his first chew and had it finished in a few heartbeats.

'Well that, ladies, was marvellous!'

'Less of the name calling,' snapped Faun, 'you should be more grateful. What does ladies mean anyway?'

'You've never been called ladies before?' said Dodd with surprise. 'What kind of a place have you come from?'

'Well you seem to know that already,' said Flow, thawing to the stranger more slowly than the others. 'Why don't you start this story of yours and then we'll see who the ladies are.'

'It's not that kind of word, it's a compliment,' said Dodd, struggling to bridge the knowledge gap. 'Although in your case perhaps it was misplaced.'

He cleared his throat again. He hadn't done this much talking for years and his voice was raspy and dry despite the juice from the pear, some of which was still glistening in his beard.

'Anyway, here's my story, for what it's worth. I grew up with a pleasant bunch of people in a village far way away from here, in time at least. I've been a rover for longer than I care to remember and its current proximity is something of a mystery to me. It could be a day's walk away or a ten year hike, either way it's not here and that's all that matters to me. I was a scout for my tribe, searching for food and potential settlement sites. I would walk on my own for days, and sometimes moons at a time, eating whatever I could find as I went. After a while I realised I enjoyed solitude more than being in the company of others and so I resolved to set off one morning and not return. It was a liberating decision and one that I have never regretted. Once you've looked after your survival for another day everything else can be forgotten, you can do whatever makes you smile, and in my case it's finding new landscapes to look at. I've slept on plains, under trees and inside mountains and they are all fascinating places to spend your time. Quite why anyone would want to tie themselves down to the same scene day after day is a baffling to me.'

He picked a lump of pear from his beard, studied it briefly and popped it into his mouth.

'So that is how I came to be here.'

'Is that it?' said Flow 'A bit of a short tale if you ask me, in length and detail.'

'You are a feisty little one, aren't you?' said Dodd, benignly. 'My apologies, I thought that was the long version. As I said, I'm a little out of practise.'

'We're on a journey of our own,' said Plum, eyeing an opportunity to recruit a potential hunter. If he has survived on his own for as long as he says then he must have some hunting skills, she reasoned. 'Perhaps you could join up with us, for a short while at least?'

'Hold your goat for a step,' said Moss, using her favourite Boardom expression. 'We have some questions we need answers to before we start inviting him along.'

The prospect of an inquisition bothered Dodd almost as much as the thought of travelling with a group. His solitary lifestyle lent itself well to his preference for keeping himself to himself. It also occurred to him that it was years since anybody had asked him a question.

'Moss is right,' said Flow. 'How d'you know Boardom, Dodd?'

Concerned glances were exchanged between Moss and Plum. The cat may not have been out of the bag quite yet but you could see its pointy ears, and the long black snake at the other end was probably its tail.

'I am a well travelled man,' said Dodd, carefully treading the line between truth and revelation, 'and I've seen many places, but there is only one named place in the direction you have journeyed from.'

That was a reasonable enough, he thought. As it happened, so did everyone in the group. It was easy for them to imagine there being nowhere else in the world past Boardom.

'What about the two men you think we're following?' said Flow, determined to find a chink in his story.

'Ah yes. As I was finding my way along this mountain range there were two men asleep near a stream. I have no interest in petty theft, nor light conversation, and so I walked on past them and found a different place for myself that night. You are the only other people I have seen in moons and so I concluded, correctly I now suspect, that you were following them.'

'So they at least made it this far,' said Flow, oblivious to the ramifications for a second time.

'Aha!' said Dodd. 'So you are following them. Not that I could give a hoot about your motivations, in the nicest possible way of course.'

It wasn't clear whether he was a nice man unused to social interaction, or a scheming charlatan with a wide selection of ulterior motives to choose from. Either way he was here now and could follow them if he had a mind to, whether they liked it or not.

Moss was keen to eliminate any doubts about their identity from her mind before she gave anything else away. 'What can you tell us about them? What did they look like?' she asked.

'One looked a lot like you, hairy and short. The other one was spread out more and had less hair, perhaps because he was so stretched.'

'Then it's likely you're correct, to a certain extent,' said Moss.

'We do know them, but we ain't following them.'

'Yes you are.'

'We are?'

'Well, if you want to survive at least. There's nothing worth travelling for in any direction bar the one they took. Behind you is Boardom, to your right is a rather large rock, to your left is Unfinished Mountain with a violent river its back. The only way is into the forest beyond the hills.'

'If it's all the same to you, we'll take a look for ourselves' said Plum cautiously. 'If our scouts agree then that is the direction we'll take. You're welcome to come with us, if you choose to. Perhaps we can help each other.'

Plum was enough of a schemer herself to realise he could make a straight line for Boardom and give up their revolution if they let him go. He appeared to her to be too much of a free spirit to be forced into joining them. He may also be too strong for them, although the ball of hair poking out from under the pile of ruffled skins gave her no clues in that regard.

'Meed, give Dodd here another pear,' said Plum. 'It's nice to be nice,' she added for good measure.

'We'll stay here for now,' she said once they had all settled into their own spaces in the dry cove. 'We can scout the area tomorrow and work out our next move from there.'

She called Pippy and Faun over to her. 'Do you need to take a rest tomorrow or do you have enough left in you to go out?'

'I'm fine,' said Pippy.

'Me too.'

'Thank you. Then you should set out at first light. There is likely no point in going out into the plain, we can see most of it from 'ere and you've already scouted far off in that direction. You should stay at ground level along the range's edge for a while before going up the mountainside, perhaps there's something we can't see from down here. Come back tomorrow if you have news, but you should take provisions for a night on your own too, just to be sure.'

'We'll walk along together but I'll go up when the time comes,' said Faun, 'I'm more nimble on my feet than you, Pippy.'

'Then it's settled. You leave at dawn.'

CHAPTER TWELVE

A SHELTER FOR NOTHING

The next day was a wash out. The bright sun of the day before was in hiding, the storm's rain had been relentless since early morning and they were doubly grateful for the day of rest. Shelter was sparse, with only the wind keeping the worst of the rain away from those tight against the rock face. With no fire and no cover they would have made a miserable crew if not for the feeling of liberation and anxiety that ran through each of them.

They passed the time swapping stories and soon realised their happy memories were mostly from their time before they were given their first chores, with those after being either sad or dull. Even Meed began to struggle to find more recent upbeat stories after a while. It served to vindicate their bold decision and steeled their resolve for what was to come.

Dodd stayed bundled in his corner. He slept for most of the day, only waking to take a piece of fruit from Meed when it was offered. They never had to rouse him, it was as though he could sense there was some free food on its way to him and would have his hand open before she reached him. Dinner was frugal and raw. Each of them ate their ration of a pear and a few berries without patience as the darkness came early. They wedged the babies into the deepest crags in the rock, wrapped up in more skins than the women, and left them to sleep. Pippy and Faun had not returned but Plum had assured everyone that this was a good thing, despite her reservations, and before long they had settled down to get what sleep they could on the cold wet floor.

Plum would have woken before the others, had she slept at all. As it was she felt more alert and awake than at any time in Boardom. For a short while she had walked away from the mountain range in the hope of finding some sign of Pippy or Faun. When that proved fruitless she clambered up the ragged sides, slipping several times on the damp rock, until she reached the inevitable conclusion that their return was not as imminent as her patience would have liked. As she arrived back at their makeshift camp she noticed Meed checking in on the babies.

'Morning, Meed.'

'Ah, morning, Plum. Looks like we'll have the sun back today, eh?'

'Aye, it's a good day for walking but there's no sign of Pippy or Faun yet. I hope they get back soon, even if it's without news.'

'I'm sure they're just being thorough.'

'Yes, I'm sure they are. It's just so hard waiting here like flies in a cobweb.'

'Don't be worrying, there ain't no chance the men will get this far. We could have left a map and they wouldn't have done anything with it. Remember when Gowie escaped from his post and Granite had to chase after him? He stopped as soon as he reached the pear trees and spent the day sleeping in the rain. Gowie had wandered back home long before Granite made it back.'

Meed had a way of putting people at ease, even during the most intense of times. Plum felt a thin smile grow on her face despite everything. If they made it to somewhere permanent they may have to struggle to survive, but they would be happy while they did and that counted for more than a cave full of food.

Pippy and Faun arrived back in the late afternoon. They had gone as far and as fast as they could, staying at ground level for the most part but nipping up the mountainside every so often. They had found nothing that could be considered a shelter, nor a natural landmark to aim for. Except one.

They set off for Unfinished Mountain with a cloud of reluctance weighing them down. None of them would have chosen it for their next goal but there was simply no other choice. It meant spending a night in the open, babies and all, and their rations were only heading in one direction. They had to get to some food soon or they would starve and so decided they must to get to the forest, just as Dodd had predicted. Unfinished Mountain was sure to be barren but it did at least offer shelter and the chance for them to rest again on their way to the trees. It was one giant stepping stone for them and they chose it for want of any other options.

Conversation dropped to a minimum and the monotony had created a sort of trance in the group. They had long since stopped walking and were now most definitely trudging, like a line of elderly ants in a hot summer sun. Only Dodd seemed light on his feet, often wandering ahead on his own and rounding back to the group. When he had finally unfurled himself from his corner in the cove Plum had been glad she had chosen to befriend him. He was a huge specimen of a man utterly unlike the men of Boardom, with the glaring exception of the amount of hair he cultivated.

They were saved the hassle of finding a place to rest for the night, at least. There were no meaningful shelters for thousands of paces in any direction so they stopped once some of them began struggling to keep up. There was a small patch of fruit bushes, a mental shelter more than a physical one, and this was where they stopped.

Fleck was ready to take the first juicy scrape of a raspberry when he saw a herd of hairy upright mammals lumbering slowly towards him.

'Well, here's something to warm the cockles of a bored spirit, to be sure,' he said with his customary sing-song lilt.

'Would you not just speak normally?' said Port, a sensible centipede with no time for frilly talk. 'You could just say 'look'.'

'Ah but where's the poetry in that now? You need to paint a richer scene to really experience the importance of the moment, to be sure.'

'And would you please stop saying that!'

'What, poetry?'

'To be sure!'

'Fine, I'll add poetry to my list of things I enjoy that you don't want me to do.'

'Not poetry! 'To be sure'!'

'Well if you don't want me to say poetry, what do you want me to not do?'

'Say 'to be sure'!'

'You want me to say 'to be sure'?'

'No, I want you to stop saying 'to be sure'!'

'Well why didn't you say? I don't even say it that much.'

'You say it at the end of every sentence!'

'I do not, to be sure.'

'There! You said it again!'

'No I didn't.'

'Yes you did, you just said 'I do not, to be sure'.'

'No I didn't.'

'You did.'

'Well if I do say it, and I'm not saying I do, it's not as annoying as your dancing.'

'I don't dance.'

'Yes you do, you thrash your feet up and down all day long. You somehow manage to keep your body still, which I have to admit is quite impressive to be sure, but you're bruising our berries.'

'I don't know what you're talking about' said Port, bending what counted as his neck to look along his belly to his feet. 'See, they're perfectly still.'

'You've just stopped doing it to prove a point.'

'No I haven't.'

'Yes you have, look you've started again.'

Their dispute was ended conclusively, if unsatisfactorily for both sides, when the raspberry Fleck was wrapped around was suddenly ripped from the bush and sent down the throat of a large hairy woman. It was a bit of a shock to Fleck, to be sure.

They stripped the bush bare in a few moments, enough for no

more than three or four small berries each, then lay on the ground in silence. Confidence was a long way away, but Boardom was further. Their only choice was to get to Unfinished Mountain and find shelter before heading to the forest. They knew how to survive in a forest, after all they had kept a whole village fed from one for as long as any living memory stretched.

Their eyelids descended with the night and opened with the sun. None of them could face another day of hard walking but their empty stomachs lifted them from the ground as they set off in fair weather.

The mountain grew imperceptibly larger until one by one they looked up in slow surprise at the rock at their feet. Moss was the first to reach the base of the mountain. She lifted her head to take it all in.

Relief was still washing over her when it was drowned out by sudden terror. She sprinted back to the group, shouting out to Plum as she ran.

'Run!' she screamed. 'Run!'

CHAPTER THIRTEEN

FILLING THE VOID

'Well ain't this just lovely,' said Granite as he casually flicked a ladybird from his hairy arm. 'I always said those women were useful to have around. I can't remember the last time my belly was this full.'

He was sitting in the remnants of his third lunch, a new record for him although far short of the tribal record of seven that Goatface the Unfillable had managed on the day of the Rock Festival all those years ago. The other men in the clearing were at various points on the gluttony scale; some snoring loudly while others still gorged from the mounds of food that surrounded them.

'Aye, I could get used to this,' said Roddo, 'and to think that young wotsisname thought we needed to hunt more!'

'Oh yeah, Nobble wasn't it?' said Plank. 'He's a peculiar sort and no mistake. Come to think of it Roddo, I ain't seen him about the place for a while. Perhaps he's off hunting mammoths for us.'

There was some generous, if slightly soporific, laughter from the more conscious members of the group.

'He's an odd one alright,' said Goober the Profound. 'He doesn't know the meaning of the word tradition. The men should be fed by the women. That's 'ow it's always been and that's 'ow it will always be. If you go upsetting the balance of things they'll come tumbling down over you and give you a pain in the head. He didn't understand that, the poor imp.'

Goober could always be relied upon to vocalise the prevailing wisdom of the day. He had been given his name as a young man after eulogising for hours on the benefits of keeping the same number of fire pits in the village.

'That's a sure thing,' said Granite. 'There is a reason that tradition is traditional. Look at us now! We have more food than we can eat, the women are doing their chores, the rumbles are still sounding reliably from Cave Mountain and all the while we are keeping the traditions of Boardom alive. This is the life, and anyone who thinks different is a fool. The women were right, we are running the perfect village.'

And so they passed the day basking in their ignorant glory, one by one falling asleep for the night in the clearing. Since most of them refused to muster the energy to move from the Meeting Patch to their caves, the idea of making it all the way home from here was unthinkable. And anyway, there was enough food left over for at least a couple of breakfasts before they had to leave their new comfort zone.

The next morning started late and drew out into the afternoon. They started by finishing yesterday's evening meal before moving on to their first breakfast.

'It's a long way back to the village, eh Slate?' said Plank between bites.

'Even longer when there is food ready for us 'ere,' said Slate, opening a single eye to be sure who he was speaking to.

'Perhaps we should finish it off before we go. It would be terrible to waste the efforts of the women, eh?'

'Absolutely!' agreed Slate as they settled in for the evening.

Day three of the feast began in much the same way as day two, only with less food. None, in fact. There was no getting away from it, they had to go back to the village if they wanted to eat. As the food ran out they also became aware of the bites and scratches from the insects that usually kept them away from the forest unless absolutely necessary and it only added to their sense that their time here was running out.

'Well that was bloody marvellous,' said Goober, 'but it looks like we've finally had our fill. I don't know about you lot but I could do with a hearty breakfast. I'd say the women will have a grand one for us back in Boardom by now. They've had long enough!' he added, with effortless prejudice.

He stood up and prepared himself for the walk back to the village. He looked around him and realised for the first time that he had taken no heed of the direction they had arrived from.

'Ah!' he said, wearily. 'Does anyone know which way the village is?'

Two by two the eyes of the men widened slowly as they began to comprehend they were lost. A peril of the tyrannical class is their dependence on those they control. All of the practical information is held by the suppressed, which is fine when a foot is on their neck but less so when the neck starts to wriggle.

'Ah!' said Rankor.

'Oh!' agreed Granite.

'Erm...' offered Old Shankswill.

"ere, how about we go that way?' said Slate, pointing in an arbitrary direction.

'Sounds good to me,' said Tark. 'If we don't find the village in 'alf an hour we'll turn back and go the other way.'

If the tribe gave prizes for logical analysis, then Tark would have been the first ever winner from the men.

They set off in groups of one, with Rankor at the head, each making their own random way through the trees like a flock of sheep after a quarrel. Those at the back were naturally, if marginally, more resistant to patient action and were the first to lose interest in the direction they were heading. Old Shankswill was the first to give in, turning to his left where the ground was easier to travel, and meandering off at his own pace. Some turned to their right, others retraced their steps. It was slow motion chaos, like pine cones being gently blown about in a moderate wind.

As the men made their way aimlessly through the forest, a pair of circling eagles watched with interest.

'Hey!' said one. 'Check zis out! Zose hairy rocks are moving!'

'Gesundheit! Look how far zey have gone! I've never zeen zem 'ere before, in fact I've never zeen them go anyvhere before,' said the other. 'I vonder if zey know zey're going ze wrong vay?'

'Vait! Some of zem are turning back. Now zey have stopped. Vait, zey are on ze move again. Zis is crazy, no vonder zey haven't made it to ze top of ze food chain.'

Rankor was first to break the cover of Green Forest, not because he was the best of them at finding a way out, just the luckiest. Even so, it had taken him several hours and he was glad of the rest as he slumped onto the grass. One by one they appeared, each dropping to the ground without saying a word. Their hunger battled pluckily for control over their weariness but was beaten back by years of convention. It wasn't really a fair fight.

It took some time, but in due course all of the men had stumbled out of the forest. The sun had already started its slow plunge by the time they were ready to move on and Rankor summoned all he had to stand up and address them.

'Right then men!' he said. 'Are we all here? Where's Granite? Has anyone seen Granite?'

'I'm over 'ere!' muffled Granite as he pulled his face up from a clump of moss. 'But I ain't going anywhere soon, Rankor, I'm bone tired. Let's just stay 'ere for now. We can eat later.'

'Yeah, come on, let's have a break, Rankor,' whined Tark. 'We can't be too hasty about this now.'

'Some of us have been here for longer than others,' said Rankor. 'Get up, it's almost dinner time and we ain't even had breakfast yet. There's plenty of time for a slumber once we're home. You can stay 'ere if you like, but I'm going back to the women and whatever they've made for my belly.'

Granite sighed. This was all very stressful, he wasn't used to decision making – that was for others to worry about – and he now had three options to choose from. Stay and rest, go home and rest, go home and eat. It was all too much. He decided against making a decision and went with the flow.

'Fine, let's go home.'

Tark was the first to suspect something was amiss. There was an abandoned feeling to the Meeting Patch, an unsettling air of vacancy.

'Rankor?' he said tentatively. 'Something ain't right.'

'What's that, Tark?'

'Look, listen. Dead silence. Even Cave Mountain is quiet.'

Rankor took in the scene. Tark was right, but perhaps the women were foraging.

'Goober, go and check the caves. Granite, go back and look in the forest. If they ain't in the caves they must be in there.'

A resigned sigh came from behind Rankor as Granite mumbled an inaudible complaint.

The mountain was quiet. The men were so accustomed to its frequent rumbling that it had become part of the village, like the sound of the river or the rustling of the leaves. It was only when it stopped that they heard the memory of it. It was a powerful change that sat uncomfortably with them.

'Erm, Rankor?' said Tark. 'I don't like this one bit. The mountain has gone quiet and the women are nowhere to be found. Do you think they know something we don't?'

'Of course they do Tark, they know where they are for a start! I don't reckon they 'ave it in them to quieten a mountain though. Get a grip of yourself, man! We'll find them soon enough and teach them never to abandon the village again. I told you they couldn't be trusted.'

'No you didn't.'

'I bloody well did, I'm always saying it! They're an odd sort, women. Mark my words, they'll be afraid to go more than a hundred paces from their caves by the time we've finished with 'em.'

Tark knew better than to push his luck further than he already had. Rankor had never concerned himself with the women, to him they were just things that looked after the day to day chores for the tribe. Tark wondered how he got away with it, but power is the master of deceit, and the powerful are experts at nudging evidence into the shadows.

'You're probably right, Rankor, I'll go and help Granite.'

Tark headed off to the forest with his mind full of growing irritation. If the women have gone, whatever the reason, then the men wouldn't survive a day. Rankor's plan was reliant on the women being nearby, and he wasn't so sure they were. Something felt wrong and the silence roaring out of the mountain didn't help his paranoia. They needed a Plan B, and possibly a Plan C too.

'Quick!' He called as he caught up with the trudging Granite. 'We need to get into the forest sharpish.'

Granite gave him a confused look. 'One thing we're not short of is time.'

'Time is precisely what we are short of! I'll explain it all when we're safe.'

'Safe?'

'Just move yourself, and if you wouldn't mind turning your plod into a trot that would be great.'

Once they had reached the cover of Green Forest Tark stopped suddenly, grabbing Granite by the arm.

'Oi! Leave it out Tark!'

'For once would you stop complaining and listen to me. There are strange things afoot and I need your help. The women have left, I'm sure of it. I don't know why and I ain't sure I want to know, but we need a plan if we're to make it to the next moon.'

'Now I'm not one for drama as you know Tark, but I think you may be getting ahead of yourself 'ere all the same. They've probably just gone off to get more food.'

'With the babies?'

'Ah. Maybe they're teaching them how to look after us men.'

'The babies?'

'Ah. Well, maybe they've... you know...'

'Left?'

'No, no! Not left. Why would they leave? They have everything they could ever want here.'

'No they don't, Granite. Think about it, what's the best thing about Boardom?'

'You know me well enough to know the answer to that, Tark. There ain't nothing better than spending a day in the sun with a pile of food. If it's good enough for me then I s'pose it's good enough for them too.'

'What would the women say was the best thing about Boardom,' said Tark with more patience than he expected. 'All they do all day is wait on us hand and foot. They don't get to laze in the sun and they have to work for any food they eat.'

'I've never really thought about it like that, Tark. I wonder what it is they like about the place?'

Tark could almost see the shaft of logic as it pierced Granite's expression. He waited.

'They must be sick of the place!' said Granite emphatically. 'They should do something about it, preferably without hampering my meal times.'

Nearly there, thought Tark.

'What would you do if you were one of the women, Granite?'

'That's a daft question Tark, I ain't a woman and I don't need to waste my time worrying about them. If you're so concerned you can spend your day here looking for them. I'm going home.'

'Wait! Granite! Listen to me. What are you going to have for dinner?'

'I'll have whatever I'm given Tark.'

'Precisely! And if you ain't given nothing, if the women really have left, then what?'

'Then someone else will make me something.'

'Who?'

'I don't care who, so long as I have a full belly.'

'Who?' Tark repeated. 'Name me one person who would know

how to find your dinner.'

'I bet that Bobble one would know how.'

'Great, go and ask him. Do you know where he is?'

'I don't keep a log of everyone's movements, Tark. Stop being difficult.'

'OK, tell me when you last saw him.'

Granite stared at a tree as he navigated through his memory.

'It was at the Obelisk, with that strange bendy thing of his. Ha!' he said with an arrogant air, 'He can sort us out. Will that do for your great plan, Tark?'

'That sounds perfect, Granite, apart from one small detail. Where was he sitting for the feast?'

'I don't know, Tark. I told you, I don't keep track of other people's lives. I have enough trouble keeping up with my own. I'm a very busy man, you know?'

'He wasn't sitting next to anyone, Granite. He wasn't there. He ain't been here for days. If a man feels the need to leave then the women certainly could.'

That hit home.

'So who will make our dinners?'

Finally.

'Which is why we need a plan. I have an idea, but I need your help.'

Rankor had gathered the men to the Obelisk. The women had left, that much had become clear. Where they had gone to was a mystery, although that wasn't saying much since anywhere that wasn't Boardom was a mystery to the men. It seemed to Rankor that he was paying the price for all the times he was given the finest fruit and the choicest cuts of meat, on those rare occasions they had some. He finally had to lead. He looked at the rag tag bunch in front of him from a different perspective for the first time. If they were to get out of this mess then they needed to use their wits, unfortunately they only had one wit between them and it wasn't a very good one.

'The women have left us,' he began, 'and there ain't no food left.'

Best to get the worst news out of the way, he thought.

'We need to find some or we will starve. I think we should assume they ain't coming back.'

Despite Rankor stating the obvious there was still a stunned silence from the crowd. They liked to have things spelled out to them before reaching rash conclusions and this time was no different.

'As you all know I am an honest man,' he lied, to stifled grunts. 'I don't have the answer to our problem. Does anybody here have any idea what our next step should be?'

The expected silence wasn't given a chance to reach their ears before a voice called out.

'I do.'

It was Tark.

'Now ain't the time for jokes, Tark. We have a real problem here,' said Rankor.

To be fair to Rankor he couldn't have been seen as unjust in his barbed response, since all of the tribe's experience of Tark in the previous hundred or so moons would point to him being a useless lump of hairy laziness.

To be fair to Tark, that could be said of all the men.

'Which is precisely why you should 'ave a listen to what I've got to say,' said Tark with confidence, continuing without waiting for permission. 'The way I see it is that Cobble and Bones – remember them? – disappeared for reasons of their own. They ain't come back yet so they're either dead or happy.'

'What have they got to do with anything? They've always been a pebble short of a mountain,' said Goober.

'Yeah Tark, what have they got to do with anything?' said Roddo, latching on to the comfort of someone else's opinion.

'I'm sure none of us would say we're a particularly proactive bunch and they have always been clever, in their own odd way.'

'Are you just here to have a pop at us or is there a point to all this?' said Rankor. 'They're both as odd as frogs and it's more likely we'll see a flying fish than do anything because they did.'

'Any more animal comparisons you'd like to get off your chest, or are you quite finished? There is actually a fish that... do you know, forget it. My point is that they have presumably given up on us and gone off to find something better. A few days later the women have gone too. What does that tell you?'

Tark knew that expecting an answer from this rabble to such an open question was like politely asking a swarm of bees to move slightly to their left, but if you hit them with a big stick they may just go in the right direction.

'It tells us that there is a good reason why they don't want to be here anymore' he continued. 'The women wouldn't leave the comfort of the village, especially with the babies, unless there was something else going on. They have all the food they could want 'ere, even if they have to get it for themselves, and it would be an 'ard road for them until they found somewhere to settle down. With them gone we have no one to gather our food, none of us know which mushrooms are safe to eat and which ain't. Does anyone 'ere know which berries are poisonous and which ain't?'

He didn't wait for an answer.

'No, we don't. We could all be dead in a moon if we don't find the women and bring them back 'ere. It's our only option. Staying 'ere will kill us, leaving might kill us. What are we waiting for?'

'I'm waiting for your sanity to wake up. You've gone and lost it, Tark,' said Slate.

Tark waited for the usual chorus of agreement. And waited.

'Rankor? What d'you reckon?' he said, going for the kill before the dissenters did.

'I think it sounds like a lot of effort, and it's only half a plan. What do you think we should do?'

Tark had scratched out a rudimentary idea in his head. Fortunately for him it was about as much detail as most of the tribe could handle.

'We should head for the Giant Sea, then across to Unfinished Mountain. There may be something behind it that we can't see from here. It could be a paradise! I'm sure the women would've taken the same route, keeping close to the water so they could bathe the babies and have a supply of fresh water for as long as they could. You know how they like to keep everything clean.'

His stunted logic hadn't worked out that escape was a more important priority for the women than clean skin.

'He's right about that,' said Granite, 'they do love to clean things.'

'You want us to leave!?' said Old Shankswill, his brain desperately clinging on to the speed of the discussion.

'Not necessarily, Shanky,' said Tark. 'We could go with your plan instead.'

'But I don't have a... oh.'

'Does anybody else have an alternative?' said Rankor.

'We could just stay here,' said Plank.

'And what will you be making us for dinner, Plank?' said Granite, falling back on the concept that had snared him.

In any group of underachievers there is always one who excels. In Boardom it was Granite. He was a master of nothing, insofar as he could do nothing for moons on end without the slightest effort. It was a real skill. If he was advocating an endless hike to a new land then something must be seriously askew.

'Let me get this right in my head,' said Plank. 'You, Granite, are of the opinion that we should leave Boardom, for an unknown amount of time, to a destination we can't see, because we need a bit more food?'

'More food? To need more food you have to have some food to begin with. It's quite an important distinction. Also, you left out the bit where you tell us what you're making us for dinner.'

Plank had nothing. Nor did anyone else.

Granite was never so disappointed to have won an argument.

CHAPTER FOURTEEN

TRIPS AND TRAPS

It had been more than a quarter moon since Cobble and Bones first arrived in Nutty Woods. In that short time they had gained more respect from the men here than they ever did in Boardom. The interest the Nutty Woodsmen showed in Cobble's abilities was as far removed from the men of Boardom as he could have imagined. Tiff had embraced the idea of them and allowed them both the freedom of the village to do as they pleased. They were looked upon as the experts in an area that had remained a complete mystery to the men for so long. When this level of respect landed on the shores of Cobble's and Bones' mind they lapped it up and filled the roles effortlessly. It was what they had always craved and they were sure they wouldn't let the opportunity pass. It was like handing a roasted boar to a starving man.

An idea had been bouncing around his head for a few days now and he had resolved to speak to Tiff about it before he and Bones started their teaching. At the village Square one evening he sat down next to the chief.

'Ho! Tiff!'

'Ah Cobble, dear boy. Please, sit.'

'I have an interesting proposal for you.'

'Oooh marvellous, I do love a bit of intrigue,' said Tiff in the manner of a man starved of variety.

'The way I see it is that we have fourteen mouths to feed, myself and Bones included, and we need to introduce better food into our meals.'

'Does this get more intriguing?' said Tiff, mischievously, 'because we already know that.'

'Bones and I can help a little, but if we want to cause real change then we need as many people as possible to be able to build the things we need.'

'My dear Cobble, I don't understand. I have already said you can use all the men.'

'That you have, Tiff, that you have, but we need as many people as possible,' said Cobble, hoping the emphasis would pull the idea out of the recesses.

'You're not making much sense here, Cobble. Perhaps you're using a Boardom way of speaking that I'm not familiar with?'

Cobble set aside subtlety once more.

'Women are people too, Tiff.'

'Oh.'

'That would give us two more people to help build shelters, boughs, arrows, traps, cooking stands, forks, tools... anything!'

'Ah.'

'Having ten men is good, but having twelve people is better.'

'Right.'

Tiff's expression managed to be frozen still and contorted in conflict at the same time, like a confused pigeon. Cobble decided that his logic was as simple as he had made it out to be and no amount of clever word play was going to help. He waited. Eventually Tiff's face defrosted.

'Cobble, you peculiar man, I can't say it's an idea I'm comfortable with. After all, the ladies have only ever prepared our meals and maintained the village. They have never known anything different and nor have we. However, your foreign ways could be a bounty for us and so I will trust your judgement. If we are to make ourselves comfortable here then we must relinquish our long held traditions. Change is a gamble, but not changing is predictable and has an inevitable end for us. You may teach the women,' he said, with characteristic pomp.

It was Cobble's turn to freeze. He had just heard a man abandon tradition for one of his more radical ideas. He leapt to his feet and ran to find Bones, calling over his shoulder as he fled.

'Thank you, Tiff!'

'Ladies and gentlemen,' Cobble began, with the beginnings of a Nutty Woods way of speaking. 'Between us we have the ability to make anything we want and the possibilities are endless. We have a long list of things to build and I will show you how to make them while Bones here will show you how to find the right parts for the jobs. I have split you into two groups. Pingo, Balcor, Fettle, Camble, Jutt and Chard, you will start with me. Tiff, Speck, Barna, Quiller, Thistle and Tarpin, you will start with Bones. Once we have all learned some basics we'll rotate the groups and by the end of the moon you will all have the skills to start building.'

They broke out into their groups as Cobble walked over to

Bones.

'Isn't this something, Bones? Could you have imagined it a moon ago?'

'It seems to me we've found our place in the world,' said Bones with uncharacteristic gravity. 'I could be happy here.'

'And so we shall, Bones. Now let's get to work.'

Cobble gathered his group together, keen to waste no time after so many years of apathy. He talked them through the basics of making some simple tools; a slate chisel and a small rock hammer, and emphasised the importance of them for most practical jobs. He showed them how these could be used to make a wooden bowl and explained how useful it would be. It could be used to carry water, hold their food, crush nuts and so on, he told them. Even this most basic of creations was met with exclamations of comprehension. Wait until they see me make a bough and arrow, he thought.

Every swipe of his slate was studied in detail, every bang of his hammer. They lapped up the revelations and Cobble had to work hard to keep them from running off into the forest in search of the right kind of wood to start their own bowl.

Bones was having similar problems. Trying to get the men to discriminate between trees was like telling the moon to stop shrinking. This was going to take time, he thought.

'I say!' Said Pingo one morning. 'This is quite the education, what!'

'Indeed,' agreed Balcor. 'This flint is a fascinating contraption too. Who would have thought it was all about having the right tools, eh?'

'Yes, it's all rather simple when you boil it down into smaller puzzles, just like Cobble said. I'd wager we'll be making all kinds of strange things soon enough.'

'Well, I for one will be glad to get something meaty on the fires again,' said Pingo. 'I'm altogether tired of those darn hazelnuts.'

Most of them had struggled at first, like chickens trying to paint a sunrise, but Pingo was as close to a natural engineer as they had. Once he wrapped his thoughts around the basic principles he was off and away. His wooden fork was almost as good as Cobble's.

Cobble had long thought about the possibility of making a trap that could be left unattended in marked areas, waiting for unsuspecting animals to be unfortunate enough to fall victim to it. The more he thought about the detail involved, the more complicated it became. He would need to have a moving part to it that only the prey could activate. This was new ground for Cobble, all of his previous inventions had been either static or manipulated by the user. If he could master the design behind getting the prey to start the motion then they could catch dozens of animals in a single moon. He had a reasonable mental picture of what was needed but had never made anything tangible as yet. He called Pingo over.

'Whatto, Cobble!'

'It's time we put your new found skills into action. I've had an idea for a trap that I'd like your help to build. It's more complicated than the contraptions you've made so far but I think you're up to the task.'

'Well, Cobble. I'm as excited as a bird in a gale, where do we start?'

'Here's what I've worked out so far. We have a piece of flat, square wood and a box with an open end, held up by a stick. We put some bait onto the lower piece of wood and then whatever wanders onto the wood knocks over the stick and the box comes crashing down and traps them. What I can't work out is how to make sure the animal can't just run off. I was hoping you might be able to help with the design side of things.'

'Ah, I see. That's the easy bit, old boy!'

Cobble felt a release of pressure in his mind. This was just the reaction he had hoped for.

'What you need to do is throw away the box, that doesn't do anything except show the prey there is a trap.'

'Ah...' Cobble wasn't used to having someone improve his ideas. He was almost sure he liked it.

'You need to hide the trap, cover the bottom part with leaves and raise the top part up high. Oh, and change the high one to a bally great spike. That should do the trick.'

'But how would they trigger the spike to fall?'

'Simple, dear boy. You tie a thin piece of string to a branch over here' he said, motioning towards a tree to his left, 'and run it past the bait just above the ground and over to... this branch here.' He was pointing to a tree on his right with several low, gnarly branches. 'You can then run it up the tree out of sight and tie it to the spike.'

'Well well, Pingo, it seems you may have a hidden talent!'

'It's very kind of you to say so, old chap, but I haven't the faintest idea how to do it. I can't see how we could be assured the spike will release and fall onto the beast. I could certainly cheer you on from here though if that would help?'

'Not a chance,' said Cobble. 'Bones is an expert at knots, he'll know how to make it work. We'll tell you what to do and you can make it. If Bones and I ever move on you'll need to show the others how it all works.'

'My dear Cobble,' said Pingo in a friendly tone. 'You're not going anywhere, we simply won't allow it. Now where do I start?'

Then came Thistle, the far less hairy woman. Such differences were not to be sniffed at when it came to young men's ambitions. A less hairy face was a lot more fun. She had captured Cobble's attention from the moment he tripped into her dinner during a particularly absent-minded wander through the Square. An unfortunate side-effect was that Thistle's first sight of Cobble was an interesting mix of pointy limbs and a dripping beard of hazelnut soup. He wasn't embarrassed, being almost entirely ignorant about how the whole 'man meets woman' thing was supposed to work. His knowledge in this field was similar to a beetle's knowledge of plate tectonics. He didn't enjoy how the mystery of it took up space in his thoughts uninvited and would have much preferred for it to take a nice long holiday with some of his other more puzzling thoughts until he forgot all about them.

He dismissed the unfamiliar feeling with a shake of his head and focused on his work. All of the men had done their rotations and it was time to select the best for each. Pingo was a natural engineer and so Cobble chose him as captain for his new team. The idea that someone else could think as he did had seemed both alien and unlikely to him, like a squirrel hoping to find a nutcracker, but Pingo appeared to be the real deal.

Tiff arrived, interrupting his thoughts.

'I say, Cobble,' he said, 'we really are most grateful for everything you and Bones have brought to us here. You are just what our little band of stragglers was missing. I wonder though if we could start, you know, using some of your things to catch some, well, food. I don't mean to sound ungrateful or anything, but the men here have had their imaginations poked and it would be rather good to cook something with a face.'

'Indeed,' said Cobble. 'I was thinking of splitting people up into the roles for which they have shown most potential. The engineers can work with me, the searchers can go with Bones. Before long we'll have a store of boughs, arrows, traps and tools to give us all the meat we could ever need. Once we find some animals with legs that is, all I have come across so far is those damned snakes.'

'Ah, yes. We had noticed that too. There were plenty of birds and rodents when we first settled here but they seem to have moved away recently. Perhaps they know something we don't, what?'

'I wonder if squirrels ever get sick of eating nuts?' thought Cobble, out loud. 'This place would turn even the most ardent of fans off them I would say.' That crystallised Cobble's plan. 'You're right Tiff, it's time to go hunting.'

Rumble... rumble... rumble...

Bones had suggested a slipping knot for the wooden spike. They tested it, making a few tweaks as they went, until they were happy it

was as good as it was going to get. They set it a few hundred paces
from the Square and applied themselves to the task of making more.
There were more than a few discarded efforts by the time they were
finished. Quiller had spent most of the time cursing the cantanker-
ousness of inanimate objects, but with fourteen eager builders they
soon had good collection and Cobble had sent Pingo and Bones
out to scatter them around the area, marking their locations with a
stripped branch staked to the floor.

The next day Cobble sent Pingo to check on them. The wait
for him to return would have been interminable if it wasn't for
the nightmare that was about to present itself. He was sitting on a
fallen tree trunk as Thistle walked straight towards him. Worst of
all was that she was making eye contact. This is awful, he thought.
He had no idea how to behave. Worse still, he had no idea how he
wanted himself to behave. Should he try to impress her? Should he
mention the hazelnut soup? In the end he chose to fumble nervously
over his words, compounding his already low confidence.

'Hi Cobble!' she said cheerily.

'Yes, yes. Hi Thimble... Thistle! Thistle! Hi Thistle. Yes, Thistle.
That's your name, so that's why I said Thistle.'

He groaned inside.

'Do you think Pingo will find anything in the traps?'

This was safer ground.

'Well Thistle, I certainly hope so Thistle,' he said, overcompen-
sating. Stop saying her name, he thought.

'What do you think might be in them? I would like it to be a
boar, I always liked boar.'

'Well I'm not sure a boar will be taken down with the traps we've
made so far. The spikes would probably just bounce off them.'

'Yes, I suppose you're right, Cobble. You would have to put a heavy weight on the spike too if you wanted to kill a boar. Maybe you could tie a small rock to the end instead of a spike, that way it might knock the poor thing out.'

Cobble's confidence vanished again. Did she just?... No, surely not. She was right though, he couldn't get away from that. If she was a woman who had a keen eye for mechanical details then he really was in trouble. He would be floundering whenever he was around her if he didn't do something about it. One minor problem was that he had no idea what something looked like. He steeled himself.

'You are good at traps. I like you. Not like that. Well, yes, like that, but not... you know. Well, actually I do mean like that.'

That was less smooth than he had hoped, but better than he expected. He had got the main crux of his message across.

'Cobble?'

Oh no, he thought. Ruined with one incomprehensible sentence.

'Do you really?' said Thistle.

'Well, I mean... It's... well... yes, I suppose so.'

'You suppose so?'

'Well you're, you know...'

'No.'

'You're a lot less hairy than me. And your nose is smaller.'

This was now going precisely how he thought it would.

'Is that a compliment, Cobble?'

'I honestly have no idea.'

He was spared any further embarrassment by the flailing arms of Pingo as he charged into the Square.

'Gentleman!' he exclaimed. 'Look!'

He held up a limp rabbit with a spike sized hole in its back.

'It worked! I had to put the bally thing out of its misery with a rock but still, it worked.'

'I say, Pingo!' said Tiff. 'That is fabulous! Fettle, quick! Get a fire going, we're sharing a rabbit for dinner.'

CHAPTER FIFTEEN

UNFINISHED BUSINESS

Barna looked at the familiar scene in front of him. He knew the patterns of the trees here as well as anyone, from the placement of roots to the undulations of the ground. There had been little to occupy them here, short of their failed attempts at engineering, and he had spent many hours meandering through the natural pathways of the forest. His mother had always told him to be wary of strangers and specifically never to accept meat from them, especially if they had gone to the trouble of cooking it. Times were different now though, they were slowly starving before the strangers arrived and meat that was given with an ulterior motive was still better than none at all. In any case, Cobble and Bones were simply strange, rather than strangers. It seemed to him that they were the missing piece of their puzzle. Quite a large and significant piece, granted, but a piece nonetheless.

He turned back towards The Great Oak, ready to do his bit for the new tribe.

An orange glow flickered across the faces of the Nutty Woodsmen. They had only a small morsel of meat each but it felt like the breaking of a dam, with all minds now focused on how to increase the food supply. It had revitalised dormant abilities and Cobble was inundated with suggestions.

'I say, we could dig a bally big hole in the ground and set those nasty spikes at the bottom. That would kill the beast at best, or trap it at worst,' said Tarpin.

'So you think they will just walk into a hole? They've survived longer than we have in this place so they can't be that stupid,' said Jutt with condescension.

'Jutt, stop your infernal point scoring, please!' said Tiff. 'We're looking for solutions here.'

'Well you won't find a solution with ideas like that.'

'We, Jutt, not you,' said Bones. 'If we cover the opening with some loose branches and leaves they won't see it coming.'

'Very good, Bones,' said Cobble. 'We could leave some food on top to attract them. That should be our next project. Pingo, Balcor, pick any two men you like and start digging. Don't forget to mark the area so we don't fall in ourselves.'

'So now we're giving away what little food we have to the same beasts we can't eat ourselves. This is spectacular,' said Jutt. 'Why don't we just leave the first animal we catch there, that way we can waste everything.'

'Do you know, Jutt, that's the best idea you've had yet,' said Cobble. 'When we catch a good sized animal we'll leave some of it on top of the trap. It will help to catch another animal and the smell of what's left of it at the bottom of the pit will attract more. We could catch several animals for the cost of one!'

Jutt lowered his head as his eyes opened wide. I'm the trapped one here, he thought. Trapped with a bunch of fools.

'You can't be serious,' said Jutt. 'That's like a freezing man throwing his coat off a cliff. It's madness.'

'No, Jutt,' said Cobble. 'It's like a freezing man burning his coat to keep warm, except we might get two coats from the deal. It's logical.'

'Cobble is right,' said Tiff. 'We may build up a constant stream of fresh meat if we give up the first few to the cause. If we catch two animals with the first pit then we use them on another two pits and so on. We may end up with more meat than we could ever need. It's genius, if it works.'

'If it works?' said Jutt, standing up to look down on Tiff. 'How can it work if we don't have an animal to set the first trap. You're all deluded! I've had it!'

He grabbed a coat, a handful of nuts and strode out of the Square into the woods. Speck stood up dutifully and followed him. They were an odd couple, both visually and emotionally. Jutt was tall and thin, with a nose that was a microcosm of his body. Speck was short, by the standards of the Nutty Woodsmen, with ears that seemed to be allergic to his head. Where Jutt went you could be sure Speck was lurking in his shadow, like an obedient servant with a fear of sunlight.

Nobody stopped them.

'I'm sure he's just gone for a walk to clear his head,' said Pingo. 'Cobble, do you think you could catch anything with that bough of yours? I for one think it's worth a shot.'

Cobble looked down at his invention and back up at Pingo. 'I've been waiting a long time to try.'

Bones rubbed his pendant as he waited for the men to leave before gently pulling on Cobble's arm and gesturing towards a cluster of small sycamore trees away from the group. There was a curious look on his face, as if he had run out of patience.

'Listen,' said Bones.

Cobble waited for Bones to get whatever it was off his chest. 'Yes?'

'No, I mean listen. What can you hear?'

'I can't hear anything.'

'Listen again, and concentrate this time. Pretend you've never heard anything before in your life and the sounds around us are the first you've ever heard.'

Cobble wondered what had happened to his friend. Maybe he had become friendly with Chard and was a bit squiggly over the whole episode. He humoured him.

'There's a rustle of leaves in the breeze,' he began. 'I can hear a bird far off in that direction, possibly a starling, and the trickling of the stream.'

'It's a thrush, but good effort. Now, what else?'

'That's it. I can't hear anything else. What's all this about Bones?'

'One more time, Cobble, please. Ignore the leaves and the birds, what else?'

Cobble didn't know how to strain his hearing the way he could with his eyes or his mind, but he tried anyway. He tuned out the birds, tuned out the leaves, and left himself with nothing. Nothing but the background hum of life. What would that be called, he wondered.

'All I can hear is the background hum of life,' he said.

'Exactly!' exclaimed Bones. 'And what is the hum of life?'

'Ah now, Bones, I don't have time for a deep and meaningful debate about the circle of life and the balancing of energy and all that nonsense! I have pits to dig, arrows to make, animals to hunt.'

'OK, OK. It's Cave Mountain, only it's not.'

'Now I am worried about you Bones, are you feeling alright? Cave Mountain is days away from here. There's no way we could hear it from this far away.'

'Exactly! There's no way we could hear it, but listen to the rumble. You know it as well as your own feet!'

Cobble strained himself again.

Bones was right, there was a rumble underneath all the bird chatter and water. It was such a part of the landscape that it took an effort to consciously hear it.

'You're right Bones, there is a rumble, but it couldn't possibly be the rumble of Cave Mountain. I assume you've thought this through though, so what are you suggesting it is?'

'It has to be Unfinished Mountain. It's the only peak for miles around and I dare say you could hear it in Boardom. What if the rumble we have assimilated into our lives isn't Cave Mountain at all. What if it is Unfinished Mountain.'

'It would be interesting, but nothing more. What difference does it make?'

'It's getting louder, even in the short time we've been in this forest. The old rumble was always the same, as reliable as the moon, but this one is getting louder. It's becoming physical. Remember the picture in Moss' cave, the one with the breathing mountain? I think that may have been Unfinished Mountain.'

'Great, so do you want us to go back to tell Moss? She'll be thrilled you've cracked the great mountain painting mystery. Bravo!' said Cobble with more needle than was justifiable.

They had never had an argument in the true sense of the word. There were plenty of disagreements about how to approach their projects, but they were always constructive.

'There's no need to be like that Cobble, I was merely pointing out that one of the great foundations of our village may have been, in actual fact, nonsense. If it wasn't Cave Mountain then maybe the breathing wasn't something symbolic. Maybe it didn't represent the life of the village.'

'Maybe it represented the hot air that all those men spouted, and that you're spouting now!' said Cobble, turning away from his friend.

'I'm going to find out for sure,' called Bones after him, 'that's what I wanted to tell you, but I can see you don't care. I'll look after it on my own, you stay here in your new kingdom.'

Cobble and Pingo were sent off with what constituted a fanfare in Nutty Woods. The remaining men and women stood to attention in a perfect line and applauded politely, wishing them jolly good luck and offering their best wishes for a swift and safe return. Only Jutt, Speck and Bones were missing.

They had determined that their route should spiral outwards

from the village, allowing them to cover a lot of ground while staying within a relatively short walk back to the village with whatever creature they were able to capture. If. They carried enough provisions for two hungry days and the rest they would forage as they went.

They were light on provisions but heavy with hope as they searched the forest for signs of movement. Neither were competent hunters, they were the pioneers of their group, but all the same their spirits were high as they began.

Over the next two days, however, pessimism encroached on hope and made itself comfortable.

The morning brought heavy rain and a sharp breeze and they were soaked, leaving them cold and grumpy despite the warm late spring sun. This was their third day out in the woods and they still had nothing to show for their efforts. They had spent a day stalking a large adult boar but the precious arrows missed their target no fewer than six times. Another day was spent sheltering from a vicious storm that ravaged the trees and swelled the streams. So far, all that their endeavours had yielded were two broken arrows and two empty bellies. They were running out of patience and enthusiasm and knew they would be heading back to the village empty handed if today's hunt didn't go well. The thought of seeing the smug look on Jutt's face if they returned empty-handed was as much a useful motivator as it was a spectre of failure at the back of their minds.

The cracking sound of a large twig echoed off the steep wall of rock beside them. Cobble gave Pingo a stern look and motioned for him to crouch. They had been tracking a young deer for over an hour and Cobble's bough was finally taut again. The animal was taking a potentially pointless drink from the bloated stream that ran along the rocks, gloriously unaware of how little future it had left. Cobble waited for a lull in the wind as he aimed his sight down the arrow.

Pfffft.

Thud.

The deer slumped to the ground, dead still, as they leapt to their feet and ran through the gushing, icy stream. The arrow had pierced the side of the animal and stuck fast. Cobble had to wriggle it more than he would have liked to retrieve it but was at least glad it was still in a good working condition. They were challenging weapons to make in large numbers, even with several of the Nutty Woodsmen helping to make a store of them for hours each day.

'Well boil my berries, Cobble, dear boy! You've done it! This is marvellous. We could set a dozen pits with enough spare to feed the whole bally village.'

Cobble was pleased to hear a hungry Pingo focusing on the big picture and resisting the temptation to try and eat the whole thing straight away.

'Yes, I have to say I'm more than a little relieved that we finally have something to show for these few days.' He was speaking like a Nutty Woodsmen more and more with each passing day.

'Let's get it home before we freeze to death.'

They found a sturdy branch and tied the deer's legs to each end, hefting it up and onto their shoulders before setting off. Pingo was a good deal taller than Cobble and an unfortunate side-effect was that Cobble's trek home was punctuated by the rhythmic thumping of the animal's rear end against his shoulder. By the time they stopped to eat the last of their food he was miserable. He tried to focus on the next part of the plan.

'How many pits do you think we could make with this?' he said.

'We could use the four legs and the head,' said Pingo, 'The rest should be roasted for the village. It will be the first time that everyone will have full bellies at the same time. I'll ask Camble to open the last of his special apple juice, although it's so weak you have to drink your own body weight to feel the slightest buzz and by that time you've skipped all the pleasant feelings and headed straight to the emptying phase.'

'Nice. I think I'll stick to water. Come on, let's get back,' he said, awkwardly getting to his feet in the manner of one twice his age. 'I could do with a different kind of back slapping.'

Bones was lost. In two ways.

He had struck out three days ago in an unremembered and arbitrary direction as his head swam with frustration. In the end, he went alone. Hunger and thirst had dropped to number three in his priority list, more pressing were the concerns he had about the rumble and the strange conversation with Cobble. He had always been Bones' only port of call for conversation or conspiracy and it was the first time they had spoken in anything approaching harsh tones to each other. It jarred with him and Bones' conviction that he was right only made it worse. There was simply no way they could hear Cave Mountain from this distance and anyone growing up in Boardom knew the feel and sound of the rumble like the toes on their feet. If he could experience it here in Nutty Woods then it could only mean one thing – they were just as close to its source here as they were in Boardom. That led to a daunting conclusion; the increasing rumble was coming from Unfinished Mountain in the Greenfields. He was unaware that his fingernails were clicking along the ridges in his pendant, although a part of his brain was quietly grateful for it.

He needed something convincing and conclusive to show the village of the danger they were in. He was sure there was a danger, but as usual he couldn't put it into words. That was always his downfall. Trying to vocalise the muddled strings of thought whizzing around his head was like trying to catch a snake with a spoon. If he wanted people to believe him then he needed to find a confident eloquence that had thus far eluded him. He calmed himself down, remembering the way Cobble had taught him to solve problems; break it down into small pieces and solve each one in turn until you have an answer.

He looked down at his pendant with its familiar shape and feel. He used to look at it with curiosity and a desire to find a meaning within it but as the years passed it had become simply his pendant. He had long since stopped imagining there was a message woven into it, some way of connecting with his unknown past, and it was now just the thing he wore round his neck. He tried to look at it as if it was new to him but all he could see was what he had always seen.

Perhaps the triangle represented the boundary of Boardom, he thought, but then why not make it more obvious? What are the lines for? Maybe it was made by a young man for his woman and showed the close bond they had. The ridges could be the years they would spend together.

None of these felt right and he knew he was trying to force an answer to a riddle that may not even exist. Perhaps there was no riddle at all, perhaps it was simply made that way because whoever created it thought it looked nice. What a disappointing outcome that would be, he thought.

He studied it again, feeling the creases and moving his finger around the edges. He lifted it up to eye level and stared at it as if it would casually give up its secret if he concentrated hard enough. His eyes tracked slowly up to the narrow point and the zigzags along the tip. He was about to consider the possible meanings behind them when a noise from behind shook him out of his reverie. Instinctively, he closed his fist around his only possession.

'Do you mind if I join you?' came the voice.

'I'd rather you didn't,' said Bones.

'Super,' said the voice, sitting down next to him and revealing its owner.

Bones took in the shape in front of him. It was impossible to know if the man, assuming it was indeed a man under all that hair, was overweight or underweight. He must certainly have been warmer than average in either case.

'I'm Dodd, a pleasure to meet you,' he said with a pat on Bones' shoulder. 'Lovely day for a stroll, don't you think?'

Bones couldn't decide which end of the peculiarity spectrum to place him. He was either thoroughly polite or calmly psychotic. In the spirit of collecting more data on the subject he made some small talk.

'Yes, it's a nice enough day. At least it's not windy,' he offered.

'Ah, yes. I'm not a fan of wind myself' said Dodd. 'That was a joke, by the way. Fan, you see?'

'Very good, very good,' said Bones noncommittally.

'So, are you from around these parts?' said Dodd, eager to strike up a conversation. After spending time with the women he had found a new vitality. He would enjoy this temporary company of others for a while before retreating back to his own world.

'This is my home,' said Bones, nodding to the whole forest with a small flinch of his head.

'So you're not from here then, just living here.'

It was a statement rather than a question and Bones was impressed, if a little uneasy, at the astuteness of this stranger.

'Perhaps.'

'Where were you reared? Somewhere less comfortable I assume?'

'It's a place far away from here. I won't see it again so there's no point talking about it,' said Bones with more passion than he expected.

He opened his hand again and started clicking his nails across the ridges of his pendant. The silence that came from Dodd thundered into his ears and made him turn to face him again.

'What?' said Bones.

'May I?' asked Dodd, offering a hand. 'You can put it back around your neck first if you'd prefer.'

Bones did prefer that. He preferred that very much. He also would have preferred the man to disappear back to wherever he had appeared from and leave him to his thoughts. He looped the string back over his neck and held out the stone. Dodd leaned forward and stared at it, dead still, before slowly straightening his back again.

'What's your name, young man?'

'Bones.'

'How many years do you have?'

'I don't know, my parents were... undefined.'

Dodd's expression changed almost imperceptibly, as if he had selected an emotional mask to cover his real feelings but got his timing ever so slightly off.

'Do you mind if I take a proper look at your necklace? I'd like to hold it if I may.'

'I'd rather you didn't, if it's all the same with you,' said Bones, putting up his guard again.

'I tell you what, you can hold something of mine while I have it, how does that sound?'

What harm could it do. He looped it back over his head and held it out. Dodd did the same, being sure to keep his hidden until the last second.

'Here,' he said, opening his fist.

Bones needed a speech.

He concentrated his efforts and formulated the beginning.

As the sun was falling he arrived back at the village Square. It had taken him hours but he was happy with his work. He repeated it in his head, over and over, until he was as sure as he could be that he could recite it well enough when the time came. He was starting to get the hang of vocalising his thoughts and it was a tangible reminder of how much he had changed in the short time since he left Boardom. Somewhere along the road home he became aware that Dodd was missing. He cursed himself before searching the area for signs of his disappearance. When he found nothing he justified to himself that Dodd wasn't important, just the knowledge he had given him, and carried on home.

'Bones, dear boy!' called Balcor. 'Where have you been? Cobble and Pingo are back from their hunt, come and see!'

Bones' shoulders sagged as he made his way into the Square and took in the scene.

They looked exhausted, but with a tired glint in their eyes. The young deer was slumped on the floor next to Tiff and the group were inching closer and closer. They hadn't seen this much meat in months and Barna and Quiller had already begun to set a fire pit in readiness for the feast that wouldn't happen.

'I say gentleman,' said Tiff, struggling to contain his giddiness. 'What a tremendous catch you have delivered. I don't suppose you picked any rosemary on your way back?'

'Now now, Tiff,' said Pingo, 'only a small part of this poor beast is going to be dripping over the fire today. Are the traps ready? We have enough here for four or five of them, the rest we can eat.'

Tiff wondered for a moment if Pingo was being insubordinate but he knew in his heart he had to think of the long term future of the group.

'You're right, of course,' he said with just a hint of childish reluctance. 'Does anyone know how to chop this plump, delicious and tempting deer up? Tarpin, Thistle, would you mind awfully setting the traps? By the new moon we will have enough meat to fill us all twice over. We will do well to remember that as we roast what is left tonight.'

The commotion was instant, the trap setters scurrying to their tools and the cooks heading to the fire pit. Only Cobble and Pingo stayed still, once they had dropped gratefully to the floor.

'Wait!' shouted Bones over the clamour of activity, emphasising the urgency by raising his arms. 'There is something we must discuss.'

'After we have set the traps, Bones, please!' said Cobble, brusquely.

'No! There is something I need to tell you all right away. It is of the utmost importance and cannot wait. The traps can be set afterwards, if you still think there is a need to do so.'

The idea that there may be a reason not to set traps won the battle of intrigue and the jostling died down. Bones steeled himself, going over the first few lines again in his head. To almost anyone else in the group the prospect of speaking to this many people at once, even on a subject as important as this one, would be taken in their stride. Unfortunately for Bones, he was standing on the edge of a cliff and the slightest step would send him careering into an abyss. There was also the worry that they wouldn't believe him. He pushed these thoughts down as far as he could and took a deep breath...

'Gentleman, we are in mortal danger!'

CHAPTER SIXTEEN

MEETING AT THE MIDDLE

'You have all gone through a lot of hard times, leaving your land, losing your friends and struggling through hunger and desperation to get to where you are now, but you all know where you came from and who you have lost. I don't. For all my life I have only had the present moment and this pendant around my neck. I don't know where it came from or why I have it, but it has always felt important to me. Now I think that I know what it means.'

The Nutty Woodsmen loved a good tale, but this one was competing against the prospect of meat and Bones sensed their curiosity was treading a fine line. He needed to fast forward to the juicy bits before he lost them completely.

'I had always assumed its shape was of no significance, just a triangle with a zigzag cut along the tip and some nice decorative touches. I now know why its meaning has eluded me all these years. The triangle does represent something. Something that could destroy everything we are all working towards.'

'Show us this trinket,' snapped Jutt, revealing himself for the first time, 'before we all die of boredom.'

Bones had planned to show them of course, but not until later in his speech. This kind of unpredictability was one reason why he avoided speaking to crowds. He would have to improvise, something that gave him an instant feeling of dread. Surely he was going to tumble over his words.

'Fine. Here.' He looped it over his head and reached out to pass it to Balcor, the closest person to him.

Balcor put down his spear and took the pendant. 'It's nice, I suppose,' he said with all the conviction of a starved trap setter. He passed it hastily along the line.

Each man glanced at it with mild interest before letting it move on to the next in line. Only Jutt held it for more than a moment, doubtless looking for something to mock Bones with. He showed no emotion as he passed it on and Bones was happy that at least one small part had gone his way. Perhaps Jutt would stop being confrontational long enough for him to get through to the other side of this.

'So as you can see, it looks fairly ordinary. If I owned anything else I probably would have flung it aside many years ago, but there you have it. Now, did any of you see anything symbolic?'

'I saw a symbol of your confounded nonsense,' said Jutt.

Speck chuckled obediently.

Bones ignored him.

'What I realised while I was away is that I had been looking at it all wrong. The top is the bottom and the bottom is the top.'

'Somebody put this man out of his misery,' said Jutt.

'Jutt!' barked Tiff, nodding at Bones to continue.

'There is another stone, one that fits perfectly into this one. The zigzags at the top slot into the zigzags of another pendant, one that tells us what is heading our way.'

'Yes?' said the group, silently.

'Unfinished Mountain! This triangle has vertical lines. That is the danger. That is what is going to destroy us. The other triangle has horizontal lines that represent the mountain and images of people running away from whatever is being fired out of the hole at the top.'

Tarpin asked the question they were all thinking. 'Where is the other half?'

This was the shaky part. Future generations would have a saying along the lines of 'a bough is only as good as the arrow that uses it' and in this case Bones had the finest bough in the land but an arrow made of thin air.

'There was a man in the forest and he showed me the other half. He wandered off on the way back while I was distracted.'

They waited as one for Jutt to make a snide comment that never came.

'There is a painting in one of the caves in Boardom that shows a breathing mountain,' continued Bones, keen to get past the biggest pitfall of his story. 'It matches the pendants when they are pressed together, there is something coming out from the top of that one too and there are tiny figures with their arms in the air. We all assumed they were dancing, as though celebrating, but I think they were frightened of something, something coming out of the mountain. I don't know exactly what it is, but whatever it is has happened before, and close enough to Boardom for someone to leave a warning for future generations.'

'You lot have finally lost the plot!' There it was.

Bones sighed as the group turned away from him as Jutt strode confidently into the centre of the Square.

'First you let these two mouths into the village when we are on the verge of starvation, then when they finally do something useful you pander to their demands and throw more meat than we've seen in months into holes in the ground. Even then you allow them to regale you with some dull story about a chunk of rock instead of getting on with cooking the damn deer! You all deserve each other. Speck, come on. I'm going to find us somewhere with normal people. Anywhere but here should do it. Come on!'

Speck looked around in the hope that someone would ask him to stay, but he was too entwined with Jutt for anyone to care enough.

'This time I'm not coming back,' said Jutt, unsure of how he wanted them to respond.

'Right-o!' said Bones, desperately trying to regain control. 'Bye now.'

Jutt gave Bones an ambiguous look before pushing past Tiff and out into the forest, with Speck bobbing subserviently behind him as they shrank into the distance.

What was that look, thought Bones. Was it contempt or confusion, he wondered. More distraction. Focus.

'Does anyone have any idea what the danger could be?' asked Bones. 'I'm only convinced of its significance, not its make up.'

'It could be a lot of bally great big birds flying out from their nooks in the mountain,' offered Fettle, with uncharacteristic reason.

'That,' said Bones, 'is a good guess, but I'm not sure it would warrant people running scared like in the painting.'

'Ah.'

'Perhaps it is something going into the mountain rather than out of it,' said Cobble, 'it could be the hail from a large storm. That would have people worried.'

'True, and that is better than any suggestion I've come up with yet, maybe that's it, but it feels like a forced solution to a puzzle rather than an event to warn future generations of,' said Bones, thawing the frostiness between them a little. 'No offence,' he added conciliatorily.

The men were now consumed by the intrigue and thoughts of roasted deer were forgotten, at least for the moment.

A silence drifted down onto the Square as under-exercised cognitive functions woke from lengthy slumbers. Each man and woman was fixated by arbitrary points in their eyeline, lost in thought.

They gradually became aware of a violent and constant scream in the distance, starting as a tiny pin prick of noise that was mostly lost in the soundtrack of the forest. In a few short moments it had lifted itself above this barrier and was now a clear and piercing presence in the Square. Pingo turned his head slowly to face Cobble, then Balcor did the same, then Tiff. They were looking at him with an odd expression that sent confusion barging through his crowded thoughts.

'What?' said Cobble.

Nothing.

'What!?' he pleaded. The looks were starting to worry him.

'Can you not hear that?' said Tiff incredulously.

'Of course I can!' snapped Cobble. 'It's clearly a scream, but I don't understand why you're all looking at me like that.'

'They're shouting your name.'

Rumble... rumble... rumble... rumble...

Moss burst into the clearing and collapsed onto the floor. She was followed by the rest of the women, albeit far behind and out of sight for the moment, and it would be some time before they made it to the Square. Moss tried to call out for the men to go to and help the rest of her group but no words came out. Instead she pointed at herself, then at the direction she had dramatically arrived from. Bones understood at once and ran out after them, grabbing Fettle's arm as he left and pulling him with him.

'Tarpin! Quiller! You too, bring water!' he called, and was gone.

'Moss! What happened? How did you...?' said a bewildered Cobble as he staggered over to her. 'Look at you. Are you OK?'

Moss shook her head slightly and pointed to her mouth.

'Water, here!' commanded Cobble.

Tiff ran over with a bowl of water and passed it to Cobble. He poured a few small drops onto her lips, being careful not to give her too much at first. His experience on the Great Grey Plains had taught him that much at least.

'Here, drink,' he said, handing the bowl to Moss. 'Not too much yet or you'll make yourself sick.'

Moss reached out to take the bowl, clasping her fingers around the rim. It fell from her feeble grip and soaked the floor beside her.

'Tiff, more!' ordered Cobble. 'Camble, find some soft fruit.'

Cobble was taking over leadership of the group with every demand, not that he realised it yet. He was to be like a swallow that had flown solo all its life, only to discover on turning around that he was at the head of a formation.

After a few minutes, and half a bowl of water, Moss was able to shuffle slowly across to a trunk and prop herself up with her elbows. Everything was an effort and she wondered how the rest of the group were doing. If Bones and the other men found them soon then there was a chance they would make it. She let herself relax for the first time in days and found that an unfamiliar feeling of relief and security was making its way through the valleys of her brain and into her consciousness. She had found Cobble and Bones, and they seem to have befriended a group of... of what? Men? They were certainly very similar, and yet altogether different at the same time. She might have thought they looked like Dodd, had she been able to establish his dimensions more accurately through the years of unkempt hair, they were certainly as tall as he was. Still, the security of the village was as welcome to her as a fire in midwinter. She warmed herself with the thoughts of it and relaxed a little more, straight into a long, deep sleep.

Balcor looked around at the scene before him. He was the only one still awake, as usual. It was a dark night with just a weak orange glow emanating from the dying fire and the usually spacious Square was cramped with bodies, each recovering from their own tribulations of the previous day. On balance, he was happy with the day's events. Meat had been won and their numbers had increased again, this time with ladies too. Strange looking ladies to be sure, but ladies nonetheless. The signs were positive for the first time since they left Cherry Woods and he let himself imagine settling down to a routine with their new company.

It was a sign of the heretofore dullness of living here that he was too excited to sleep. The women were exhausted and starved and their story had to wait until they were rested enough to deliver it. It would be exhilarating at best and intriguing at worst, but either way it would surely be worth hearing. Growing up in Cherry Woods, he was reared on the power of stories, of entertaining the mind and piquing the imagination. That pastime had fallen by the wayside as they busied themselves with surviving and living through future stories. It would be good to be a listener again.

CHAPTER SEVENTEEN

PILES AND TRIBULATIONS

'It's not like they're going to achieve anything there,' said Jutt, as much to himself as to Speck. 'If you have meat you should eat it, not throw it away. It's common sense. You'd think they would have learned their lesson from the lost hunters of Cherry Woods, but no, they finally get to a good spot to settle down and ruin it all by trusting in a pair of damnable strangers. The fools deserve each other.'

'You're right' said Speck.

'Of course I'm right!' snapped Jutt 'Why else would I leave? No-one else was going to look after me. I should have made Tiff send them away the day they arrived.'

'I look after you.'

'They'll be the ruination of all we had worked for.'

'We didn't really work for much though, did we? We just about scraped by on nuts and water.'

'Shut up Speck!' snapped Jutt, finally acknowledging his presence.

'Right-o!'

'And don't say that either.'

'Sorry Jutt.'

They walked in silence and noisy thoughts for a time. Jutt played over the events of the last few days in his mind and stretched them to meet his memories in the middle. He dredged his past and something glinted at him from the murky depths.

'We have to find the Giant Sea' he blurted. 'Come on, stop dallying.'

'Is there a reason we're hiding behind this rock?' said Speck.

'Yes.'

He waited for Jutt to elaborate. When an explanation wasn't forthcoming he shrewdly chose not to rephrase the question. They had been walking for days on minimal rations and the hunger was starting to pinch. Earlier that morning they had found a small snake pit under a patch of pink heather and Jutt had captured three of them by throwing a heavy rock into the hole. It required no skills of any note but was effective nonetheless. Speck looked again at the peculiar man crouched beside him. If he hadn't been afraid of him already he certainly would be now. What kind of man wears dead snakes around his neck, he wondered.

In a flash Jutt leapt to his feet and sprinted across the green floor to the edge of the water. He unhooked two of the snakes, throwing them on the ground before turning to run back to the safety of the boulder. As he turned he stopped dead and stared at the floor. He bent down and seemed to Speck to be studying something carefully, in stark contrast to his otherwise rushed behaviour. He picked up whatever it was and resumed his sprint.

'This way man, and be quick with it, you lumbering baboon!'

They ran back to the water's edge, passing the snakes and continuing along the shoreline. Speck wondered why Jutt had brought them out into the open like this. There was no spot where they would be safely hidden from their invisible followers. Speck knew better than to question Jutt but his curiosity was becoming quite convincing.

'Stay here,' Jutt said without waiting for an acknowledgement.

He ran in a different direction this time, and slightly slower. He arrived back and barked more orders at Speck. 'This way, come on!'

Over the next couple of days they zigzagged their way back towards Nutty Woods with calculated inefficiency, leaving precious morsels behind them as they went. Their luck in finding meat was ultimately short lived and so they resorted to giving away their rations, although they also dried up quickly.

'We have to go back to the woods, we need more food,' said Jutt one morning without explanation. 'Come on man!'

'Er, Jutt?' said Speck bravely. 'You know how we're a bit, you know, hungry?'

'What of it?'

'Well, it's just, well, erm...'

'Spit it out man! I haven't got all day.'

Speck chose not to correct Jutt on that particular point. They had, in fact, all the time in the world.

'It seems a bit odd that we're foraging lots of food in the woods and then leaving it in piles in the middle of nowhere. Could we not just, you know, eat it?'

'Speck, Speck, Speck,' said Jutt with lashings of condescension. 'Do you really think I went to all that effort of finding dead animals only to leave them on the ground for nothing?'

'Well, it did cross my mind. It is what you were mocking the men for after all. If a man opens a snake pit with nothing but a rock then he must also have a plan, otherwise he's just a lunatic,' said Speck with uncharacteristic lucidity. 'And I know you're not a lunatic,' he added wisely.

'Of course I have a plan, but I don't expect you of all people to understand.'

'Maybe some of the other people who followed you out here would understand. Shall we ask them?'

This was a gamble, possibly a terrible one and certainly ground breaking. Jutt considered something unsaid for a moment.

'I'm gathering up a force that will restore some... tradition to our new home. Maybe even knock some sense into our trusted leader.'

'Who, Cobble?'

'Not Cobble, dammit! Tiff! You're as bad as the rest of them, now shut up and find some fruit before I knock some sense into you myself.'

'Right-o!'

'And stop saying that!'

'Are we there yet? Are we there yet?' said Goober for the fourth time since they had left Boardom.

'We've only been gone ten minutes,' said Rankor. 'We can still see the damned Obelisk! Get a grip of yourself or we'll leave you behind.'

The decision had been made that they would rest at the Meeting Patch for the remainder of the day, despite the critical lack of food. The battle between laziness and hunger had been won by inertia and indecision. The preparations had been surprisingly straightforward, their great plan didn't need much boiling down, it was already a well reduced jus. Since they had no food and no way of getting more they simply stood up at first light and walked towards the sea. Any dissenting voices quietened down with a speed that was inversely proportional to the noise coming from their bellies. They were to walk along the edge of the Giant Sea where they expected to find the women cooking and cleaning. If they weren't there then they would strike out for Unfinished Mountain and find whatever was behind it. Its simplicity meant that most of them understood what was happening, although none of them knew what they would do for food during the journey.

The hungry groans calling for a halt began after about an hour and continued right up until lunchtime. They then became groans that asked for the break to be called something other than lunchtime.

'Stop saying that, please!' said Goober, stretching out the syllables like a teenager. 'My stomach is about to pop out of my mouth to see what the problem is. Let's just call it a stop.'

'Fine, fine,' said Rankor, 'let's stop for a short while.'

Two flies landed on the prone figure of Tark.

'Don't be stupid Fuzz, they're not mammoths. They don't have any tusks.'

'They are hairy though,' said Fuzz, 'and mammoths are hairy.'

'I'll give you that, they are hairy.'

'And they have eyes. Mammoths have eyes.'

'Yes, yes they do.'

'And legs.'

'I get the gist, Fuzz, thanks. You'll notice they only have two legs though, mammoths usually have four.'

'Usually, yes. But maybe not always. Or they might be half a mammoth.'

There was a certain quality to Fuzz's logic. Asking him to assess a situation meant filling in a lot of the gaps yourself.

'I'm not sure half a mammoth would be quite so... alive.'

'Why? Have you seen any half mammoths before?'

'Well, no, but... you know... half a mammoth? How would it eat, for a start?'

'Depends which half it is.'

'Fair point.'

'It's strange there are hundreds of them though. I wonder where they all came from?'

Fizz flapped his wings in frustration. He had gone over this with Fuzz countless times before.

'Remember what I told you,' he said patiently. 'You have to divide everything you see by sixty four. That's how your eyes work. You're a fly, remember?'

'Right, right. Sixty four. Yes. How many is that again?'

A swift flash of a hairy hand allowed Fizz to avoid the pain of explaining the basics of fly life to Fuzz again. To his brief annoyance it was replaced by a very fatal feeling of flatness.

The stop lasted three hours.

'Does anyone know how to catch fish?' said Plank. 'I could sure go a nice crispy fish skin right about now.'

'Would you stop talking about food, you damned nuisance?'

'Oh I don't know,' said Slate. 'The thought of it might be cruel but I can almost taste it in my mouth. It's better than lying here wasting away.'

'No it ain't,' said Granite. 'I can't take it anymore, I'm off. There must be some food out there somewhere.' He stood up awkwardly and trudged off along the water's edge. Tark followed him. If Granite was motivated enough to do anything then following him was probably the right course of action.

An hour later they were back with two snakes in their hands. They had found them being lapped by the gentle waters of the sea and had leapt onto them for fear they would slither away. As it turned out they had recently expired without any clue as to the cause other than a small dent on their heads. They didn't worry about it for long, after all they were ostensibly at the top of the food chain. They were ready to rip the skin off them when Tark asked the hitherto unspoken question.

'Should we take them back to the tribe?'

'Oh yes, we should,' said Granite, 'but are we going to? That is the real question 'ere.'

'We are, ain't we?' said Tark.

'Looks that way.'

It was neither tasty nor enough, but to the men it was the most satisfying thing they had eaten in a long time. It had an unexpected side-effect too. In the oversimplified minds of the men, continuing the walk meant finding food lying on the ground. The evidence was irrefutable. Tark and Granite had gone ahead and found food. Simple.

They walked with a greater urgency now, even Goober keeping up with the pace without a grumble. About two hours after they had eaten the snake, with the sun setting to their right, they found three frogs. They were stripped and eaten in minutes. An hour later, and a little further to their right they found another snake. Nobody thought this was strange. Perhaps this was how the women found so much for them.

'I don't know why those women left us. This foraging malarkey is easy.'

They chose a very specific sleeping place. As luck would have it, it was right beneath their feet. There was no shelter but they had drunk their fill and had at least eaten something. They slept like men who placed the pastime right at the top of their list of favourite hobbies until the sun woke them with a sudden glare over the horizon.

'Right men, off we go,' said Rankor with more enthusiasm than he felt. 'We 'ave foraging to do and I think I can see a dark shape over 'ere.' He pointed off to his right, towards the sun.

Their trail turned continually, but gradually, to their right until Unfinished Mountain was directly in front of them, albeit at a distance. It was punctuated by small piles of food. The only meat they found was on the first day and as the days passed they stumbled across small piles of fruit at even intervals, sometimes mixed with nuts and occasionally mushrooms.

A journey that would have taken just a couple of days, even for the women, took them five. Their haste was quickly replaced by curiosity, although none of them questioned where the food was coming from. They only spoke of what food they would find next.

As they closed in on the mountain they found their path was being bent to the right again until it met the beginnings of what might have been a forest. It was still a day's walk away at best for the lumbering remnants of the tribe but they were in no rush. The fruit, and by extension their stoppages, were growing as they went. When they were within a few thousand paces of what was now clearly a forest, they found a bounty of food that would see them through a normal evening back in Boardom. It thrashed the possibility of making it to the cover and comfort of the trees into the ground and their forward motion stalled for a day. They were neither familiar with nor inclined towards exercise of any kind and the trials of the last few days enveloped them completely.

The next day they rose late and stood up even later. By the afternoon they had made it to the forest and the feel of the pine needles under their feet was too tempting to resist. They found the most padded parts of the floor and settled down to a day of apathy.

For the time being none of them wondered where their next meal would come from.

Jutt looked down from his lofty perch in the tree. He had been watching and listening to the Boarders for a full day and was surprised to learn how good they were at idling, particularly for men who had just crossed the entire Greenfields with nothing more than an empty belly and hope.

He motioned to Speck to climb down and head back into the woods. They crept along, thankful for the dark sky and soft pine needles. When they had moved out of earshot Jutt turned to Speck, choosing this moment to let him in on a plan. Not the plan, naturally, but rather the part of the plan where he needed his help.

CHAPTER EIGHTEEN

TALES AND FEATHERS

The days were now becoming perceptibly warmer and the long-awaited summer would soon be in full bloom. This day began like many before it with sunbeams finding gaps in the trees with the precision of practice. There was no birdsong, although this wouldn't be noticed by anyone for a little while longer. The effects of the recent downpour had now receded and the leaves were crisp once again, creating a rhythmic noise in the still air that followed the men as they walked. It had taken some time to get all of the women to the safety of the Square but they had managed it. Bones, Tarpin and Quiller had found the women quite soon after leaving, the distance being far shorter for them than it was in Moss' mind. They gathered them all together before Quiller ran back to get more help. Two men kept watch over them at all times while more groups of two carried the women, one by one, to the village.

Once they were all safe the men decided to get back to the work of setting the traps while the women slept. Four of their traps, far apart from each other, were chosen for the first real test and the men were glad of the distraction from the previous night's events. Camble and Barna were the first to make it to their trap. Camble chose some suitable branches to act as a false floor before covering it with leaves and other forest floor detritus. Barna placed the hind leg of the deer carefully on the trap. A strange feeling of loss mingled with hope as they stood back to inspect their work. It was as good as they could manage and they walked off with a spring in their step and a glance at their backs.

They had only gone a few paces when they heard a shrill voice to their left.

'Fools! Fools!'

They looked about for the source of the voice but saw no one. They scouted around the backs of a few trunks but still there was no sign.

'Shut up Speck! Shut up Speck!'

This time the voice came from above them.

'I say! Did you hear that?' said Camble. 'That must have been Jutt, but it wasn't his voice.'

'It also came from high above us, old boy. How peculiar.'

'Giant Sea! Giant Sea!' said Budge as he landed in front of Camble, startling him to the floor.

'Goodness!' Quiller exclaimed. 'It's those bally birds again. It seems we are crow magnets. What confounded mischief makers they are.'

'Let's leave them to it,' said Camble as he got back to his feet. 'They're just playing tricks with our tired minds.'

'Fools! Shut up Speck! Giant Sea! Fools! Shut up Speck! Giant Sea!' squawked Spike.

'Did he just say that with more... emphasis?' said Quiller with a doubtful look.

'Yes, I believe he did,' said Camble with a concerned glance. 'Although it is a bird, so there is a pretty good slice of probability that says I'm wrong.'

'That's only a minor consideration though, when you actually hear the bally thing, what?'

'Fools! Shut up Speck! Minor! Giant! Shut up! Minor!'

'Did it just say minor?'

'If it is, in fact, talking, then yes, I believe it did.'

'They're going to think we've gone mad, aren't they?'

'Eccentric, dear Quiller, eccentric.'

'Say otter over and over.'

'What?'

'No, otter. Ott-ah.'

This would normally be the strangest thing to happen to Camble in any given day, but not this day.

'Otter. Otter Otter. Otter. Otter. Otter. Otter.'

'Is that enou…'

'Otter! Otter!' said Spike.

'It's mimicking what we say,' said Quiller. 'It must be repeating what Jutt was saying to Speck.'

'I wonder what a Giant Sea is?' said Camble.

'I'm more concerned with what he's up to.'

'So that's it,' said Cobble. 'Now we wait.'

'And hope,' said Fettle. 'Maybe there's something we could do to help our chances.'

'Unless you're going to dress up like a fox and herd some rabbits into the traps I don't think you can help,' said Cobble.

'That's not a bad idea.'

Dozens of raised eyebrows turned to him in confused unison, each trying to work out if he was joking.

'...or not, whichever,' he said.

'We could have a jolly good jig, that would give us some entertainment and might keep the prey away from here at least?' said Tarpin.

'We may as well talk to an invisible man,' countered Balcor. 'Perhaps he can help if we ask him fervently enough?'

'...or an invisible fox,' said Fettle, consolidating his mastery of misjudged one-liners.

'Anyway,' said Tiff diplomatically, ' it looks like we'll be entertained soon enough gentlemen, the women are stirring.'

It was late afternoon before all of the women had woken. The rejuvenating qualities of their sleep varied greatly and some were still borderline catatonic. The babies seemed to have been affected least and their resilience, while noisy, was the sturdiest. Some water and a couple of raspberries each were all that was needed to bring them back to full health. It was assumed that Daffy would be the worst affected of the women, although her latest lethargic episode was difficult to distinguish from her usual sullenness. When all of them were awake they joined the expectant Nutty Woodsmen in the Square.

Cobble had explained his connection to the strangers but Tiff was keen to have the mystery of their dramatic arrival explained and asked Moss to tell them the events that led up to it.

She began, as all good tales do, at the start. From the very beginnings of the Boardom Revolution, to meeting the strange hairy man who seemed to have enigmatically and inconveniently disappeared, right up to the time they reached the base of Unfinished Mountain. It was at this point that she stopped, hoping they wouldn't ask her to go into too much detail. Desperation has a way of focusing the mind on the negative and she was sure they would ridicule her and send them all away into the wilderness. Unfortunately for Moss she had built an accidental crescendo and the men were not going to allow her story to finish before the end.

'I was scouting ahead,' said Moss, fidgeting nervously with an apple core, 'when I rounded an outcrop of rock. I was looking for shelter and it seemed like a promising possibility.'

She was being more defensive than she needed to be, and less than she felt she should have been.

'When I looked into the crevice there was something there that froze my bones, I can tell you.'

'There was ice there?' blurted Bones.

'No, not ice. Something else, something slow but violent, hot but chilling, obvious but mysterious.'

The men didn't know whether to snap at her for being a torment or congratulate her on teasing out a good old fashioned yarn.

'I should point out to you, just in case you missed the signs, that you are not being enigmatic here, you're being annoying,' said Tiff with more decisiveness than the others could manage.

'I didn't mean to be unclear, I just don't know how else to describe it, if you catch my drift.'

'Let's start with the basics,' offered Pingo. 'Was it an animal or something else? Was is hard like the mountain or soft like muddy ground? What colour was it? Why did you run?'

'It was the colour of an orange but with a black crust. It was like water but not as... thin. It was so hot it would probably burn your skin if you got too close and felt like it would destroy anything that stood in its way.'

'Will that do?' added Plum, using her last risky drop of defiance.

There was silence as the men took in this bizarre development. Only Bones looked alert.

'What did the man look like? What was his name?' said Bones.

Of the list of questions Moss' story had conjured in the minds of her audience, these two were quite a long way down. They were in the vicinity of 'What did you have for dinner?' and 'Had the daffodils sprouted yet?'

'He was an exceptionally hairy man and called himself Dodd.'

'That's it!' he squealed. 'It's the missing link!'

The heads turned from Moss to Bones but their expressions remained the same.

'Don't you see? That's the same man who has the other half of my pendant. He knows what's coming out of the mountain!'

It was the women's turn to look bemused. It was like watching a show whose puppeteer had a nervous twitch.

'Did you say 'coming out of my pendant'?' asked Faun.

'Look,' he looped it over his head and passed it to her. 'That's the tip of Unfinished Mountain and I think that,' he said, pointing to the vertical lines, 'is what Moss saw.'

'But Moss said it was at the bottom of the mountain?' said Faun, failing to take the small step of conjecture.

'Remember the painting in the cave? The mountain with the dancing men?'

'Yes, but...'

'Well they weren't dancing, they were fleeing from whatever it was that Moss saw.'

'Ah.'

'Moss, do you think you could draw the painting on the ground here? You'll remember it better than any of us' said Cobble. 'Here, use this stick.'

Moss knelt down and scraped a rough version of the painting into the soil. When she finished she stood up, satisfied it was as accurate as it could be.

'What's this?' said Balcor, pointing at the forest in the drawing.

'That's a river,' said Moss with a liberal dose of sarcasm. 'It's a forest, obviously.'

'And what's this?' he said, pointing at the highest point in the middle.

'Really?'

'Yes, really.'

'It's a tree'

'Then it's a picture of Nutty Woods. That must be the Great Oak.'

'How can it be Nutty Woods when neither of our tribes have ever been here until recently?' said Thistle.

'What if they have been here before?' said Bones, laying the tracks of his hypothesis in front of him as he spoke. 'What if people lived here but had to escape whatever that orange thing is. They may have headed to Boardom and settled down there instead. Maybe Boardom is out of the reach of the mountain's anger?'

'That's a lot of maybes, Bones' said Camble. 'Maybe it's just a badly drawn picture?'

'Maybe you should stay here to find out for us?'

'Ah well, yes.'

'So what do you suggest we do?' said Pingo to Bones.

'I think we take some time to digest it all. Perhaps we should get far away from here, or perhaps we should stay. Who knows? We need to find this man too.'

'If we're going anywhere then we need to recover from the last few days first' said Plum. 'There ain't no way we could make it through another long trek yet, my feet ain't stopped screaming for a start.'

'Then that is what we do,' said Cobble. 'We wait and make a decision tomorrow. We should gather up as many provisions as we can, just in case, and check the traps before sunset and again in the morning. If they work then we will need to reset them quickly if we are to get enough food for all of us. If we need to leave quickly then at least we will be prepared.'

Tiff was becoming aware that Cobble was quietly making decisions for the group. He assumed there should have been at least a passing flutter of annoyance that this young newcomer was usurping his authority but the overwhelming emotion for him was one of relief. He had never wanted to be a leader but circumstances had gone against him. The difficulties they had encountered over the last few months were quite enough for him. This young Cobble is welcome to the job.

The problem with life, he thought, was that it was terminal. Sooner or later there would be animals tramping around your once favourite places without a second thought for your well-being. He should spend more time doing things that made him happy, and that meant practising his storytelling now that there were new ears to listen.

'Agreed,' he said, and headed off to wash the purple stripe from his face.

CHAPTER NINETEEN

SORRY STORIES

The four pairs of men spread out as they left the Square, each heading to their own trap. Their mood was buoyant and full of hope, perhaps they would be eating their fill of meat tonight. They were the lucky ones, the rest of the group had to sit on their hands until news returned. Tiff chose this interminable waiting period to regale the women with some of his stories, starting with the great river rescue of Wappo the Wet.

It was a good choice and the women lapped it up. All of the men in Boardom would consider themselves bards and were good storytellers in their own way, but they didn't have much material to go on. Most of the tales were ancient and all of them were much repeated, another by-product of generations of lazy Boarders, and it was liberating for them to hear something new. As he reached the climax of the story, when Bonk the Heavy was standing knee-deep in the fast running river, braced for the impact of Wappo, he even got an 'oooooh' from his enthralled audience. This beats being a leader, he thought to himself.

He was halfway through 'Hoppo And The Dancing Duck' when his audience gradually shifted their attention away from him to something happening behind them in the woods. Two figures were approaching, carrying something on a large branch at their shoulders.

'Tarpin!' he called. 'What is it?'

'Ladies and Gentlemen!' announced Tarpin proudly. 'May I present to you one fat badger!'

The group jumped to their feet and surrounded their dinner, but before they could do any more a call came from their left.

'I say, everyone! Look here!'

Camble and Pingo strode into the Square and flopped a young boar next to the fire pit, followed quickly by an empty handed Barna and Quiller.

Nobody was quite sure where to look, until Cobble and Bones arrived with another badger.

'Well boil my apples, this is marvellous!' said Tiff triumphantly. 'You did it, Cobble, you really did it!'

'It was a great team effort, Tiff. We couldn't have done it without Pingo's changes or Bones' knots.' He looked sheepishly over at Thistle. 'Or Thistle's heavy weight. I mean, the weights she suggested we use. Not that she is... never mind.'

Bugger.

'Now let's stop the back slapping and get that fire lit,' he said, recovering a little. 'We have a lot of meat to cook.'

They had to dig a bigger fire pit to fit in all the fresh meat. They wanted to cook and chop it as quickly as they could in case they had to make a speedy exit. The memory of the mountain and its secrets stifled the joy a little, but not so much that it took the smiles from their faces.

Against all known tradition, the women were given the larger share of the food. Cobble had ordered this because they were the most in need, and to him this was the only consideration. Conveniently, it also reinforced his vision of how any new tribe should be run. Equality for all, even women.

Rumble... rumble... rumble... rumble... rumble...

'I'm sorry, Bones,' said Cobble as he sat down next to his friend.

'Because I was right, or because you're sorry?'

'Does it matter?'

'Yes.'

'Then I'm sorry I doubted you. I should have listened but I got caught up in our adventure. You were right, there is something odd about that noise.'

'Thank you, not that it changes anything. We're still in trouble, I'm sure of it.'

'What about Dodd? We should go and find him.'

'Should we? I thought that at first but what difference would it make? If people believe what I'm saying is true then we don't need him anymore.'

'Don't you want to know who he is or why he has the other half?'

'Yes, but everything is relative. When you've had a lifetime of unsatisfied curiosity, as I have about my parents, then a stranger in a forest is of no consequence at all.'

'So what do you want to do?'

'Are you asking me what I want to do, or what I think we should do? I can give you two separate answers.'

'Both.'

'Then I want to stay here, with our new tribe. They are friendly, sensible to a point, but most of all I feel at home here.'

'I feel the same, especially now that meat is back on the fire and the women have joined us. Plus I think I might have an admirer.'

'Oh, Thistle? Have you only just worked that out? We've been talking about it since the day we arrived.'

'We?' said Cobble, unsure of which emotion to vocalise first.

'All the men. She's always staring at you, it's obvious. I'm pleased for you.'

Cobble felt a pang of something that wasn't quite sympathy. He realised he wished that Bones could meet someone who would make him content. Happy, even. Perhaps Chard would take a fancy to him. There was nothing he could do about that now though and the talk of womanly things was making him anxious again. He decided to change the subject.

'So what do you think we should do?'

'You won't like it.'

'Try me.'

'Really though, it's the last thing you want to do.'

Cobble knew the answer before having to be told.

'You think we should go back to Boardom,' he said with finality.

'I think we have to, Cobble. The way I see it we can't stay here. While I was in the forest on my own I saw something that sent a chill down my legs. I was a long way from the village, towards the mountain and close to the edge. There was a wide tract of hard, black land that was utterly void of life. Nothing was growing for a good forty paces wide, running from the boundary of the woods near the mountain and right through as far as I could see in the opposite direction. Whatever caused it came from the mountain and destroyed everything in its path. I don't fancy waiting around to see it in action. I crossed it and reached the far end of the trees where the widest river you can imagine cuts through the landscape. It was wild, deep and perfectly impassable. Whoever drew that picture and made this pendant must have seen it and escaped to Boardom. Now I think we must to do the same. We can't go back to where Tiff and the men came from, they've told us already there is nothing worth travelling for that way. We can't cross the river or head towards the mountain for obvious reasons. The only way is back to Boardom and I suggest we cut right across the Greenfields to get there all the quicker.'

Cobble took a moment to process it all. He had vastly underestimated his friend. Nutty Woods had changed him too, it seemed. Gone was the blundering misfit who could trip over his own voice. Bones was much further ahead of the game than he was, and could explain why in smooth detail. It would be a shame to change the scene again when they were both thriving so much in their new home. Still, Bones was right – they had no choice.

'You should tell Tiff.'

'Why? He'll do whatever you tell him too.'

Cobble didn't believe him but didn't want to argue with him again.

'Then let's go and see him.'

CHAPTER TWENTY

THREE TIMES IS A CHARM

'If I tell you something do you promise not to laugh?' said Camble to Bones.

'No.'

'Right. Well, the thing is, Quiller and I saw something rather strange when we were setting our trap.'

'Should I laugh yet?' said Bones.

'Well, not saw precisely. More like heard.'

'OK.'

'Remember those two strange birds we saw the day you arrived here?'

'Is this a different story now, or did the birds start talking?' said Bones, laughing at his own joke.

'Have you heard them too?'

'Oh dear, you really do think the birds were talking!'

'I know what you must be thinking, old boy, but they really were talking. Well, not talking, more like mimicking. We even tested it out and I got them to say 'otter' over and over.'

'Otter?'

'We got it to say 'minor' too, but that's not important. It was saying something else,' said Camble, ploughing on to the good bit.

'It was repeating the words 'shut up Speck', 'Giant Sea' and 'Fools' over and over.'

Bones considered this for a moment.

'So Jutt is heading to the Giant Sea, eh?'

'It seems that way, although I've never heard of the place before, have you?'

'I have, but I don't know how Jutt has. No doubt he's up to something but we have more important things to concentrate on. Starting with these mushrooms, come on.'

'Bones has an idea,' said Cobble to Tiff as they entered the Square.

'Bravo! Do tell, do tell. Here, take a seat old boy and rest your bones.'

'Very funny,' said Bones with the neutrality of a man who has heard the joke a thousand times.

'Funny?' said Tiff with genuine puzzlement. 'Ah, of course, my apologies. I wasn't thinking.'

These may just be the most polite people I'll ever meet, thought Bones.

He explained to Tiff his reasoning behind escaping the mountain, though he used more flowery language than with Cobble and exaggerated the scale a little to be sure the message hit home. He stared at the trunk of the Great Oak as he spoke, trying to keep his words flowing and his mind clear. When he had finished he looked up at Tiff for the first time. The first thing he noticed was his colour.

Tiff was as white as a summer cloud and his expression was as still.

'Tiff?' said Bones. 'Are you OK?'

'Dammit, Bones!' he snapped.

Maybe they weren't the most polite of people after all, thought Bones.

'Thank goodness you're here old boy. Cobble, would you be so good as to gather up the men? We should make our plans together.'

'So that is why we must leave,' said Bones, finishing his story for the third time that day.

'What about the men back in Boardom?' said Pippy. 'If we arrive back in Boardom there will be a price to pay for our disappearance.'

'On the contrary, Pippy,' said Cobble, taking another linguistic step towards the Nutty Woodsmen. 'There will be a price to pay for their behaviour all these moons. There are more of us now than there are of them, and we have all the skills. If they want to live with us they'll have to start joining in with the work. Gone are the days where only the women are made to provide for everyone else. We will hunt and we will gather and if they don't like it then it will be them who will be forced to leave this time.'

'This guy is going to make a bard of me yet,' said Tiff.

'A bard?' said Fettle 'What do you mean?'

'What?' said Tiff, unaware for a moment that he had said it aloud. 'Oh nothing Fettle, nothing. Shush now, Cobble is talking.'

'I know you have all travelled a long way to get here only to be heading straight back, but the place you'll return to is not the place you left. Things will be different. You can eat well and rest for a few days before we leave. If this goes well then it will be the last big journey any of us will have to make.'

Any other dissention was minimal and perfunctory, more as a gesture to vindicate their decision if it all went squiffy than a serious concern. They began to plan their grand journey and they were each given a part to play. Chard and Balcor would look after the meat, slicing and packing it in large leaves. Tarpin, Fettle and Camble went off for apples, nuts and mushrooms while Cobble and Bones visited each of the traps to reset them. They would go back the next morning in the hopes of finding something to bring with them. They would then pack up those elements that could be carried easily and reused in Boardom. Thistle had shown an aptitude for tool making and she, along with Pingo, was charged with making as many arrows as she could in the time that was left. The Boardom women rested themselves, knowing just what lay ahead of them. Meed set herself to finding a way to carry the babies more easily, settling on slings made of tough strands of ivy and animal guts.

That evening they ate well and retired early. It was decided that they would rest for three days to be sure they had the best chance they could have of making it back to Boardom. The following few days would be testing for all of them and this would be one of the last times they could sleep comfortably. Only Cobble stayed awake. His mind was racing with the infinite possibilities that lay ahead of him. What was in the mountain? What would the Boarders say when he arrived back with more mouths in tow? What was going on with Thistle? Did they have enough food to feed them all for days in the fields? Was he now the leader of this group? Did he want to be leader? Would he still be leader when they got back to

Boardom?

He went for a walk to try and put these errant thoughts into an orderly queue. It was the first time since leaving Boardom that he was able to wander aimlessly and he was glad of the solitude. He let his mind fumble over the problems in his mind until he could make some sense of them. After a time he sat down against a trunk and took in his surroundings.

Tap. Tap. Tap.

Thistle could wait. He also wasn't sure if he wanted to be a leader or not and so had conveniently deduced that this issue would sort itself out naturally enough. He really didn't mind either way, much to his surprise. Whatever was in the mountain didn't matter, all that mattered was that it was widely agreed it was a bad thing and should be avoided if at all possible. That left just one consideration, for the moment at least. He had to find the best way to get the group home to Boardom safely and quickly. The 'quickly' part was easy, a straight line across the Greenfields. Decision made. The 'safely' part was trickier, since he didn't know what dangers they may face there. The best he could come up with was that the biggest threat to them was hunger and thirst and so he resolved to find a way for them to carry as much food and water as they could. His mind was now singularly focused and ideas were conjured and rejected with reasoned haste.

He looked up absent-mindedly at a rustling in the trees, thinking nothing of it until a small black monkey plopped down about a dozen paces in front of him. He had never seen anything like it before. They stared at each other for a moment before they were both startled by a much larger monkey with a silver streak on its back landing between them. It looked back and forth between the two strange looking versions of itself; one smaller and one larger, but less hairy. None of the three knew quite what to do next, their fight or flight reactions cancelling each other out for a brief, but perfectly balanced moment.

The silver monkey looked at Cobble, then past him at something unseen. Cobble turned and startled slightly at the sight of Pingo. All four of them exchanged glances, none of them wanting to make the first move.

'Oo-oo!' said the small monkey.

'Grrrr!' agreed the silver monkey.

'Erm...' said Cobble.

'I say!' said Pingo.

Cobble was the first to move, in slow and smooth backward steps towards Pingo. He curled his fingers over Pingo's wrist and the two men backed slowly away and around a tree.

The large silver monkey swayed over and picked a flea from the head of the smaller monkey.

'They must be cold with those bare patches,' he said.

'They need to relax a bit too,' said the smaller monkey, 'their backs were dead straight, did you see that?'

'What funny looking creatures,' agreed the silver monkey.

'What funny looking creatures,' whispered Pingo. 'I've never seen anything like them before. Did you see how stooped their backs were?'

'Me neither. They were oddly familiar though. I suppose they must have an intelligence of sorts, enough to stay hidden from us all this time at least. Doubtless they could outwit some of the Boardom tribe. They didn't even take any bait.'

'I think the best course of action is to ignore the whole thing and pretend it never happened. If we're leaving anyway then what difference does it make, we'll most likely never come across them again. I for one will be quite happy with that particular outcome, I didn't like the look of that silvery one, he was huge! Let's get away from here.'

'What are you doing here at this time of night anyway,' said Cobble, letting go of Pingo's wrist. 'I thought I was the only one awake.'

'Me too, I couldn't sleep so thought I'd check on the traps. There's one over here, come on,' he said, gesturing towards a small clearing.

They peered in the darkness at the trap but all that was showing was the hunk of badger leg. They moved on towards the next one.

'So what do you think is inside that mountain, old boy?'

'I don't think it matters really, does it?' said Cobble. 'All I know is it's something hot and destructive and probably enough to have forced a whole tribe to move all the way to Boardom. That's all I need to know. The bigger problem is how we get everyone safely to Boardom, and then how we deal with the incumbents when we arrive.'

'Oh don't worry about them. From what I've heard of them they're a useless bunch. If they haven't starved already they'll be glad to see you and your traps.'

'Maybe you're right, but they're an odd bunch. Don't underestimate their stubbornness. You could smack them in the face with a rock full of logic and they would still say that tradition was the safest bet, all things considered.'

'Well then we'll just have to bally well cut them out of the decision making process.'

'Now that is more like it!' said Cobble as they neared the second trap. 'Come on, let's see what's in this one.'

They arrived back to a dark and silent Square, with the occasional sound of Balcor's snoring the only noise puncturing the black air. Pingo stoked the fire while Cobble skinned the hare they had found at the third trap. As the meat began to sizzle Cobble picked up his bough and arrow. He hadn't used it as much as he would have liked, but then he hadn't needed to either. The traps were working well enough to keep them fed for as long as there was prey to find them. He cursed the mountain silently. Maybe they could just stay here. Perhaps Moss had seen something perfectly explainable. If he could disprove Moss' story then perhaps they didn't have to leave. He could live a contented life here, settling down with Thistle and surrounded by his new friends. He had a vague idea of a sort of permanent shelter he could make. Something like a cave, but built wherever they chose. They could create a perfect oasis here; dry, warm, welcoming, and with food and water aplenty.

A spit of fat on his arm woke him from his daydream.

Another pipe dream.

Although perhaps not. His last pipe dream had come alive so why not this one? There was Bones' pendant and the painting in the cave back in Boardom, that was why.

He debated back and forth with himself until he reached the best outcome for all concerned, as far as he could tell. He could indeed build his oasis, just not here. That meant going ahead with the journey to Boardom, and a confrontation with Rankor and the men. His father was able to rule over them, in a neutral sort of way, so why not him. The Cobble that left Boardom was not the same Cobble that now guided a band of men, women and children. More importantly, they seemed to respect him and his decisions and respect can travel further down a difficult path than fear.

CHAPTER TWENTY-ONE

A CHANGE OF PLANS

'They're not moving anytime soon,' said Speck, skipping a little to keep up with Jutt's wide gait. 'There are plenty of berry bushes near their camp and they'll find them soon enough.'

'Thank you, Speck, I'm well aware of that.'

'So where are we going?'

Jutt sighed.

'If we can't tease them to the Square then the Square will have to come to them.'

'I'm not sure we'll be able to move the whole Square, not with just the two of us anyway.'

Not for the first time, Jutt wondered if it was Speck was worth keeping around.

'Obviously I don't mean the actual Square, you fool. We have to get one of those charlatans to find them.'

'Why?' said Speck, cowering a little.

Jutt wondered how much of the plan he should let Speck in on. A little knowledge could quench a thirst for curiosity, he knew, but sometimes it paid to drown a man in it.

'Those newcomers are polluting our little tribe. None of them have the capacity to see the damage they're causing so we need to introduce a new perspective to the group, or rather reintroduce an old one. Our traditions have worked for as long as time, with a couple of insignificant exceptions.'

'Like the catastrophic demise of Cherry Woods?'

'Shut up Speck, I haven't finished. The only way we can stop them is to force the issue and make them see sense so we're going back to the Square to do just that. When we get there we'll tell them we've found something dangerous at the edge of the wood. They'll go and investigate until they come across those men. When they find them they'll bring them back to the Square because they're soft. Then we can begin to impose the old traditions again until we have a new Cherry Woods right here in Nutty Woods.'

Even to Speck this didn't sound quite right. For one, he wondered how the lazy bunch they had coaxed all the way across the Greenfields could change anything, they didn't seem the pro-active type, but he knew better than to question Jutt when he was like this.

'Right-o!'

'I swear if you say that one more time...'

'Sorry.'

They were still a few dozen paces away from the Square when it became clear to them that all was not as they had left it. There were more people for a start, lots more. As far as they could tell they were all women too, with a look of Cobble about them; larger noses and hairier everything. Jutt screwed up his eyebrows. He wasn't certain if this made things easier or more difficult, and wouldn't be until he had more information.

'Quick, up that tree,' he said, pointing.

They climbed a large, tall conifer to maximise their cover and peered through a small gap in the thick branches. There was a flurry of activity all around the camp. After a few minutes he realised it was the men doing all the work while the women lounged around, some sleeping and others simply chatting and laughing.

'What is this madness? The men are behaving like women and the women are behaving like men. Look!'

'They're packing for a journey,' said Speck. 'Cobble is doing something with an animal skin and Chard is doing something at the fire, looks like she's ripping up a badger.'

'So it would seem,' said Jutt, closing his eyes a little more. 'This is perfect.'

'It is?'

'Of course it is you dumb fool! Come on, we have work to do.'

Jutt climbed down from his perch, being careful to keep the trunk between him and the eyes of the crowd. He didn't wait for Speck as he jogged into the Square, panting as though at the end of a long run.

They had been resting and preparing for days now. The women had spent the time recovering their energy while the men gathered up provisions and cooked the meat from the traps. They had proved to be a great success and were quickly becoming a reliable source of food, even at this early stage. Cobble knew he could make improvements to them once they were back in Boardom and was sure they could bring down an adult boar in time. He wondered how his father would feel about that. His memory sent an empty feeling through his stomach. For all that his life had changed so much recently he would always have that emptiness inside him somewhere. That was the problem with the past, no matter how hard you tried to move on, as soon as you turn around there it was staring back at you.

He stood up, keen to occupy his mind with something new. He walked over to Moss and sat down next to her, patting her on the shoulder as he lowered himself.

'How are you all feeling, ready to make a move?' he said.

'I reckon so. Daffy is still a little fragile but I ain't sure any amount of rest would fix her. She'll just have to keep up as best she can.'

'How are the babies?'

'Like nothin' has changed. They're the envy of the group.'

'Hopefully they'll make it back to Boardom just as easily.'

'The worst part of the journey 'ere was having no food and no home, not to mention the secrecy. At least this time we can stride as we like across the Greenfields without a care.'

'What are we going back to though, that's what I'd like to know,' said Cobble with more than a little concern. 'I'm not sure if Rankor will run us out of the Meeting Patch or be grateful to see us again.'

'If he's hungry he'll be glad, I can tell you. Even if he's not I can't imagine him doing much about us. He'll probably just glance over with a smug look in his eye and slouch a little deeper.'

'You might be right, but what if our departures, your departure, has changed them? They might be ready for a battle and things could end up worse than they were before.'

'No they couldn't. With respect, Cobble, you don't know what it was like 'aving to cook and clean after those ungrateful slobs. Nutty Woods has given most of us the first day without work in a hundred moons. All we want is somewhere to do our fair share with time to enjoy good company. If that means going back to face Rankor and his cronies then that is what we will do. We will win too.'

'I'm hoping there won't be any winning happening at all,' said Cobble, 'So long as they don't interfere then there are enough of us to look after ourselves. If they don't want to contribute then they can find their own food. Let's see how long that lasts.'

They sat in silence for a moment.

'Enough of this seriousness now, let's get back to work. There's a lot to be done before we set off.'

They made their way through the busy Square, stepping over piles of food and a variety of carrying equipment. Cobble had shown Tarpin and Pippy how to use the skins from the trapped animals to make bags for food, scraping the wet underside with a flint and letting them dry in the sun before tying strings through each corner. There weren't nearly enough of them but they would help a little. The rest would be carried by the ivy slings Meed was making. Moss checked in with each of the women, asking after their health and readiness. She was pleasantly surprised by their upbeat spirit. They had come so far, only to be going right back to where they started, but none of them saw it as simply as that. They may have been going back to the same place, but they were sure they weren't returning to the past.

'All right Plum, how's the sling making business these days?' said Moss with renewed humour.

'Better than boiling mushrooms.'

'How's Daffy? Do you think she'll be OK to make it back?'

'She'll be fine, there's more man in her than she'd like to admit. She has a bad bout of laziness, nothin' more. Once we start off she'll be right there with us, moaning as well as ever.'

Moss chuckled, not so much at what Plum had said exactly, more at the tone of the conversation in general. The women had been serious for too long and hearing some humour, as light as it was, was like dipping her head into a cold river in high summer.

'I was just 'aving a word with Cobble, he thinks we should leave in the morning. What do you reckon?'

'I think that suits me fine. The sooner we leave 'ere the sooner I can see the faces of the men when we march into the Meeting Patch like beetles on dung.'

'Beetles?'

'Like we belong there more than anyone or anything else. We'll be setting the rules and they can join in or bugger off.'

Moss was almost sure she had never heard Plum use that kind of language before. The men didn't know what was coming.

As it happened, nor did the women.

CHAPTER TWENTY-TWO

RETURNING FIRE

'Men! Men!' Jutt called, as he stormed into the Square. 'I have grave news!'

'Is it grave for the women too?' said Cobble, not missing a beat.

'Shut up you!' snapped Jutt, pausing briefly before adding, 'My apologies, dear Cobble, I meant no offence, but there are pressing matters I must discuss with you all.'

'Where have you been,' said Tiff, 'while we have all been busy in preparation for tomorrow?'

This was not part of Jutt's plan. He was used to the comfort of predictability but it seemed nothing was sacrosanct to these confounded newcomers.

'Tomorrow?'

'We're leaving, but you are welcome to stay.'

'Leaving?'

'Yes, leaving. Now if you don't mind there are slings that need to be made and food to be collected.'

'Slings?'

'You sound like one of those birds,' said Camble, 'repeating everything you hear.'

'Birds?'

'Why did you go to the Giant Sea, Jutt?' said Bones.

Jutt's jaw flopped towards his chest. How could they possibly know? He had been so careful to be sure they weren't followed. He wasn't ready to give up his secret just yet. Soon, but not yet. His instincts took over, knowing that the how was not as important as the fact. Bones somehow knew he had been there and judging by the looks on the faces of everyone else he was the only one. Except maybe Camble. There was a story here that he was desperate to hear, but curiosity would have to wait, he needed to dig himself out of this hole quickly.

'What do you mean? I haven't been anywhere, just around the woods here looking for something to help feed us. Do you really think I've been doing something else?'

'How do you know about the Giant Sea?' said Bones, pressing on.

'I don't, I've never heard of it. If I have, if, then maybe I heard about it from the tale of your journey here.' Jutt allowed himself a little pat on the back for that one.

'But we never journeyed past the Giant Sea, we never even mentioned it, did we, Cobble?'

'No, no we didn't. Pingo, have you ever heard of the Giant Sea?' said Cobble, sensing an entrapment.

'Not until Jutt said it just now. Is it important?'

'It's on the border of our home, at least three days hard walk away from here,' said Bones, 'and the birds told us you were talking about it.'

'Is it really? Golly!' said Jutt, feigning ignorance. Quite badly as it turned out. He would have been better advised to question the queerness of talking birds.

'Explain yourself, Jutt, what have you been up to?'

'Up to? I don't know what you mean. Now, how can I help with the preparations?'

That sealed it for Tiff. One last show of leadership was required.

'Jutt Cragnose, we know you know about the Giant Sea and you've been gone for days. Now you turn up out of the blue with exclamations of doom and offers of help. You haven't even asked us why we are leaving. I know you well enough to know that you wouldn't offer help without first knowing what was in it for you. Now stop hiding behind improvised ignorance and tell us what you've been up to.'

While everyone was looking at Tiff, Moss was staring at Jutt, as if trying to remember his face so she could describe it in detail later.

'OK, OK,' said Jutt, thinking furiously, 'I didn't go to the Giant Sea, wherever it is, but I did find something while I was gone. That is why I came back. I was on the edge of the forest foraging for mushrooms to share with us all – very generously I might add – when I saw a group of men sitting in a clearing. They looked a lot like you actually Cobble. Very hairy. I erred on the side of caution and came straight back here to warn you.'

'Where are the mushrooms now?'

'Well, they were... I ran back, yes, and haste was more pressing than hunger so I dropped them in a thicket. I can show you later if you like, but now isn't the time as I'm sure you can appreciate.'

'What about the Giant Sea?' said Fettle, his slow wits finally paying dividends.

'And don't think you can talk your way out of this one,' added Bones. 'How do you know about the Giant Sea?'

'Can we please focus on the immediate peril here? There is a band of dangerous men in Nutty Woods and we're playing semantics with the very person who bought us some time to plan!'

'So they're a band of dangerous men now?' said Moss, 'And how would you know that?'

'Who are you? I'm speaking to my friends here, if you would be so good as to keep quiet.'

Moss put two and two together in her head and came up with something that might have been four.

'I'm your worst bleedin' nightmare,' said Moss.

'Are you indeed? How delightful. Now, can we please discuss the matter at hand? Tiff, let's begin with why you are leaving?'

Tiff thought it prudent to remove this line of questioning from the interrogation by giving up the answer.

'There is a great danger heading our way.'

'So you believe me?'

'No, a very different danger. One that has the power to flatten the forest and destroy our home. We are escaping, back to a place where we think we will be safe from the reach of the mountain.'

'The reach of the mountain?'

'Don't start that again,' said Camble.

'Wait, you said back to somewhere. You're not seriously going to take us back to Cherry Woods? There is nothing left for us there.'

'Indeed there is not,' said Tiff. 'Though you are correct to say we are going back. Our family has grown since you left us and we have more than one back to head for.'

Jutt looked at the women properly for the first time.

'I see you have drawn the same conclusion,' continued Tiff. 'The only safe place for us is in Boardom, where we guess we will be safe.'

'You guess?'

'Yes, guess. My sight doesn't yet extend to the future.'

'Enough of this nonsense. There are better places than that over-grown cesspit to head for, and closer too!'

'Overgrown cesspit?' said Cobble. 'And what would make you say that?'

Jutt was losing his grip on the situation, maybe now was the time to give up his secret.

'I was being poetic, dear boy. You didn't seem to think much of it when you left, according to your version of things at least.' At-tack and distract, he thought. 'Why would you want to go back to somewhere you've just wriggled free from?'

'Because imperfect safety is better than perfect danger.'

'Now who's being poetic?' said Speck, half hidden behind Jutt.

'Shut up Speck! I told you to keep quiet!'

'Shut up Speck! Shut up Speck!' said Budge.

'Giant Sea!' said Spike.

Camble looked around at Bones. 'There they are! Look!'

'Bloody birds!' said Jutt. 'Now would be a good time to show off your bough and arrow again.'

'On you, maybe,' said Meed, joining in the fun.

'Get up Tark! Get up Tark!' shrieked Spike.

'Otter! Otter!'

Moss decided to gamble. She glanced over to Jutt. His secret, if he had one, was about to become something else.

She passed a look of sorrow to Bones.

'There is something you should know.'

CHAPTER TWENTY-THREE

MYSTERY AND HONESTY

'It was more than two hundred moons ago I would say,' began Moss, 'and I was working at the stream washing the babies' coats. The wind had been blowin' all morning and it was good drying weather so I had taken some of the mens' coats too, thinking they could dry quickly before the cold dusk set in. It's important not to waste good drying weather, that's what Old Willow always used to say. I had been working all morning in a wind that would cut your legs in 'alf so when it came time for lunch I took shelter under the bridge and was glad to hide from the biting air. I was almost finished when I heard voices nearby. I was a good distance from the Meeting Patch and, as you know, the men would never normally 'ave bothered to travel so far. I was curious, so I crept out from under the bridge to see who it was. I don't mind tellin' you how surprised I was to see two figures, one a full head taller than the other, standing by a rocky crag at the foot of the mountains. They looked to be out of earshot but the wind carried their voices over to me so I strained my ears to listen.'

'I told you not to come back' said one. 'You did enough damage the first time.'

'That's not true now, is it?' said the other. 'You told me not to come back unless I brought something... important.'

'That was a dozen moons ago. Times have changed.'

'Times may have changed but the terms of our agreement have not, old boy.'

'Then show me.'

The taller man stepped behind a crag and picked up a bundle of animal fur.

'We have skins. Not many, perhaps, but we have enough.'

'Our agreement is inside. Look.'

'I couldn't make out what was inside,' said Moss, 'but I could see that the smaller figure didn't move, other than to put a gentle hand into the bundle. The wind changed direction and I lost the thread of their conversation. A few minutes had passed by the time the smaller man began walking towards me with the 'agreement' before stopping still. I couldn't say that they saw me exactly, but I'm sure they saw something. They placed the bundle at their feet and turned away, back towards the crag before changing direction again back to the Meeting patch. It felt like an eternity before I broke cover and my walk became a jog as I got closer. The furs were as good a quality as my eyes had ever seen and whatever was inside them wouldn't have felt a single breath of the wind that circled them.'

She paused, realising that as she spoke she had been staring intently at a solitary pine needle in the midst of hundreds on the floor. She looked up at Jutt, she couldn't bear to look at the other. He had a pleading look in his eyes, desperate even.

'Well that's a fine tale, friend.' He said, heavy with hidden instructions. 'What say we get back to this business of the men encircling us with spears.'

'Oh, they're encircling us now, are they?' said Cobble, nudging

Bones. 'Next time they'll be charging at us on boarback.'

Bones didn't react.

'Moss?' he said.

She didn't turn.

'Moss?'

'You tell him, Jutt.'

Bones looked from Moss to Jutt and back again with increasing panic.

His voice was low and terrifying as he shot a look of impending rage at Jutt.

'Tell me now before I make the mountain the least of your problems.'

Jutt knew this was one corner he couldn't escape. Moss was right, she was his worst nightmare.

'There were two things inside the bundle,' he admitted. 'A baby...'

'And?'

'And a triangular pendant.'

The chaos of questions careering around Bones' head was overwhelming. He needed space to make sense of what he had been told, but was instantly desperate to get answers.

'I'm sorry,' said Jutt with a sincerity he had never shown before. 'I should have told you as soon as I saw the pendant.'

'Shut up Jutt.'

'Shut up Jutt!' squawked Budge.

Jutt kicked the bird across the floor.

In all of history there is one phrase more than any other that sends an emphatically opposing message to the one intended. Jutt chose this critical moment to use it.

'It's not what you think.'

As it turns out, it wasn't what Bones thought, though that wasn't much of a comfort to Jutt.

Bones stumbled out of the Square and into the anonymity of the forest. Jutt followed discreetly, kicking out at Speck who had instinctively tried to follow him, catching his shin and making him hop like an excited rabbit.

'I say, that was all rather dramatic, what?' said Pingo when the hubbub had died down.

'Rather!' said Balcor. 'I have to say though, I'm a little confused as to where we focus our efforts now. There's a mountain about to destroy us and a band of strangers loitering at the edge of the woods, possibly violent, possibly harmless but certainly hairy.'

'I'll help you,' said Plum. 'That bird was saying the name of one of the men in Boardom. Unless they have long memories or can fly faster than the wind then the men wandering about on our lands are the slobs from our home.'

'Are they dangerous?'

'Normally I would say they're as dangerous as rain on a rock, but if they've travelled this far then I reckon the rules 'ave changed.'

'And that helps, does it?' said Pingo, grinning at Plum like a young boy telling a rude joke.

'Well it means they're desperate. If they're in need of something that we can give them then we have 'alf a chance to change the way we live there. With your help, naturally.'

'I'll help to the best of my ability, old girl. What can I do?'

Plum blushed for the first time in her life.

'You can help me with these slings,' she said as Balcor slinked quietly away.

Bones stared at the floor, then at a root, then the floor again. It would help if he knew where to start. How could he untangle the mess in his head if half of the information was in someone else's?

He looked into the distance to an eye and an ear sticking out from behind a tree.

'Jutt, get here now!' he called.

Jutt walked over and sat down next to him. Even in his gait he seemed like a different Jutt from the one that had stormed into the Square just a few minutes ago.

'I'm sorry,' said Jutt.

'So you said.'

'I should have told you earlier.'

'So you say.'

They sat in a silence that would have been uncomfortable had they the mental space for it.

'I want answers,' said Bones.

'And I will give them to you.'

'The real answers, Jutt, not some game of facts to suit your agenda.'

'Agreed. What do you want to know?'

'What do I want to know!? Really? How about starting with why you carried me all that way to dump me with a tribe of bald monkeys?'

'I'll tell you what I know, someone else will have to fill the gaps.'

'Which someone else? Someone from Boardom?'

Jutt ignored the question.

'First of all, it wasn't me Moss saw, it was my brother. I can only tell you what he told me, any gaps are there because I don't have the information, just like you. I wasn't always as you see me now. I was a happy, pleasant man before fate conspired against me. My brother was a pretty good scout as a young man and would often travel with the hunters to find prey for the village. On one occasion, near the desperate end of our time in Cherry Woods he decided to head far to the west to the very edge of the mountain range, then north to where the hills are coated in thick purple heather. It took him longer than any trip he had done before and he found nothing. He headed back south until there were signs of a village up ahead. Before he could reach it he was spotted by a young woman collecting pears. She came up to him as if he was a friend and started telling him all about herself, how she was from the village at the eastern end of the mountain range and that it was her job to collect the fruit for the special drink that one of them made. She said it made them dance and sing, although he didn't believe her, obviously. She said she would get some for him if he came back to the same spot the next day. He was grateful for the chance of some food and the company so he agreed. She gave him some of her crop and was gone.'

Bones studied his face for signs of deception, or possibly conceit, and found only sadness. He hadn't known Jutt for long but even so he could tell that this story had been hidden deep below his cold, harsh exterior.

'The next day she came back with a large animal skin, pulled up at each corner. She explained that she couldn't stay long, she had stolen the skin and it was one of only a few that the whole village had to share. Its absence would be discovered once the sun went down and the men called for their drink. He believed her about that much at least, despite his doubts about the side effects of the juice. They drank the whole batch, swapping stories of their homes and ways. Before long they were dancing and singing, although her songs were a little coarse for his taste. Anyway, you can probably imagine what happened next. Afterwards she said she wanted to travel back with him to Cherry Woods and that she couldn't go back to living in that overgrown cesspit of a village – her words, not my brother's I should add.'

'So what happened then, what was all the talk of an agreement for?' said Bones, curious in spite of his fear of the ending.

'Before they could talk any more about it they were shaken from their daydream by the calls of a man running down the gentle grass slope towards them. He grabbed my brother and flung him against a tree, pinning him against it despite his protests. He spat accusations at him and insisted he be dragged back to the village to have his fate determined by the leader of the tribe. He knew that if he reached the village it would be the end of him, so he used the only thing he had left at his disposal; his wits.'

'What was the leader's name?' said Bones, now glaring.

'I don't remember, does it matter?'

'It all matters, Jutt.'

'I'm sorry, I don't recall.'

'Then what happened?'

'He had little to bargain with, so he used the only thing that could get them out of there. He explained that they had decided to go back to his home lands and that they would stay away for good. He asked why he should let him run off with one of their women, a valid point to be fair to him. My brother had to gamble, so he told him that they had been meeting up for some time and that the woman was pregnant. He was telling a truth he was ignorant of at the time. He said he would take her away until they had delivered the baby safely. Once that was done he would return with both her and the baby and give them back to the village. He lied about the resources we had at Cherry Woods, telling him that there were villagers who tended to pregnant women and looked after the babies in the first few weeks. He bought the story and let them go.'

'Just like that?'

'No. He took some convincing, with a promise of retribution if things didn't go according to their agreement. My brother explained that the guarantee of a new tribe member was worth being without one for a few moons. He also offered something invaluable to him, to show his sincerity. He gave the only possession his father left either of us.'

Bones' expression asked the question for him.

'Yes, the pendant. It was your grandfather's, then your father's, and now it is yours.'

His head swam with a nauseous cocktail of questions and answers. Jutt, to his credit, stayed quiet. After a time Bones steadied himself enough to release a question from the murky soup.

'Why did he not return the woman... my mother to the tribe?' The words sounded foreign.

'I'm afraid she was a victim of our famine. I'm sorry Bones, we did everything we could to save her but when I returned one day from scouting she was gone. You would have liked her, she was more like you than me or my brother.'

'What was her name?'

'Coren.'

'What name did she give me?'

'They didn't name you, I'm ashamed to say. They knew they would have to give you up and decided it would be easier if there was less to remember you by. They were wrong, they should never have given you away.'

'Who was the man who pinned him against the tree?'

'As far as I know he went by the name Willie, although that may not have been his real name.'

'Is he in the band of men at the edge of the woods?'

'I don't know, I've never seen him before. I had hoped he was with them, but now I'm hoping he isn't.'

'Why are they here?'

Jutt described his journey to the Giant Sea and back using only the facts and none of the motivation.

'I said why, not how,' said Bones with a confidence he had never felt before.

'When I saw the pendant I panicked. I have held this secret for so long that the thoughts of it escaping petrified me. I thought if I could find Willie and give you back to him then it would compensate, in some small way, for the loss of Coren.'

'So you were just looking after yourself again. I'm just a bargaining chip to you.'

'You've been many different things to me, Bones. You were a bargaining chip at some points I'll admit, but you were also a joy, a burden, a mystery and a hole.'

'Why didn't your brother just keep me?'

'We couldn't feed ourselves, let alone another mouth. You had a better chance of surviving in Boardom than you did with us.'

Bones had had enough. He hauled himself up to search for a place to sit alone, turning around for one last question.

'What is your brother's name?'

CHAPTER TWENTY-FOUR

CHANGING MEN

They were finally ready. Preparations had gone well and each person knew the jobs they had to do along the journey. Cobble orchestrated the men, and Moss the women. Tiff helped out to an extent, but his mind was busy storing up the imagery to be retold at a later date around a firepit he had yet to see. Pingo and Plum had become each other's giddy shadow and they had already decided to walk together all the way to Boardom. There were already a lot of mock eye-rolls between the other members of the village but their blossoming relationship proved to be a good tonic after the drama of Jutt's revelation hours earlier.

Cobble wondered if he would ever be as relaxed when he was with Thistle. That was a nice problem for another day, he procrastinated. There were piles of slings, some for the babies but most for the food. They had struggled to make water carriers that would last long enough for the whole journey. He could only make three of his complicated wooden flasks in the short time they had available to them and they would have to rely, for the most part, on fruits and streams for their water supply. There was no need to plan the route as it would be a straight line out of the woods and across the Greenfields.

Almost everything was on track. Almost.

Bones had been gone for hours now and there was no sign of Jutt. Once they were back they would be set, with one last sleep in the comfort of Nutty Woods before they left to complete the circle.

RUMBLE... RUMBLE... RUMBLE... RUMBLE... RUMBLE... RUMBLE...

Everybody stopped. They would have been dead still if it wasn't for the movement at their feet. A roar unlike anything any of them had heard before assaulted their ears and some fell to the floor in a dizzying combination of shock and fear.

The sky darkened and a gentle heat permeated the air.

Jutt knew he should leave Bones alone to digest the news, but he had nowhere else to go so he followed him.

'Leave me alone, Jutt,' he snapped. 'I've heard enough from you for a lifetime.'

Jutt's reply was stifled in his throat.

RUMBLE... RUMBLE... RUMBLE... RUMBLE... RUMBLE... RUMBLE...

The roar wasn't as polite as it could have been, ripping the air between them and throwing a distracted Bones to the floor. Jutt's expression shifted from concern to fear and finally to neutral as he offered a hand to his nephew. Bones ignored it, leaning on his fore-arm and pushing himself up and onto his feet. He ran towards the Square as if he was alone.

'The mountain!' screamed Bones as he careered into the Square.

'Yes, thank you Bones, we had noticed,' said Pingo in a tone that Bones couldn't decide was impatience or humour.

'Are we ready? We have to leave!'

'We're ready,' said Cobble, throwing a sling to him. 'Gather the men, I'll get the women.'

Cobble scanned the crowd as they gathered in the Square. Every-one was there except for two.

'Bones, where is Jutt?'

'Why should I know? I'm not his keeper!' said Bones, a little too frostily. 'We don't need him anyway. Come on, let's get going.' He patted a few shoulders as he made his way out of the Square. A few of the men adjusted their burdens in preparation and set off.

'Wait!' called Cobble. 'You're right, we don't need Jutt. But I'm not leaving without Thistle, has anyone seen her?' He had said the thought without passing it by his brain first, but it was true.

'She went off that way,' said Pippy, pointing away from the Square.

'Right then. Tiff, take everyone to the edge of the forest that way,' said Cobble, pointing back towards the Greenfields. 'I'll find Thistle and catch up with you. Don't leave the forest without us.

Now go, before Bones' pendant comes to life right in front of us.'

ROOOOAAAAAARRRR...

Cobble ran out of the Square. Bones let out a resigned, but pleasantly familiar sigh and followed him.

'There's no need for you to come,' said Cobble. 'I can look after this, you look after yourself.'

'No, my place is here,' said Bones. 'I'm sorry we fell out, let's not do it again.'

They had always been light spirited together, even in the worst times in Boardom, but the last few days had seen them be more serious than either of them would have liked and it was time to move on.

'Enough of that nonsense,' he said. 'Let's focus on our impending doom instead, eh?'

'Sounds like a good plan.'

'We'll find Thistle and get back to the group as quickly as we can. Then we'll skip over that little patch of grass and be in Boardom – New Boardom – before we know it. Come on.'

They found Thistle on her way back to the Square, carrying a squirrel by the tail. She looked petrified.

'What was that!?'

'It's Unfinished Mountain giving up its secret at last,' said Cobble, grabbing her by the arm and quickening her from a walk to a run. 'The rest of us have left, come on.'

They ran back to the Square and passed straight through in the darkening forest.

'What was that?' said Balcor at the head of the formation. 'It sounded like a man's voice.'

'I didn't hear anything,' said Fettle.

'It could be those other men,' said Tiff, raising an arm to stop the line. 'Let's not charge into them until we can see what kind of threat they pose.'

'They don't pose anything,' said Plum. 'That would be too much effort. 'Come on, we're going straight through them.'

The Nutty Woodsmen were not used to a woman ordering them around, but then they weren't used to exploding mountains either and Tiff, for one, was glad for someone else to take control of the decision making process. They set off again, the sounds of the Boardom men getting louder as they went.

'Oi! Rankor, something's comin' this way, look!' said Tark, pointing into the heart of the forest.

'Don't be stupid Tark, we're the only ones here. When was the last time you saw anyone you didn't recognise?'

There was that Boardom logic again.

'The last time?' said Tark, nodding into the forest. 'I'd say about five seconds ago.'

Moss had a hundred lines ready for when they met the men again. All of them were sharp, some were funny, but all were better than the one her brain selected from the very bottom of the pile.

'Rankor,' she said.

'Well, well, well. What 'ave we 'ere,' he said. 'Look who's come crawling back.'

'Have we?' said Moss 'Are you sure about that?'

'You're 'ere, ain't you?'

'Yes, but not for long. We're going back to Boardom now and to be honest I couldn't give a badger's foot whether you come with us or not. If you do, you'll need to bring your own provisions, we've only got enough for us. If you're not, then goodbye.'

She stepped over the prone leg of Granite and continued her way through the tribe. Rankor would have fallen over had he not been lying down already.

'Now wait 'ere young lady...'

'No.'

'Ah.'

Pingo walked up to Tark. 'Pardon me, kind sir, but would you mind awfully moving your leg out of the way so I may pass freely?' he said, taking the opportunity to get in an almost gentle kick on his way past.

Rankor stood up, his curiosity over the terrifying roar overpowering both his pride and laziness.

'Please, wait. What was that noise?'

'Who wants to know?' said Cobble, striding through the crowd and right up to the face of Rankor.

'Robble! There you are! We were so worried about you. Will you tell these damned women to stop and explain their behaviour. They're acting all strange. And who are these men? They sound like they 'ave a chunk of apple in their mouths.'

'One, it's Cobble,' said Bones, stepping in front of Cobble and up to his former leader. 'Two, no you weren't. Three, they're not the women who escaped all those days ago. Four, most of these men are ten times the man you will ever be. Are you keeping up? I know four is a big number for you to manage. To be fair, I'll give you a warning that five is next, and it's worth listening to.'

Rankor could have been given an hour to choose how his face would react and still wouldn't know which expression to choose.

'Five. Are you listening Dankor?' He inched closer until their noses were almost touching. All the pent up frustrations of a lifetime of irrelevance collided with the anger of Jutt's revelations and his falling out with Cobble. 'Five. There is an enormous mountain over there, you may have seen it on your way here. It's full of a boiling orange liquid that moves at the speed of an injured boar, but nothing can stop its progress. It has destroyed part of this forest before and is about to do so again. For now it is only noisy but soon it will spray its deadly venom as far as you can see. It will kill us all if we don't get away from here. You are welcome to stay, in fact please do. We, on the other hand, are not going to stay. We are going to get as far away from here as quickly as possible. We will get to Boardom and we will remake the village you so carelessly destroyed. There will be culture and dancing, equality and happiness. We will all play our part in making our lives there full of joy and laughter. If you follow us you will not be leader, you will all do your fair share, you will all cook, you will all clean and you will all treat the women as you would the men. If you refuse to do your bit then you will not be fed the meat that we are now able to produce at will. That's right, Rankor, you should have listened to Cobble. His bough and arrow worked, his hunting traps work, and his leadership will work. Now if you'll excuse me, I have a long journey ahead of me and a violent mountain to escape.'

'Bloody hell, he's got you there,' said a voice from behind Rankor.

'Shut up Granite,' said Rankor, and with the last of his pomposity called out to his tribe. 'If they're going that way, then we're going this way.' He gestured away from the Greenfields with one arm, picking up the last of the fruit with the other and marching off deeper into the woods.

'This should be interesting,' said Plum to nobody in particular.

Those who knew the Boardom men studied them for signs of individual decisions being made. Those who didn't studied Bones instead and wondered where that outburst had come from.

One by one the Boardom men stood up and followed Rankor. Despite the height of the stakes, or possibly because of it, they found themselves slinking back into the well worn grooves of tradition and habit. Only one of them was still sitting where they had been all along. Old Shankswill creaked himself upright and looked at the dozens of eyes staring back at him. He walked up to Rankor and gave him a slow, deliberate look.

'You're a fool,' he said and turned to Cobble. 'I think we should get away from this mountain, leader.'

'Then let's go.'

They broke out on to the Greenfields and immediately spread out, glad to be out of the confines of the woods. Cobble didn't know whether to go over to Bones or Old Shankswill first. In the end, the decision was made for him. Shankswill was busy in his own thoughts, walking a little to the side of the group. Bones skipped up to Cobble and put an arm around his shoulder.

'So, our glorious leader, how long do you think it will take us to cross this little patch of grass?'

'Depends whether we come across any badgers or not. And don't call me leader.'

Bones gave a chuckle. 'Oh, but you are Cobble. You got us into this mess so you can get us out of it.'

'I may end up being their leader' he said, nodding towards the small throng behind him, 'but not yours.'

'So you say, friend, so you say.'

'Here comes Jutt, look. So is now a good time to tell me?'

'No.'

They had gone about two thousand paces from the cover of the woods. The roar of the mountain was still at the forefront of their minds, but only as a recent memory. It had been quiet ever since. Had any of them seen a volcano before they would have known it was a threatening silence, but as they hadn't they chose to ignore its absence, for the time being at least. While the danger was neither audible nor visible they would keep their feet pointing to the far side of the Greenfields and their heads light with conversation.

There were plenty of untold stories and unexplored personalities between the new group and they had all slunk to a steady pace, both at their feet and in their voices. Plum and Pingo were filling in the considerable gaps of their relative histories, both engrossed in the other's background. Moss walked with Balcor, and Fettle with Daffy. For once, Daffy was speaking in full, inefficient sentences and for his part Fettle was enjoying having someone listen to his ramblings on the endless possibilities of the usage of ivy. He had been able to wrap his head around the concept, unlike most others, and it was now his favourite subject. Thistle was with Faun, but spent most of the time glancing over at Cobble. Aside from Old Shankswill, only Jutt and Speck walked on their own. When Speck trotted up to his side Jutt had sent him away with a sharp comment and a clip around his head.

Bones needed one more answer and knew where he could find it. He walked over to the hairy old man, smelling the rotten fruit long before he got there.

'Why did you give me away?'

Old Shankswill shook himself from his thoughts and looked up at Bones.

'What makes you think it was me?'

'Come on, Jutt has told me everything. I know you were checking on your pears when you caught his brother and... the woman.'

'Then it seems Jutt hasn't told you everything.'

'Then why are you here?' said Bones, not buying the denial.

'I'm here because Rankor is a fool. The future lies with those who can feed themselves, not with a band of talentless oafs.'

'Of which you are one.'

'Am I indeed? You may detect I have escaped their clutches.'

'For a thousand paces, maybe. There's a long way to go yet. Now tell me, why did you give me away?'

'As I've already told you, I didn't give you away. Not me.'

'Then who?'

'It's not for me to tell. And anyway, nobody believes Old Shank-swill, he's just a confused drunk.'

'A confused old drunk who has enough wits about him to abandon his tribe for the sake of his future. You are more cunning than you would have people believe.'

'Which is why I won't tell you who gave you away. Now if you don't mind, I'd like to be left alone for a while.'

It was an absolute statement rather than a request.

Bones looked around at the group, choosing to fall back to the rear to give him space to think.

They spent the first night in the open, no closer to the mountain than was necessary and not so far away as to make their journey longer than it needed to be. Real motivation is a powerful catalyst and they were making good headway towards Boardom. As they walked with a morning breeze at their backs, none of them thought about how they were a collection of people unique in all of history to that point; a mish mash of cultures colliding for the first time. An inconvenient absence of context meant that this defining moment in the life of the world passed by them without so much as a murmur of feigned interest. Had they been aware of the significance it would soon have been pushed back into second place in any case.

The seconds turned into minutes without getting any longer. Unfinished Mountain gave its biggest rumble yet, wobbling their legs and forcing their arms out for balance. A great rush of boiling hot air hit them like a wall, sending them to the floor. Almost in the same motion some of them sprang back to their feet and headed for the nearest prone figure. Each of them were helped up and Cobble yelled for them to run. Jutt took more than his fair share of slings, bounding clear even with the extra burdens. Cobble and Tiff stayed at the back, closest to the mountain, making sure everyone was moving. They ran at full tilt until the first of them started to struggle. Gradually they all slowed to a brisk walk, some looking back in fear, others staring straight ahead.

'We have to get away from it, far away,' said Cobble to anyone who could hear. 'Looks like a straight line isn't the best way home after all. This way, come on!'

They jinked to their left, perpendicular to the mountain now and causing it to shrink behind them as quickly as they could manage. After a time they had to stop, they had no way of knowing if they were far enough away but they had to stop.

The mountain went quiet, briefly and ominously. As one they turned to face it and felt the roar before they heard it, a great explosion of power that rocked them backwards. Liquid the colour of a summer sunset, but not as pleasant, bounced violently from the top of the rock, splashing over the edge and sending great plumes of smoke into the sky. What followed was unlike anything they had imagined. A huge orange cylinder shot up as high above the mountain as the mountain itself and landed all around the mountain causing several steady flows of the mysterious liquid to begin their journey down the slope. They heard a different, more desperate roar to their right. It came from a smudge of brown on the green landscape.

Goober was the first to reach them. The laziest people are often the quickest to react when there is danger to be avoided.

'Did you see that?' he said, holding his knees and panting.

'No,' said Bones. 'What did we miss?'

'There's a giant orange... thing in that mountain, look!'

'Oh that? Yes, we saw that,' said Pingo. 'We were just fleeing for our lives when you arrived actually.'

'Which way are you going?' said Goober, happy to be a parasite to knowledge. 'I'll come with you.'

'Oh really?' said Cobble 'And what would Rankor have to say about that? Ah, here he is! Let's ask him.'

'Cobble, Bones and... the rest of you,' said Rankor. 'We're travelling with you to Boardom. When we get there I will decide how our cosy little village is going to work.'

'Is that so?' said Bones. 'It's going to be a hungry journey for you, we're not giving up our food to a bunch of self righteous oiks. It'll give you a chance to get used to the feeling, since you can't hunt.'

'We'll take our share, you can be sure of that. You will give up the food just like we gave you up all those years ago.'

Bones stared him down.

'Listen, Rankor,' he said, vitriol dripping from his tongue. 'You're all as bad as each other. So what if I don't know precisely which one of you abandoned me to the wolves, what does it matter? Who it was is not important. I could go through the rest of my life without the knowledge and it would be of no concern to me. What does concern me is the future of Boardom, of these people here. The old men of Boardom could burn in the mountain for all I care, but if you insist on coming with us then you will play by our rules. There is no food for you – you did nothing to earn it – but if you help when we are back home then you can have your share. If not, then you can starve like a stream in summer. Either way, I don't care.'

As the different groups stared as one at Bones, and more specifically at the change in Bones, Unfinished Mountain exploded once more. A great river of orange splashed violently a few thousand paces in front of them, blinding their vision for a moment and freezing their muscles. The ooze kept coming, sliding down the gentle slope of the Greenfields and setting light to the bushes dotted around them. Their path was quickly becoming blocked, the flow reaching past their horizon towards the Long Mountains.

Without a word being said they started off as a single band of escapees, hoping to reach the mountain range before the boiling rivers. They had no way of knowing how quickly the gap was closing, just that it was. Their desperation fought against fatigue and stretched them out in a long line of fear.

The dark sun had passed its highest point when the first of them started to drop. They became a scattering of still blobs on the green floor, wide apart. They had no choice but to stop again and rest. Balcor and Pingo set off to the back of the line to help bring whoever was there to the front. As Cobble stood up to do the same he looked for Rankor to gather his men to help. None of them were near the front. Only as he reached the far end of the line did he realise that it was they who were the backmarkers. He knew he would help them out and it was too tempting to resist being the one to help Rankor.

He found him slouched over Tark, eyes closed. Putting his arms under his armpits he hauled him off and dropped him gracelessly to the floor.

'Are you going to get up or do I have to drag you all the way to the front?' said Cobble, savouring the moment.

'Help, please.'

Cobble grabbed a wrist and pulled, walking backwards to get a better footing in the thick grass. It was harder work than he thought he was capable of but he gleaned an odd pleasure from it. When they had all gathered at the head of the line they stopped, limbs slumped over limbs and faces pressed into bellies. They lay there, still as the sun. In his swirling head it occurred to Bones that all the people most of them had ever seen, discounting the dead, were here in this mass of exhaustion. Whatever lay ahead of them would be determined by the actions of this motley crew, but Cobble was as good a leader of them as he could imagine.

An hour or more had passed when the first of them began to regain enough energy to haul themselves up onto their haunches.

'I'm going to scout on ahead,' said Jutt as he looked down on Cobble. 'Hopefully I'll find a route through.'

He was back before sunset. If his body language wasn't enough evidence, his face told them all they needed to know. The flow had reached the range and they were trapped.

CHAPTER TWENTY-FIVE

A CHOICE OF ONE

The rain was torrential now, spitting walls of steam all around them. It had come out of nowhere, the rainclouds hidden by the dark, imposing clouds of the mountain. Had they not been at their lowest ebb already, it would have been a bloody nuisance. As it was, they hardly noticed. Only a few of them were able to stay positive, in a hopeless sort of way.

'I say!' said Camble. 'This is quite a lark, what?'

'That's just what I was thinking,' said Meed. 'There's nothing quite like being trapped between a molten river and a forest that's just caught fire, I said to myself. Being soaked through is just a nice bonus.'

'Well ain't you lot just great at keeping the spirits up,' said Rankor through narrowed eyes. 'Perhaps you 'ave a good song that will help us pass the time while we wait for the mountain to throw its load this way?'

'Shut up,' said Tiff.

'Shut up!' squawked Spike.

Camble turned to the birds 'Ah, hello there little ones. Want some nuts?'

'So you're giving our food to birds before us now?' said Rankor.

'Of course. They've done more for us than you have, dear boy. Why should we give you anything?'

Rankor had nothing. This change in the group dynamic was both new and frightening to him. All the certainties of his life seemed to have packed a bag and gone for a long walk. He felt as though the ground was moving under him, which it was as it happened. The mountain was preparing to speak again.

This time the plume was wider and higher than before. Part of it broke off and headed for the woods. Another part of it was aiming more in their direction than they would have liked. They were facing their moment of truth and they had nothing. The slow river crept along towards their last camp and none of them moved. There was a little more space between them and the Long Mountains that they could have moved into, they could even have gone a little way up the mountain range, but the hope was slim and their legs were bone tired.

'It looks a bit slippy,' said Roddo.

'Slippy? Slippy?' said Balcor, his eyes almost popping out. 'I'd say it's a little more than slippy, young man. It looks like it'd take your toes off just for looking at it.'

'We should go up to the mountain range a little way if we can,' said Tiff, voicing what they were all thinking.

'I've climbed it before,' said Pippy, 'and there is no way even I could make it up the sides in this rain. They're just too steep and are slippy enough in a dry sun.'

Rankor had something.

'So, Bobble. As our unquestionable leader, what d'you reckon our next move should be? Should we walk that way into the hot river, or that way to the burning woods? Perhaps we could sit here swapping stories of how we came to be in this sticky mess. As I recall it begins with you abandoning the safety of Boardom. Please, do tell us.'

Cobble had a nagging doubt that Rankor was right, in a round-about kind of way. If he hadn't left Boardom then nor would the women have. The men wouldn't have followed them and they would all still be in Boardom, miserable but safe. All he had wanted was a bit of respect, and perhaps excitement. He thought back to those dull days growing up around the Obelisk. He was right to leave, he was pretty sure about that. What others did after that was not his concern, they chose their own paths. He scanned the Long Mountains absent-mindedly as he retraced his only, and likely final adventure in his mind, enjoying the fleeting sense of freedom it gave him.

He suddenly leapt to his feet, something that took everyone by surprise.

'The conifer! This way! Hurry!'

Buddy folded his wings against his pale green body, rubbed his legs together and gave his friend a look of encouragement.

'Well?' he said.

'What are you doing now?' asked Grub, a cricket whose patience had gone past running thin and was jogging towards oblivion.

'If I told you that there'd be no point in playing the game now, would there?'

'Can we not do something else? I'm too hot now for games and

I've heard every tune you can play. I'm bored.'

'You can't be bored with talent like this on show, its cracking stuff. Listen.'

It wasn't cracking stuff, but that didn't stop Buddy. The only thing capable of stopping him was a guess. Even then, once you had offered one you needed the reactions of light to distract him quickly enough to stop him launching into another round.

'It's 'Rock Around The Rock' again, isn't it?'

'Wow, you're good!'

'No Buddy, no I'm not. You're just very bad.'

'That's not what you said when I did 'The Fat Leaf'.'

This was a valid point. Buddy's rendition of The Fat Leaf was very good, at first, but the lustre had worn off after a thousand or so performances.

'I'm sick of it now.'

'Why don't you lighten up a bit?' said Buddy. 'You should try making a tune yourself. It'd help with that fatalistic attitude of yours.'

'What's the point? I could be run over by a rabbit tomorrow.'

'But imagine the fun you could have in the meantime.'

'I'd rather not. It makes me queasy.'

'There's no talking to you sometimes, Grub. You can really bring a cricket down, do you know that?'

'It'll be nice to have the company.'

As Grub looked at him for signs of agreement a hairy foot replaced Buddy for a moment before disappearing again, leaving a flatter, and presumably deader cricket half buried in the ground.

'See,' said Grub 'I told you.'

It couldn't be said that the group hurried, per se. They certainly moved more quickly, relative to their recent behaviour, but only in the same way a tree moves quicker than a bridge.

'I ain't moving until you tell us where you're trying to take us,' said Rankor.

'OK, best of luck with being burned alive,' said Bones cheerily as he hoisted up a couple of slings and headed over to Cobble.

'He's got a point there,' said Granite.

'Shut up!' said Rankor.

'Shut up!' squawked Budge.

'Women, come on,' said Plum, offering a hand to Faun. 'If there's a choice between being boiled and going for a walk, even if it's a short one, then I know what I'm doing.'

One by one the women stood up and followed Cobble. The Nutty Woodsmen were already on their way. Only the Boardom men remained where they were, struggling between loyalty to Rankor, ingrained laziness and a fear of the orange rivers encircling them.

'Bugger this,' said Goober, rocking up onto his feet. 'If we stay here, we're dead. If we go, we're probably dead. I prefer probably.' He set off and followed the others.

'He makes a good point, Rankor,' said Roddo. 'It does feel a bit like we'll die here quite soon if we don't do anything. Don't get me wrong now, I ain't a fan of Hobble, his rabble or settin' off for another damned walk, but I do prefer all of those things to losing bits of me one by one in a sea of liquid flame.'

'Keep it light, Roddo,' said Tark. 'This might be our last day and I don't want to get all down in the dumps about it. Where's Goober? He could tell us a good story to pass the time.'

'To pass the time? We don't have any damned time, look!' Roddo pointed to a new foot-melting stream heading their way 'I'm off!' Rankor could only scold him metaphorically, the ooze would be far more literal about the whole thing.

That was enough, even for Rankor. The area around them that could confidently be described as safe was now no bigger than the Meeting Patch. There was a route out of the trap, but it was narrowing fast. They ran through the last dry channel as if their lives depended on it, which they did, and headed off towards the lesser of two evils.

The flame was spreading everywhere and now covered most of the Greenfields. One of the lesser, and as yet unidentified problems the group faced was the renaming of this once lush landscape. If they had laid wagers on it then Blackfields would be the overwhelming favourite.

Fear defeated fatigue and curiosity as they followed Cobble to the mountain range. Each of them carried a burden relative to their size, so the strongest of the men were struggling with the heaviest of the burdens while the slightest of the women struggled with the lightest of weights. It meant that they were all at the absolute limit of their resources when they finally reached the base of the range.

'Up here!' called Cobble, gesturing to an opening just a few small steps up the mountain. 'We'll be safe there for now.'

They clambered up to the dark hole and crawled inside. It was a large enough opening for the tallest of the men to stand up straight in, but crawling was all they were capable of.

'What good is this?' said Rankor. 'Now we're trapped like fish in a tree.'

That was the thing with solutions, they were always unlikely. If they were simple and obvious then they wouldn't be solving anything at all.

'Are we really?' said Cobble, with a nugget of derision that could have been mined from a mountain of condescension. 'And what would make you think I would bring us all the way here just to escape a bubbling field of liquid fire? Perhaps we should have stayed down there. Would you be so good as to pop back down to the grass there and see if there's another way out?'

'Well haven't you come a long way from the forgettable little runt we remember?'

'Forgettable yet memorable?' said Cobble, pausing to let the words float around the group. 'No wonder your leadership sent the tribe into a downward spiral of doom.'

'Says the man who has us perched over a sea of fire.'

'No, Rankor. Says the man who can get us all back to Boardom without burning alive first.'

Rankor let out a mirthless laugh.

'If you get us back to Boardom I'll personally cook your meals for a dozen moons.'

'Oh there's no need for that,' said Cobble, 'if I get us back to Boardom safely all I will ask of you is that you do as I say for the rest of your life. In fact, you can add Bones to that too. If he asks you to do something you must do it. Actually, Tiff, Moss and Plum too. Yes, that should do it.'

Rankor looked about him. It occurred to him he was surrounded by the revolution. It also occurred to him that he was also surrounded by an ocean of black and orange death with no way out. Bar one.

'Fine. Get me back home and you're welcome to this rag tag brigade of misfits.'

It might have taken a day to deconstruct the complexities of the glance that Granite sent over to Tark. It could also be summed up in one compact little phrase. So be it.

Rankor's reign was over. He slunk back to the privacy of a nobody.

'Would you like to lead the way?' said Cobble to Bones.

'"ang on a minute,' said Pippy. 'Where exactly is Bones leading us to?'

'Through the mountain, of course! We came this way when we first left Boardom, only from the other side, obviously.' said Cobble.

'Erm, Cobble?' said Tiff with the lucidity of a man who remembers every detail of a good yarn. 'Remind me again what it was you saw while you were in there.'

'We never actually saw anything,' he said, truthfully.

'Yes, yes. What was in there with you?'

'It was an animal of some sort but they fell down the... ah... yes. It fell down the gentle slope. They won't be bothering us this time.'

Tiff took a second to select which flaws in the story he would address first.

'If it was a gentle slope then why wouldn't they be bothering us?'

'OK, it was more like a gentle cliff.'

'And the mammoth? You told us there was a giant mammoth and an army of smaller mammoths.'

'Yes, well. I may have miscounted.'

'Miscounted?'

'Let's not dwell on the details. In any case, what difference does it make which version is true? Either way it's our only option.'

He had a point, Tiff conceded.

'Right-o!' said Bones, keen to move away from the molten mountain bubbling up around their feet. 'If we are all agreed, we will take the only option available to us. Hold hands please, it's a little on the dark side and rather narrow.'

'Aha!' cried Tiff. 'I knew it!'

CHAPTER TWENTY-SIX

THE DARK NEEDLE'S EYE

The clear, present and very hot danger of whatever was oozing behind them had prevented any more dissent and the widest steps they took in the tunnel were the first. Rankor stood at the front, despite the protests. If he was going to give himself over to the loss of power then he could at least give one last show of defiance. For a while it was easy going, the path was wide enough for three men to walk abreast as it gently lowered them into the rock. He could hear the murmur of stunted conversation behind him and was surprised to hear the voice of Granite talking to one of the strange men. He couldn't make out what they were discussing, nor imagine what it may have been about. Being a leader meant putting up a certain amount of barriers and it became apparent to him that he would find it difficult to break them down. Perhaps this could be a good thing. He despised change, but then so did the rest of his men and they seemed to have finally embraced it. What would happen if he didn't? He would be left alone at the edge of the tribe, fending for himself and feeling miserable, like a dung beetle in the desert. As the darkness enveloped him he made his decision.

They had been walking for some time when the path narrowed suddenly. They walked in single file with Rankor still at the front, the catastrophically hot air downgrading to merely unbearable as they went. They had heard nothing from the possibly-dead mammoth, nor his possibly-never-alive army. Cobble found himself longing for the very thing he had mocked not so long ago. A boring walk through to the Great Grey Plains would do just fine. The sound of falling rubble hit his ears, followed briefly by a dusty sliding sound and a quiet, gentle thud.

'Help!' called Rankor.

The voice came from below Cobble's feet, and slightly ahead of him, which threw him momentarily. He looked down but saw nothing. The blackness in the heart of a mountain generally behaves that way.

'Are you OK?' called Cobble. 'Don't move!'

'Are you sure? I was thinking I would do a bit of a jig while I'm just 'anging around doing nothin'.'

Cobble would look back on that pivotal moment and wonder where the humour came from. Rankor was not a man known for his joviality so he was either scheming or had given in to the revolution. Either way, Cobble wasn't the sort of person to leave a man dangling, even if it was a cantankerous old stick-in-the-mud like Rankor.

He handed his slings to whoever it was beside him, dropped to his knees and fumbled around the floor. He found Rankor's hairy, and probably white, fingers gripping perilously to the edge.

'Nobody move!' he called out to the blackness. 'Who is closest to me?'

'It might be me,' came Balcor's voice. 'Here, can you find my arm?' he said, waving slow circles in the air.

Cobble reached out and found him.

'Now, crouch down carefully next to me and hold my ankles in case this goes pear shaped.'

He leant down and a little way over the edge, grateful that he couldn't see how far the fall would be. He gripped Rankor's forearm and began to haul him up, struggling with the dizzying combination of probabilities that only the possible prospect of probable almost certain death can offer.

'I have an idea,' said Cobble, raising an unseen eyebrow.

'It had better be the same as mine!' screamed Rankor, now desperate.

'I suspect not. Does yours involve apples?'

'Lift me up, you crazy fool!'

His panicked shout echoed off the stone, bouncing around before gradually diminishing to a brief hum.

'Now, maybe this is just me, but I wouldn't think it wise to call the man holding your life in his hands a fool, would you?'

'No, no. You're quite right, of course. Now please, if you don't mind!'

'Just one thing,' said Cobble, more slowly than was absolutely necessary. 'You must promise me one thing.'

'I already did,' pleaded Rankor. 'Well, sort of,' he added, hoping to prevent any additional chat about whether he had, in fact, agreed to Cobble's demands outside the mountain. A debate about semantics was not on his list of immediate priorities.

'Forget those, they were just bluster,' said Cobble honestly. 'I have only one request, well arguably two but let's not dwell on the details. They can be so tiresome, don't you think?'

'Yes! Yes! Very tiresome. Come on, spit it out!'

Cobble cursed inwardly. The problem with trying to be a good and just man was that you generally had to lean towards the indiscriminate side of the moral fence, to the eternal consternation of that part of your brain that wants you to shout 'hang them all, hang them all now!' When the opportunity presented itself to mete out a deserving justice, you were expected to be forgiving and forward-thinking.

'You can do whatever you please, within reason. The only thing I ask is that you make something new each day and bring it to me, together with a single piece of food you have foraged yourself that same day. They needn't be impressive, an arrow and an apple would be fine, just so long as they're the results of your own work. Oh, and you can't bring me the same thing twice in the same moon. Yes, that should do it.'

'Fine! Fine! I'll do it, now haul me up for goodness sake!'

Balcor lay down on the ground and braced himself against the wall behind him, closing his grip on Cobble's ankles. Cobble strained himself before pulling up the former leader of Boardom and shoving him onto the flat ground.

'Now, is everybody here?' said Cobble, slipping into the role of leader with more ease than he would have anticipated. 'Thistle, are you here?'

'I'm here, near the back I think,' came a voice.

'OK, let's go. Carefully now, if my memory can be trusted this ledge gets narrower as we go, and there is a rather terminal crevasse somewhere ahead.'

This time it was Meed who led the way, feeling her way along the rough stone wall as she went. They moved along more slowly than before, the threat of falling proving to be an effective dampener to their craving for fresh air and sunlight. Nobody spoke, each focusing solely on their next step. They hugged the wall to their left, not daring to test the width of the path to the right. In any case, the unending darkness meant they weren't entirely convinced which way right was. For all they knew they could have been going round in circles, so slow was their progress.

There was a scuffling noise coming from somewhere up ahead. Not the gentle, playful scuffling of a squirrel preparing a place to store their nuts for the winter, thought Meed. It was more like the guttural, soul-freezing scuffling of some unseen beast with nails that could do with a good trim. She pounced on the opportunity to inject some humour into the hitherto quite serious journey through the mountain.

'... could do with a good trim' she finished, turning to the blackness behind her, despite the pointlessness of it.

Nothing.

'I said,' she called, raising her voice a little and adding a dash more emphasis, 'it sounds like its nails could do with a good trim.'

Blimey, this lot were a tough crowd. She knew a thing or two about jokes, especially ones delivered with inappropriate timing, and she was pretty sure this was a cracker. She stopped and listened. When she heard nothing she stepped tentatively back along the path, holding on to the wall that was now to her right.

'Hello?' she whispered at the nothingness. 'Helloooo?'

'Be quiet woman!' snapped Rankor. To her surprise he sounded no more than a couple of inches from her face.

So they heard the scuffling too, she thought. At least a couple of them could have stifled a laugh. It would only have been polite.

Nobody was quite sure what to do next. There were no cues to take from other people's body language, usually the safest bet in times of mortal peril, and they had no idea how much path they had left to them if they stepped away from the wall. It seemed to Meed that the unspoken consensus was to remain stock still until something else happened, which it did, rather sooner than they had hoped.

There was a sniffing noise now, a sound that could only have been made by sharp, prowling teeth with a wet nose. It reached Meed and drew in a great, and presumably quite satisfying, sniff. Having thought she was frozen to the spot, it was something of a surprise to her to feel her muscles tighten a little more. Whatever it was now stood right next to her in the pitch blackness. It rubbed what she assumed was its snout against her arm and whined. Not an evil whine, it didn't have that other-worldly howl woven into it. It was more like the whine of a lost pet. Instinctively she put a hand out to pat it on what might have been its head. It snuggled closer.

Wolves are usually big. Not if you stand one next to a mammoth, of course, but then everything looks small next to one of those. In the normal run of things around these parts though, there are few things larger. Perception is reality, to all intents and purposes, and when you are ambling along a death-dark cavern in the Long Mountains, even the slightest perception of a wolf often doubles its size. Aldo was a small wolf, but a wolf nonetheless. He repeated his mantra over and over, just as Brannan had taught him.

'Stay in the shadows and prey on the minds of the blind, stay in the shadows and prey on the minds of the blind, stay in the shadows and prey on the minds of the blind.'

It was a good mantra, simple and dependable. It taught him not worry about his size, to never leave the mountain and to wait for dinners to pass him in the darkness. There were two rather significant downfalls, however. The first was that when his pack left the mountain to search for a new territory to monopolise, he stayed in the cavern on his own, unable to put a paw into the sunlight. The second was the level of footfall. He would sometimes wait for days on end for his supper to wander into the mountain. It didn't have to have four legs anymore, he wasn't a committed limbophobe like the elders. They wouldn't be seen dead eating anything that had the audacity to paw along on two legs, it just wasn't proper.

Aldo's ears pricked. His eyes were sharper in the darkness than anything in here but his hearing was bordering on the ridiculous. Something was moving along the tunnel far above him. He could hear grunting noises similar to those he had heard recently and the memory of the sudden drop to the long, slippery fall to the cavern's floor came back to him. That was an embarrassing episode, even for him. A wolf shouldn't be outmanoeuvred by... anything. He hadn't seen anything like them before, their proportions were all wrong too. They seemed to be permanently hoisted onto their hind legs, while flopping their front legs along their body, which were altogether too vertical for Aldo's liking. Still, he hadn't eaten in a while and had long since removed any fussiness from his diet. He was also quite lonely, although that itch would have to be scratched another time, food was more important for the moment. He scrabbled up the wide, rising path that led to the cliff face. It was a small wall, only a fraction higher than a dangling man. Calling it a cliff was a little like saying a puddle was a lake; justifiable from a certain point of view, but thunderously misleading from most. He padded around to the right, where the slope rose more steeply to meet the lip of the ledge, remembering to prowl in just the right way. He scraped his claws on the dusty floor, increasing his perceived size a little more.

He sniffed the air. There were more of them this time. Lots of them. There is a tipping point for every carnivore, when the size of their intended dinner becomes so great that it triggers a fight or flight debate. Aldo was close to this point as he gave another long, drawn out sniff. The grunts increased in volume, in both senses of the word, and it became clear to him that it was probably for the best if he didn't aggravate whatever they were. He was used to living on his instincts, his lifestyle didn't require much more than that, but he had a strange feeling of intuition at the back of his mind. This differed from instinct insofar as it involved a decision making process of sorts. If this band of creatures could survive in such numbers then they must have ways of finding food that he could only dream of. He resolved to try and tag along, perhaps they wouldn't notice him and they could slink along, stealing small mouthfuls of food as they went. He played this out in his head, quickly realising that they would spot him as soon as they left the darkness of the mountain. He would have to join them. He would also have to get out of the mountain, but he would leave that particular battle for his future self to sort out.

Somewhere deep in the evolutionary back catalogue of his brain he told himself he should be cute and cuddly. He didn't understand how that would help, but that wasn't important. What was important was to respond to the impulse. He gave a pitiful whine and nudged one of the dangling limbs. To his pleasant surprise it patted him gently on the head rather than trying to eat him. This might just work, he thought to himself.

'I think it wants to be our friend,' said Meed, now rubbing the furry top of the animal. 'Look, it's letting me stroke its head. Well, you can't look, obviously, but you know what I mean.'

There was an almost silent shuffle far back down the tunnel. Someone cleared their throat gently, the kind of noise some people make just before they nervously vocalise a well organised thought.

'Does it feel... friendly?' asked Barna, rather more sheepishly than he intended.

'I'm not familiar with the fur friendliness rating scale but I would say it seems harmless enough.'

'Well I ain't taking another step until I see whatever it is with my own eyes,' said Rankor stubbornly.

'Why don't we light a fire?' said Bones. 'If it's something friendly we'll know soon enough.'

'Not as quickly as if it isn't,' said Tark, not entirely unfairly.

'Well staying still isn't going to get us very far now, is it old boy?' said Pingo. 'I say we do it.'

'With what?' said Goober. 'Are you going to rub two apples together?'

'I have some sticks and dried leaves here,' said Thistle from the back of the line, nudging the arm of whoever was in front of her. 'Pass these to Quiller, he's the best firemaker we have.'

Cobble wondered where she had been all these years.

They were passed along the line until they reached Quiller. He set himself to the task of lighting a fire in the dark while everyone else tried to surreptitiously edge away from the beast of unverified friendliness.

Soft sparks flew from the floor and Quiller blew at them until a small flame licked his fingers. He added some more dry material and stood up. A dark yellow glow revealed the very edge of the wolf's face. If they hadn't known better, they would have said it was trying to give a look that was teetering on the edge of being adorable. If it was, it needed to practice a bit more. Its fangs still showed themselves malevolently, emanating precisely the kind of aggression it was trying to hide. As the sticks caught light their surroundings were revealed for the first time too. They were in a large chamber, bigger than any cave they had ever seen. The crevasse that Rankor had dangled over was just a short drop and there was a wide, flat floor that dropped benignly into the darkness.

'See!' said Cobble. 'I told you it was a gentle slope.'

'Is that a wolf?' said a voice from the back. 'It seems a bit more docile than a wolf should be, don't you think?'

'It's the eyes,' said Balcor. 'They look like they belong to something else, something less deadly.'

'What about those teeth?' said Granite.

'You always have to focus on the negative, don't you?' snapped Tark. 'It can't help it if has a pleasant disposition and bloody scary teeth. It's like Block used to say, 'a woman can't dance and cook your dinner at the same time', ain't that right, Slate?'

Slate remained silent, partly out of diplomacy but mostly because he could never quite get the hang of proverbs.

'Let's move on,' said Cobble, trying to restore some form of order to proceedings. 'If it was going to attack it would have done so by now. It can follow us if it wants, it may prove to be useful to have around the place.'

Quiller picked up a small branch from the fire as they set off again. It was as close to being an unlit piece of wood as it was possible for a torch to be but it felt like the right thing to do all the same. Aldo padded along beside Meed, rightly assuming that if she was prepared to pat his head then it was unlikely that she would try to kill him. She may even give him some food.

As she moved along the tunnel at the head of the train, Meed leant some of her weight against the wall for balance and security and its disappearance was something of a surprise. She fell sideways into what was presumably a rather thorny bush, based on her squeals of pain. Balcor was behind her and tripped over her heels as they flew through the air, landing with an oof as the wind was taken from his breath. It seemed they had reached the other side of the mountain late into the night. They could tell this by the absence of moonlight glinting off the rocks and the dry, heavy air of the mountain was replaced by a cool, slightly damp one. They sucked it in gratefully, thankful to have put a rather large rock between them and the burning Greenfields.

Lupine mathematics was more subjective than most other forms. Aldo tried to do the sums in his head. Did probable food minus painful sunlight equal more than improbable food plus comfortable darkness? He decided there was only one way to find out and stepped across the threshold into the blinding light of the plain.

'They're making heavy weather of this,' said Budge as he pecked hopefully at the rock floor below him. 'Why don't they go over the top?'

'They can't fly Budge, do I have to explain this again?'

'What do you mean they can't fly?'

'They don't have any wings,' said Spike, shuffling impatiently from foot to foot. 'You need to have wings to fly, remember?'

'Right, right,' said Budge unconvincingly. 'And they don't have any.' It was a question wrapped half-heartedly in a statement.

'No, they don't have any. They're going through it, look.' Spike waddled towards the tunnel's entrance and thrust his beak back and forth.

'They didn't have a wolf when they went in,' said Budge. 'Maybe it'll be our friend.'

They flew down to Aldo, being careful to land as far from his teeth as they could, and pecked him playfully on his back. The wolf craned his neck to see what was happening but could only make them out in his peripheral vision no matter how hard he tried. He spun around and tried in vain to catch his eyes off guard. The upshot was a curious combination of a spinning grey mass and two startled birds trying desperately to maintain a grip on his fur.

It continued long after the men and women had left.

CHAPTER TWENTY-SEVEN

FROM PAIRS TO PEARS

T he next morning Cobble gathered everyone around him. Were they his people now? He still wasn't sure, or at least wasn't comfortable with the idea. He looked at them in the pale sunlight. There was Plum, Moss and the other Boardom women. They would be happy with him in charge. After all, they did follow him, from a certain point of view, into the unknown. The Nutty Woodsmen seemed happy to follow him, Tiff more than most. The passing of responsibility seemed a little too easy there, but perhaps Tiff was a reluctant leader of their group in the first place. They had integrated themselves into the group well, seamlessly in some cases. He looked over at Pingo with Plum sitting at his side. It was already inevitable. Even the wolf was lying snugly up against Meed.

He looked over at the Boardom men. He couldn't quite make his mind up about them. Had Rankor given up, or was he calculating one last gamble for power and tradition? Granite and Tark seemed to be happy enough with the new world order. They weren't quite as friendly to the Nutty Woodsmen as they might have been but it was still early days. Under normal circumstances the best way to measure their revision of an opinion would be in generations rather than days. These were not normal circumstances, however. He put these thoughts to one side as he stood in front of his future.

'Morning!' he began chirpily. 'I'll keep this brief. We've made it through the worst of it and now we have to put our trust in a cave painting. If our deduction is correct then we'll be safe there.' He decided not to point out the alternative. 'We should be home in a few days. We can then get to setting traps and building up a store of food for the colder moons.'

There was a general mumble of agreement. The kind you get at the end of a long journey when someone points out there is still the matter of tidying up the mess you made before you left.

'It seems we may have another member of our little assembly,' he said, gesturing towards Aldo. 'Would anybody like to be our first wolf handler? We can come up with a snappier name another time if it helps.'

'I'll do it,' said Meed. 'I think it has taken a shine to me, my arm is covered in wet nose residue already.'

'Good. Congratulations Meed. One last thing,' said Cobble, raising his arms slightly in a pre-emptive calming motion. 'I think we should walk in pairs for the last stretch across the Great Grey Plain. If we're going to be living together then we should at least be able to talk to each other.'

It felt to Cobble as though this was what a leader was supposed to do. Find something that is stopping something else from happening. Then do something to make that something go away. Something like that anyway. He matched up each member of the group, being sure not to put those from the same group together where possible. When he had finished he asked that they each prepare their loads for the last stint. He wasn't ready to order just yet, so asking would have to do until he worked it all out.

His face was buried in a pile of arrows and a sling when a nervous voice behind him said 'What about me?'

'Ah, Thistle. Hello! Did I not pair you up?' he said with as much innocence as he could muster.

'No, I think you must have forgotten about me.'

'That is one thing I can guarantee you with some certainty that I did not do. Will you walk with me?' Had he been asked, he would say he was probably wrinkling his eyes in nervous anticipation.

'I'd love to.'

'Phew!' he said, quite a lot louder than the thought that it was supposed to be. 'I mean, erm... great! Do you need help getting ready?'

She didn't, so she lied.

They made their way along the edge of the range, just as Bones and Cobble had done all those days ago. This time there were thirty seven of them all told, meandering in and out of the vast crags, each in their own new world. Pingo had been paired with Daffy, who had changed so much over the course of her adventure that she occasionally offered an original thought for discussion. That was the power of enforced captivity, as she saw it. The longer the conversation had to last, and in this case it was days, the more time you spent thinking about what you were going to say next to fill the gaps.

Meed walked with Fettle, producing a quality of conversation that spanned the full humour spectrum. Granite was with Camble, a pairing that took half a day to get going but was finally thawed by Camble's tale of the talking birds. Balcor told Tark of the new ways they had learned to trap animals, a topic that was of no interest to Tark at the start, but by the end of the second day it had spawned an unlikely advocate. Each couple talked about everything and nothing, with two stark exceptions. The first was the only grouping other than his own that Cobble had put much thought into. He had chosen to put Moss with Rankor. It was a gamble, but one that would pay dividends if it went the way he hoped.

The other exception was Thistle. He would have preferred to have been pecked by the vulture again than spend days trying to talk coherently to her but it was a trial he had to pass if he was to make a life with her. For the first hour they stumbled and stammered over their lines, each secretly grateful that the other was suffering as much as they were. When Thistle told him of some of her ideas around how to make a machine that would fire arrows automatically at passing quarry they finally relaxed onto common ground. From then on they were in their element, as comfortable with each other as trees in a forest.

They were almost within sight of the Obelisk of Boardom as the sky began to darken around them. The sun was slinking away for the night and they were broadly excited to be reaching the end of the road in time for a well earned sleep. Bones was at the head of the line discussing the benefits of figs with Keera. They had gone through most food types and were struggling to keep the conversation going. Just as Keera was about to cross a line by suggesting ways in which the leaves could be put to practical use Bones put an arm out across her chest and stopped still. He turned to the snake of people behind him and called out in a harsh whisper, just loud enough for enough of them to hear.

'Stop! Get off the plain! Quicker than that, come on!'

He dragged Keera behind a crag and immediately ran back out to pull Faun in after her. As he was hauling Pippy in he could see they had all got the gist of the message, if not the reason for it. He found Cobble and whispered in his ear.

'We're almost at the Meeting Patch.'

'I know that, why the sudden panic?'

'Anyone who we've ever seen there is either here or dead.'

'Yes. And?'

'Take a look for yourself.'

Cobble peered out from their hiding place towards Boardom. In the rapidly darkening light there was a flickering orange glow.

Bugger.

'It could be the mountain flame, although I'd be surprised if it had made it this far so quickly. The only other possibility is...'

'Quite,' said Bones, cutting him off before he could say it out loud. That would somehow make it more real and him absolutely certain. There is only one person who isn't here but knows where we may be going. They have even been here before, if the stories are to be trusted, although neither of us have any memory of it.'

'Then we have nothing to fear from his presence. It looks like there may be one last rogue to knock into line before we're done. Would you like to do it, or shall I?'

'I think we should all do it, it could be fun.'

He stared thoughtfully into the fire, poking at a half-charred log. He had endured a hard journey to get here so swiftly and was grateful for the rest, physically, at least. His mind wouldn't slow down and sleep had become like an old friend he hadn't seen for days. He had trekked around the end of the mountain range, just as he had done all those moons ago. This time he cut across the Great Grey Plains rather than heading far to the north, using his rusty scouting skills to find his way.

He went over it all again.

He knew better than to follow Bones. He let him go to where he wanted to be. After a while he stood up and went to where he wanted to be – away from the cacophony of the village. He headed in the general direction of Cherry Woods, although he was unaware of it. He gradually veered to the right, towards the very furthest edge of the Long Mountains and lost himself in his thoughts. He hadn't intended to go so far at first, his journey sort of evolved as it went, like a spider who decided to weave a simple tightrope between two leaves but couldn't help but add a few frills to the edges.

He hadn't always been the version of himself that people saw now, he thought to himself. As a child he was normal; sometimes helpful, sometimes troublesome. He did all the usual things and played in all the usual ways. He would be subjected to the range of motherly cries that all children endured.

'I've told you before, you're not to play down in the valley after sunset,' and 'Come here young man,' as she licked her hand to rub vigorously at a patch of muck on his face.

He knew precisely when it had all begun to change. That hot summer night when he returned to Cherry Woods with Bones' soon-to-be mother. Her arrival was met with consternation, what with her being a peculiar sort to look at, not to mention the fact she brought with her a mouth that would need to be filled. He always thought they had overreacted, so he did the same. For every cold shoulder they were offered he would offer two. At first his bitterness was raw but undeveloped and he put their reaction down to the look of the girl, rather than the girl herself. Every time a new baby was born there was a celebration, but wasn't that also just another mouth to feed? His conclusion was that they were wary of the stranger. After all, they had never seen anyone before who didn't look more or less like them. Granted there were a few large noses and perpendicular ears, but on the whole they looked the same. This arbitrary prejudice only consolidated his resolve. As the moons went on they became more and more detached from the rest of the village until the breaking point arrived.

She had become undeniably pregnant. He reasoned that they would be happy for a new baby to arrive, as they were for all other babies. The contradictory nature of their prejudice, however, resulted in the very opposite reaction. Jutt lobbied for the baby to be born and taken away, with or without his brother and his peculiar looking woman. He had argued vehemently to the contrary, but it was apparent that there was no way around the will of the village.

He left a few days after the boy was born. Bones' mother was too weak to make the journey and so he was forced to leave her behind with no more than a half hearted commitment that they would look after her until his return. Jutt placed a triangular pendant in the bundle of skins and the baby's mother kissed his forehead one last time.

His hollow lie to the man in Boardom was to become a prophetic truth.

When he returned to Cherry Woods his woman was gone. They said she had succumbed to the fevers that had taken several of them that moon but he wasn't convinced. He raged against them, demanding to be taken to her, but they simply said she was laid in the river, as was their custom. He had nowhere to go, and so remained, his bitterness growing with his detachment until he resolved to never again trust or help the men of Cherry Woods.

As the days and moons passed, so did their numbers. Survival became more difficult and his resolve waned. When death is staring you square in the eyes it is easy to be distracted from what was once important. He thawed a little towards those who were left, like a glacier melting inch by inch. But as with all good glaciers it grew again in the face of extreme cold. In his case it was the frosty interactions he had with them all, particularly Jutt. The feeling became mutual and he left, happy to be rid of them and on his own.

Now it had come full circle, his son had returned and helped save his former peers from a rather short life of nuts and dull stories. He had given no thought to a destination and was surprised to discover he had reached the end of the mountains. He could go back to Nutty Woods to see Bones, although he was sure he wouldn't be welcomed. None of them would hold any affection for him, he was sure, and why would they? He had been a tetchy naysayer for so long that he was of a mind to think they had forgotten what he was like before all of his troubles. What was it his mother used to say to him?

'Better to be a fish in a man's fire than to fire a fish at a man.'

He was never quite sure what it meant exactly but he thought it may have been something to do with how people appreciate what you do for them, not what you are.

He couldn't survive on his own anymore, he knew that much. It had become harder and harder to get past the survival part of his day and he was spending less time doing as he pleased. He span a good yarn to the women, he was happy with that one, but it had been more about hubris than reality. The only people he was sure existed were those who were likely to dislike him quite a lot. So that was it, he would have to make amends for all the moons of absence. It rankled with him even now. While he wouldn't have said he held the moral high ground, he at least had the moral foundation, even if it was a long time ago.

It had meant getting to Boardom before them. They would be slow in a group, weighed down by provisions and people. He had flown around the mountains and up the Great Grey Plain, reaching his new home long before they made it, despite their straight line across the Greenfields. How he would win them over was something else entirely. They had seemed happy despite the impending doom. He wondered where they would find safety from the mountain. Would they really head to Boardom?

If he was to prove himself worthy of a place in the new world order then he had to do something tangible for them, with a heavy dose of altruism to hide the ulterior motive. If he was good at one thing, he knew, it was at manipulating a situation to get what he wanted. The difference now was that he was trying to do something good. He certainly wasn't use to that, but if he reached far enough through the dark memories of bitterness and resentment he could just about make out a younger version of himself waving pleasantly back at him in the distance.

All he needed now was something to show them.

They made their way along the plain as a scattering of disparate individuals morphing gently into a cohesive lump of community. Aldo and his feathered companions had caught up with them and padded along beside Meed.

As the rock became shallower and more familiar Bones was sent scrambling up to scout over the peak at the burning Greenfields. As he neared the zenith he wondered what he would see. His instincts told him that there was simply no chance the liquid flame could have stretched this far but none of them had any experience of this kind of mystical mischief before so he assumed anything was possible. It had either reached Boardom or it hadn't, the probability of each outcome was only relevant if he had to check on a thousand mountains spewing towards a thousand villages. There was only one mountain and one village that mattered and so it came down to a fifty-fifty chance. This train of thought didn't help his insecurity. Suddenly there was a greatly improved chance their new home would be destroyed before they could wipe the dust from their feet.

He paused before pulling his head over the top. Maybe he would just wait a few moments longer, at least that way the ooze would not have visibly reached Boardom. The thought relaxed him a little, just long enough for a practical, if slightly irritating trait of his to pop along and say hello.

Whenever he found himself in a situation where he had to do something he didn't want to do, he would take himself by surprise and get his body to do it before the rest of him had a chance to explain why it wasn't a good idea. His legs thrust upwards as his elbows got a grip on the rock and hauled him over the top. To his right was a worrying mix of charred, black ground overlaid by a sizzling bright orange network of still rivers. Straight ahead of him was the most vivid green he had ever experienced. The starkness of the contrast took him by surprise as he studied the movement of Unfinished Mountain's innards.

He waited patiently in the hopes of finding a definite pattern in its movement. Along the edge of the verdant grass was a wide seam of blackness that grew almost imperceptibly as he watched. The orange was being coerced down to the base of the Long Mountains, building up there but unable to break the dark barrier. He couldn't tell from his vantage point, but he assumed the ground must rise ever so slightly at that seam, just enough to keep it from making it any further towards Boardom. This fitted nicely into his theory that Boardom was safe from the mountain's anger and so he decided he had collated quite enough data to arrive at a sweeping conclusion. He dropped back over the edge and made his way down to the expectant crowd.

Cobble had the somewhat childish idea that they should arrive in Boardom in one long, horizontal line. Once he had explained to Fettle that he meant a wide line of people, rather than for them to be horizontal individually, they were ready. They crossed over the small stone wall and picked their way through the fruit trees. Under normal circumstances they would be within smelling distance of the Meeting Patch but the abandonment of the area had the rather pleasant side effect of eliminating that particular idiosyncrasy.

To some, the sight of the Obelisk was a sign of home, to others a sign of change. To the Nutty Woodsmen it was a sign of an Obelisk. As they finally reached the Meeting Patch they closed in a wide circle around the flames. There was a bent figure, still prodding logs as if unaware of their arrival. The orange glow flickered across their faces as he looked slowly up at them with a doleful expression. He scanned them, looking for Bones.

'Friends, I have prepared us a feast,' Dodd said, pushing his hands on to his knees to stand up. 'Some of you don't know me, but I can guess what those of you who do must be thinking. Here is a rat that has run out of choices, trying to weasel his way back into the group. Doubtless there are other creatures you would gladly compare me to. I would think the same, but before you cast your judgment, I would ask but one thing; that you allow me the duration of a feast to explain myself. When I am done, you can choose to cast me aside or welcome me home.'

Jutt felt compelled to be the first to speak, despite his reservations.

'You are a scoundrel and a ruse, Dodd. Why should we believe anything you say?'

'You shouldn't.'

'Then why are you here?'

'All the evidence to date would tell you not to believe anything I say. All I ask is that you believe the sentiment and sincerity of my reasons.'

Cobble considered the future of the village. In the grand scheme of things it would do no harm to hear what he had to say. They could always send him away regardless of the power of his story. He also didn't want to lead unilaterally, that wasn't how his vision of the future worked. He would pass this decision over to the best barometer for the occasion.

'Then I will give you your chance. When you are done, Bones will decide whether you stay or go.'

CHAPTER TWENTY-EIGHT

FULL CIRCLE

Dodd would leave Bones for last. He had decided his best chance of success would be to speak to each member of the group individually. Crowds had an annoying habit of finding momentum in the face of all logic and he only had one shot at this. He had gone over his lines for hours on end and was sure they were as good as they could be, as persuasive as they could be. Even so, he wanted to practice before he got to his son.

The least influential person would be his first audience, and he had chosen Fettle for that particular honour. He sat down beside him, handing him a chunk of meat from the fire. This was more for show, since everyone was watching his first move. They would soon get bored and he could stop some of these more extravagant displays of altruism as he went on.

The meat had been hard won, as it had always been. They say a man can lift a mammoth if his favourite coat was trapped beneath it, and so it proved with hunting. There was so much at stake that he found himself able to lurk in the trees, as if hiding from snakes, and drop on to unsuspecting animals of varying sizes. Some he had to finish off with a snapped branch, but he just closed his eyes and thought of fluffy clouds on a summer's day before plunging. Before he knew it he had a haul that was unique in all of Boardom's history. He had gathered up what mushrooms he could find and knew to be safe and added them to the berries he had picked when he first arrived.

Fettle looked like a man who would be quite happy not to be involved in this whole process, let alone be the first victim. Dodd sat him down on Cobble's bench, still standing where it was left in the Meeting Patch, patiently waiting to be used. He was trying hard to resist the urge to put a friendly arm around him for show. This couldn't be a caricature of a gesture though, it had to seem real. It had to be real. Fettle blankly endured the entire speech, from Dodd's early years as a normal boy through to the events that led him to prepare the feast. When he had finished he simply said, 'so that's it.'

'I understand,' lied Fettle. It was all far too complex for him.

Dodd worked his way through them all, alternating between the Nutty Woodsmen, the Boardom men and the women to give himself time to revise small parts for each demographic. The food had run out by the time he got to the last two. He walked over to Bones and Cobble, who were leaning against the Obelisk away from the rest.

'Cobble,' said Dodd, nodding his head with what might have been respect.

'No need to tell me, Dodd. I trust Bones to do the right thing for all of us.' He stood up and walked back towards the fire.

'Bones,' said Dodd, a little more nervously than he had expected.

'You've gone to a lot of effort just to make a point.'

Dodd wondered how he could counter him without coming across as confrontational. He was making a point to a certain extent, that much was true, just not a sinister one.

'Sort of,' he said. 'You're right, it would have been a lot of effort just to make a point, but I am trying to explain a point. To show one.'

'Semantics will be the death of you.'

'Perhaps, but I hope to have more than the length of a meal to show you. Now isn't the time for you to hear the story I've told the rest, you know most of it in any case. Unless you need me to fill in the gaps now?'

Bones ignored the question, instead laying out the trap he fully expected Dodd to career headlong into. Untrustworthy people have an ability to conjure grand, complex and ultimately unrealised schemes on the spot, it's what makes them so untrustworthy. The part of Bones that wasn't dealing with the gravity of the situation was curious to discover what he would come up with.

'How will you show me?' he said.

'I have no idea.'

Cobble gathered the group together. He stood by the Obelisk, as was right and proper. He didn't want Boardom to be the same place he had left, but some traditions were important, even here.

'Friends! We have arrived at our new home. To some it is in the same place as our old one, but to all of us it is new. Gone are the days when women do all the work and men do nothing. Gone too are the days of prejudice and cynicism. Bones has decreed that Dodd's honour is true and is welcome to stay here until the end of his days, if he chooses to do so.'

He was worried that he might take the fancy language too far, but he would only have one inaugural speech and it was sure to be repeated many times by bards through the generations. A simple 'Welcome home everyone, let's get drunk' would simply not do. There was none of Old Shankswill's funny pear juice ready anyway.

'This will be a place of laughter and freedom, of shared work and shared responsibility.' A few of the women cheered. 'We will raise our children where they will be happy and healthy. We will hunt and we will feast, we will dance and we will sing.' It was the mens' turn to cheer now, even Rankor. He raised his voice above the noise. 'We will live!'

He stepped down from the dais and into the arms of Thistle at the front of the appreciative crowd. It was his crowd, his village. He decided there and then he would never let himself look so much like a leader as long as he lived.

EPILOGUE

It was a cold and clear winter's morning and he was the first one there, as usual. He used an old worn spade to dig another small square of earth from the ground and put it to one side. Picking up his trowel he scraped the edges of the hole until they were just the right size. He took the last of the special stones that Cobble had made and placed it in the last hole, tapping it with the tip of the handle.

He stood up and admired his work. The path stretched from the Meeting Circle, as it was now known, all the way down to the stream. It had been Granite's idea to build something that would stop the water-walk from being a muddy slide. The sense of achievement in completing it would have been a surprise, had it not been for the myriad projects he had completed since his return. Jutt had proved to be a willing and able partner and the Cobble Stones was their greatest success yet.

He packed up his things and headed back towards the obelisk, wallowing in the immature pleasure it gave him to be the first one on the new road. The first road.

'Morning, Faun!' he called out as he passed the Obelisk.

'Morning, Rankor. Lovely day, ain't it?'

'How are the orchards coming along, any crop yet?'

'I'm just off to check. Goober says the pear trees will be ready any day now.'

'Marvellous, I'm anxious to sample Shanky's special dancing juice again. Let me know how you get on, will you?'

'Of course, bye for now. See you at dinner.'

He trotted on towards the Meeting Patch, looking about as he went. There was a pleasant combination of light work and relaxation being done. He had to hand it to Cobble, he knew how to make a village work.

It had surprised Rankor to discover that the times he was resting were made all the more enjoyable for having worked beforehand. He always completed his jobs in the morning, allowing him to fully relax into the afternoons and evenings and had even begun to enjoy the work he was doing, to his eternal surprise.

The village looked very different from the one he left; there were the Cobble Stones, obviously, but there were also the wooden shelters they had begun to move into. They surrounded the Meeting Patch and gave a cosy community feel to the place. Each shelter had its own fire pit that encircled, at a polite distance, the Tribal Fire Pit in the centre. The Nutty Woodsmen would have called it all very modern indeed, although they weren't referred to as the Nutty Woodsmen any more of course. They were all part of the new world, part of the new Boardom, part of Corenstown.

He took in the scene. Dodd was where he always was, processing the spoils of their hunt to be distributed to the various pockets of enterprise that had sprung up. Moss would take the skins and prepare them for clothing, carriage and general backside comfort. She had refused to look after the cooking, as did all of the women. Those days were over and now it was down to Pingo, Tark, Balcor and Granite to prepare the tribe's dinners each day. Fettle worked with Goober in the orchards, a natural assistant if ever there was one. Speck still shadowed Jutt on his scouting missions, but was increasingly on the receiving end of his impatience. On the face of it this was nothing new, but any keen eared observer could tell that the clips around the ear were more often given when Speck said something snitty about the others. The old Jutt would have appreciated the disdain, but not the new, evolved version he had become. The others were either working at their daily tasks, or resting in the Meeting Circle.

Cobble and Bones were playing with two small children.

'Don't let her play on those stones,' called Chard, stroking her belly. 'I'm not tending to cuts anymore in my condition.'

'Yes dear,' said Bones, in a tone only used by downtrodden fathers.

He turned to his daughter. 'Coren, listen to your mother, get down from there!'

'Same goes for you, Cobble,' said Thistle, giving him a cheeky wink.

Cobble lay on his back and raised his arms to the sky, hoisting a bundle of animal skins above him.

'Now then, Lava, what adventures will we get up to, I wonder?'

THE END

Printed in Great Britain
by Amazon